DICTATOR

Donald Kozlosky

Book cover design by Alexandra Covaleski

Printed in the United States of America

ISBN 978-1-7333244-0-3 (paperback)
ISBN 978-1-7333244-1-0 (ebook)

For Jane

ERGO JENNIFER

In the attic of an old four-gabled house lived a tenant named Jennifer Golembeski. Her short-cropped hair was nearly black and splashed with streaks of purple dye. Her eyes were slate blue. At 22 years old, Jennifer was on her own and struggling to make ends meet. Her job in a warehouse at a manufacturing plant paid peanuts, and what with rent to pay and bills and the cost of almost everything going up she had no choice but to start moonlighting. She did this three nights a week, tediously steam-cleaning rat shit out of cages in a toxicology lab. Not that such toil could ever rival the ambitions of poised and well-educated young men and women, but it did keep Jennifer out of hock, and not only that, it also provided wondrous pickings from the supply room—bottles of disinfectant, sponges, plastic garbage bags, all of which Jennifer would discreetly pocket, for she did, indeed, prize such items as one less thing to spend money on.

Through hard work and an eye for scavenging, Jennifer managed, albeit just barely, to keep her head above water, even launching a little layaway plan, the success of which had as testimony a brand-new mattress that lay on the attic floor, made up snugly with burgundy sheets and a calico quilt and topped off by a smelly foam pillow on which Jennifer would lay her head at night. Yet such extravagances, mind you, never got the better of Jennifer. She remained thrifty. She cut costs. To obtain privacy, she had used

1

clothespins to attach faded beach towels to the curtain rods above the windows. Likewise, when a floor lamp she had bought from a local Salvation Army store needed a shade, she fashioned one out of aluminum foil, a crude but effective piece of handiwork that she would later boast of to Amber Lamphere, her confidant and drinking buddy.

Clearly Jennifer's life was marked by struggle. Stoically she slogged on and did her duty by that precious grind called the work world, yet nonetheless she was always ready to blow off a little steam, to belt back a few drinks, to go a little wild. She thrived on louche crowds and tumblers of gin. She also had a vulgar streak and liked a good dirty joke. An all-around live wire, she possessed robust animal spirts. As far as anyone could tell, she might have been living out some free-spirited creed, though nothing so definite as a creed had ever crystallized in a mind like Jennifer's. Highfalutin' ideas, for the record, were not her strong suit. She lived for the moment and kept her pleasures simple—be they bar hopping or partying or, just lately, getting it on sexually with her closest friend, Amber.

Their first intimacy, in fact, involved a case of highly erotic oral pleasure, the incident taking place after each girl admitted that none of the guys they knew really seemed that interested in going down on them. And so, while up in Jennifer's attic one night, the two friends came to the conclusion that guys, for all their horniness, could be notorious prudes. Then, after downing the last of their gin and tonics, they looked into each other's eyes and took matters into their own hands. Not only had a specific sexual fantasy come to the fore, but it now took on a life of its own as Amber, getting to her feet, leisurely removed her jeans and dropped her panties. Jennifer, meanwhile, crouched eagerly before her, nestling her nose in a patch of blond pubic hair, a slow lap of her tongue following. Soon, breathless with giggles and soft moans, each girl took turns returning the other's favor, working their tongues in prolonged and exquisite ways. The whole experience made for a delightful and earthy form of arousal. Not lost on Jennifer, of course, was that this absolutely delightful indulgence could be had for absolutely nothing out of pocket. It was free.

Although no one ever would have predicted the intimacy that flared up between Jennifer Golembeski and Amber Lamphere, it was, all in all, not surprising. Strange and unexpected encounters would often, as they say, follow Jennifer around. Wherever she showed up, things were bound to happen. Her mere presence could somehow alter an otherwise humdrum situation. People reacted to Jennifer. They were affected by her. They found her intriguing and felt different around her. People knew instinctively that she was always at the ready, somebody who had no compunctions about letting herself go. And if she got carried away? So what? If she went a little too far? So be it. What was it to Jennifer anyway? She'd merely dismiss the matter by saying: "Whoopee shit! Who cares?" And who, really, in all sincerity, did care? Jennifer was a nobody. All anyone could discern about her was that she was unpredictable and at times had an unsettling influence on people.

On one particular day, Jennifer was in the midst of a week's vacation. She had slept late and was now heading out to the food store when she noticed that the left rear tire of her old Impala was nearly flat. Since she hadn't been able to come up with the money to fix this flat just yet, every two weeks she had to fill it, and so she drove over to the Red Apple Kwik-Fill. She climbed from that old clunker of an Impala, zipped up her jacket against the cold, and then popped the required number of quarters into the air machine before grabbing the hose and doing what she had to do. It was a cold day and when her task was over and the tire firm, she blew on her hands to warm them, once again telling herself that she really ought to buy a pair of gloves, but once again putting it off because of those flimsy green pieces of paper called money, of which she never had enough.

So for now Jennifer resorted to blowing on her hands and rubbing them together when, in a flash, she thought of how good it would be to have her hands folded around a cup of hot coffee, a large coffee, a coffee she could buy right now simply by walking into the Red Apple.

Jennifer almost never spent money on something she could provide for herself more cheaply, but then again, hey, she reasoned, it was her vacation after all, and while it wasn't a friggin' trip to the Bahamas, exactly, that cup of coffee would taste good and feel good on her hands, and so she walked into the Red Apple and drew herself a large cup of black Columbian coffee, snapped on a plastic lid and then walked up to the counter to pay.

As she stood in line at the cash register, Jennifer's eye meandered over to a nearby rack of newspapers, the headlines jumping out at her, but as she shifted her gaze directly in front of her, there at the checkout counter she found herself staring squarely at an array of scratch-off lottery tickets, all of them spooling off of individual rolls. The names on the tickets were tantalizing: LOOSE CHANGE, MONEY IN THE BANK, LUCKY TRIPLER—all ridiculous come ons, Jennifer knew, and yet, the odds of winning aside, one ticket stopped her cold: GOLD RUSH. WIN UP TO $100,000! How it beckoned to her, this ticket, its gold letters bright and shiny, its little stacks of bullion set off richly against rays of bright purple. What Jennifer could not ignore was how the purple color of this ticket matched the streaks of purple in her hair, a detail she construed as an omen, a good omen, telling herself she simply had to have this ticket, even though it cost five dollars. But if she actually won something? If this little gamble paid off? Well-well, Jennifer reasoned, such an outcome would be justice for having to spend money on something as dumb as air— "Air for fucking Christ's sake," she grumbled to herself.

When it was her turn at the cash register, Jennifer paid for the coffee and plunked down a five-dollar bill for the GOLD RUSH ticket. Quietly obliging her, the cashier, an older man with a grizzled beard, tore the ticket from its spool and pressed it into Jennifer's hand. Staring at it, Jennifer nodded, perhaps to the ticket, perhaps to herself, perhaps to the man behind the counter, it's impossible to say. She simply never said a word and walked quietly back outside, the cold air pinching at the flesh inside her nose as she pushed the GOLD RUSH ticket deep into the pocket of her jeans.

Hustling over to her car, Jennifer got inside and slammed the door, holding the cup of coffee between her hands like a sacred offering. Steaming up into her nose, the aroma of the coffee was rich and heady, and as she gingerly sipped the dark liquid she thought: Yes, this is what a vacation is, relaxing in a parking lot sipping a tasty cup of coffee and knowing that the slow leak in that damn tire won't be a bother for another couple weeks. Yes, she considered further, it was a perfect treat not to have to be anywhere or do anything, but instead to simply feel free and daydream. And Jennifer wondered if maybe, just maybe, that GOLD RUSH ticket tucked inside her pocket would pay off, if by some long shot she'd score with it, and were that to be the case, were she to actually win $100,000 dollars, well, as Jennifer exclaimed out loud: "Wouldn't that be the dog's bollocks!"

So with her coffee now placed in the cup holder and an Inkubus Sukkubus CD loaded in the CD player, Jennifer turned the key in the ignition and the song "Wikka Woman" began. With the old Impala having jumped to life and the music blaring, she flung the car in reverse and hit the gas, whipping the car backward at a sharp angle, then braking, then throwing the shift forward as she gunned the engine, shooting past the gas pumps and the other cars in the parking lot before flying out onto the road. Hooting loudly as she cranked up the music, Jennifer, out of sheer exuberance, slapped her thigh, the impact of which landed square on the spot where the GOLD RUSH ticket lay in her pocket, causing a sensation that was like a hot spark burning her skin, a hot-cold tingle that momentarily puzzled her.

When she arrived at the grocery store, Jennifer had a spring in her step, wheeling her cart up and down the aisles, her eyes peeled for bargains, her hands snapping up the simple but satisfying goods she relied on. Often in the produce section she would take her time, poring over the apples and Bosc pears, smelling the potatoes, lightly squeezing the red peppers. Yet today she moved about briskly, collecting quickly the various fruits and vegetables she needed and, of course, buying the limes and tonic water that would go along with that brand-new bottle of Beefeater gin that she and Amber planned to break open that very night. Wow, if only every week could be vacation, thought Jennifer, if only every week allowed the time to while away the hours and not have to be doing some half-assed job, to just be gadding about free and easy. It was possible, she reminded herself, to stay out late at the local bar and listen to the Steamin' Jimmies, watching that mean saxophone player with the yellow-tinted sunglasses. To be sure, she had the whole damn week to kick back and break the routine, and the thought of doing so made her feel juiced up and ready.

The fact of being free, at least for several days, unleashed in Jennifer a brash desire to relish anything she could. Things were, for the moment, pretty good for her. Her hard work and frugality had enabled her to carve out a small niche of breathing room for herself. Despite her hand-to-mouth existence, she had at last gotten herself out of that nasty flophouse she had been in, and however close she cut it with paying her bills she still, nonetheless, paid them, and somehow, by some wicked stroke of luck, she had even managed to hoard away a little dough that she could fall back on—and fall back on just for the fun of it if she wished. But the real kicker was that now, on top of everything, she had a week's paid vacation, a concept so novel, so unprecedented in her life that she couldn't help see it as a dastardly way of beating the system, a coup of sorts that she had pulled off simply by being a working drudge day in and day out. She didn't owe anybody any money, there was a little extra cushion in her checkbook, and she could rightly proclaim she was ahead of the game.

On getting back home from the food store, Jennifer marched up a musty stairwell for three whole flights to her attic loft. Lugging groceries that grew heavier and heavier with each step, she could hear the dull thud of her boots resounding with a weak echo. Entering her digs, she did not remove her jacket but stored away her groceries until everything was quickly in place. Then she left again and flew down the stairwell at a rapid clip, her steps unbroken until she had reached the ground floor, and as she went out the door she had one thing on her mind—recycle bins. For today was recycle day, and whenever she had the chance, Jennifer would roam the streets of her neighborhood targeting the familiar green bins that lined the curb. Specifically, she would rummage about in the brown paper bags that were stuffed full of paper products. Rifling through junk mail and cereal boxes and whatever else, she would soon enough turn up some recent newspapers or a few magazines, *Sports Illustrated*, maybe, or *National Geographic* or *Rolling Stone*. It hardly mattered what she found so long as she got her hands on something to read, so long as she had something to pass the time with, for Jennifer could never afford the monthly bill for cable TV, and so she didn't even *own* a TV.

As she explored the contents of one particular paper bag, she spotted a magazine and grabbed it, its cover so slick and glossy it seemed impervious to water or any other damaging fluid, and as she fished this magazine out into the daylight she gave a start, her heart plummeting downward like a stone before quickly bounding back, beating fast, for there on the cover was one of the most well-known women in the world, the Dictator's wife, in fact, Primo Bimbo herself. With her grip on the magazine tightening, Jennifer felt herself getting riled up. She despised Primo Bimbo, who was, in

Jennifer's opinion, an uber-whore, a slut-bucket who had held her nose and married the Dictator so she could reap the windfall, a windfall of billions of dollars, a point which the magazine cover made egregiously clear, for this was not the typical photo of Primo Bimbo, not the usual leggy pose in which her high-altitude pumps made it look like she was forever walking around with a stick up her ass. No, not at all, this was a photo in which Primo Bimbo had outdone herself, an up-close image of the woman feasting, literally feasting from a bowl of jewels, her fork dipping into a stew of rubies and emeralds and other gems that floated languidly amid strings of pearls and creamy opals and all sorts of baubles bubbling up from sapphire depths.

Stunned, even confounded, Jennifer stared at the picture of Primo Bimbo and could not help voicing her feelings out loud right there on the street: "Is this some kind of friggin' joke? Is Primo Bimbo really such an asshole she thinks it's like clever to be eatin' from a bowl of jewels?"

Jennifer narrowed her eyes and looked closely at Primo Bimbo, attempting to discern just what the woman meant by posing for such a photograph. But Primo Bimbo offered no clues, her face a mortician's still life, a death mask of dolled up perfection whose lips were bloodless and algid, whose whole expression was a masterstroke of makeup, mascara, eye shadow, while her long mousy hair swept the air so freely it might have been staying aloft by a perpetual thermal. But all of it, Jennifer concluded, was just another display of Primo Bimbo's cheesy front, for Primo Bimbo was zombie chic at its best, a woman who looked out at the world with eyes so dead they might have been popped into her head by a taxidermist.

However upbeat Jennifer had felt, after seeing Primo Bimbo her spirits dipped. On a level she could not fully explain, she felt inadequate, irritable and offended, putting the question to herself of just who was this rich bitch that she could have so much money and then get in people's faces about it. As far as Jennifer was concerned, Primo Bimbo was little more than a prop for the Dictator, a piece of eye candy who did nothing but preen about and look good and maybe fawn over the Dictator when he was screwing up his little pig eyes and bellowing at people—and no doubt bellowing at Primo Bimbo as well, Jennifer supposed, for the Dictator was just that kind of dumb lout who would shout her down at every chance he got, an idea which was not farfetched and which was borne out by the fact that whenever Primo Bimbo appeared with the Dictator she displayed a singular air of dread. There was something ill at ease about her, some morbid vexation that ran very deep. What this vexation was exactly, Jennifer could not, of course, know, but she clearly chalked it up to living with the Dictator, a fate worse than death to Jennifer's mind, but one which Primo Bimbo had obviously embraced. Uber-whore that she was, she got all the perks of being a rich man's moll, she got to walk around in six-thousand-dollar outfits that she might wear only once and then hang up in a closet the size of someone's living room where the outfits would never see the light of day again. But money aside, Jennifer just couldn't get her mind around how Primo Bimbo went through life being at the beck and call of a creep like the Dictator. How did she do it without retching? And how did she crawl into bed every night with such a bloated and perverted piss weasel?

Jennifer shuddered to think of such things. As far as she was concerned, the Dictator was the equivalent of having dirt under her fingernails, a man forever spouting off crazed and ludicrous lies, a blundering halfwit who did nothing but berate and belittle other people. To read about him was quite enough, making Jennifer glad she didn't own a TV, because to think of the Dictator's long face and yacking jowls appearing large as life right in front of her was enough to make her puke. While watching him one night over at Amber's (where there was a TV), both she and Amber found themselves gaping in disbelief as the Dictator, shifty-eyed and glum, stood hulking over a podium and glowering, his snout flinging at the air as he spluttered on and on about how he would make the nation safe by banning all Muslims, Jews, Hindus, Buddhists, agnostics, atheists and Pygmies.

Yes, Jennifer, like many other people, was of the firm conviction the Dictator was a dangerous crackpot, and she deemed it wise to limit her exposure to the man. No one wants to see or have to listen to a flaming bummer like that man, after all, but on this particular day Primo Bimbo had proven to be a bummer as well. To see her in all her filthy-rich glory eating out of a bowl of jewels was like a sharp dig in Jennifer's ribs, because Jennifer had to sweat every penny to eke out a living, and she just couldn't fathom why the Dictator and all his cronies wanted to squash her and keep her down when in her mind she wasn't even worth keeping down. She was simply jarred by all of it, all the conniving, all the dirty dealing, all the shit she couldn't keep up with thrown in her face by the Dictator and that sleazy clan of his, forever giving her the shaft and yet talking through their hats like they were all doing her the biggest fucking favor. It all began to weigh on Jennifer and she began to wonder if she had been shortchanged by fate somehow, because it was pretty damn clear nobody had left her a legacy of millions of dollars like the Dictator got, doled out when he was still a little snot-gobber wet behind the ears no less. Millions! Imagine! And so why wasn't she born rich as sin or smart or looking like a supermodel? It was a conundrum that had started to eat at Jennifer ever since the Dictator came to power, and it needled her even more seeing Primo Bimbo on the cover of that magazine, for she had begun to second guess everything. At times, she even went and stood before the bathroom mirror, wondering why the bridge of her nose bumped out slightly at a certain point and why her hair had no body and was just simply dark, and why whenever she pulled on her jeans her ass seemed packed too tightly into them even though she didn't eat much at all. Was her ass really that big? Was she putting on weight? What in blue blazes was she doing with her life anyway?

Overcome by a wave of despondency, Jennifer wondered if she was doomed to be stuck in a rut forever, nickeling and diming it to the grave. All the vim and vigor that had pepped her up earlier had drained away, and that scratch-off lottery ticket she had bought, that GOLD RUSH ticket she had felt so good about and which still lay snug in her pocket, she simply didn't have the heart to rub off. She didn't care to see if she had won anything—or lost. On arriving back at her attic loft, she simply pulled the ticket from her pocket and walked into the kitchen, where she stuck the ticket firmly on the refrigerator with a magnet designed as a pentacle.

By evening Jennifer was animated and feeling herself again, a change due in part to the fact that Amber was coming over to have a few drinks and celebrate the start of Jennifer's vacation. At one point, as she and Amber stood at the kitchen counter squeezing limes and mixing gin and tonics, Jennifer produced the magazine she had found featuring Primo Bimbo on the cover. She wanted very much to hear what Amber had to say about it, and Amber, on seeing Primo Bimbo, jumped back and threw her hands to her head, exaggerating the impact of what she saw.

"My God!" Amber cried, laying her arm around Jennifer's shoulder and tugging her close for emphasis. "Don'tcha see, Jen? This here magazine explains it all, it explains just why the Dictator thinks his shit don't stink, because him and all his rich cronies, they're all eatin' jewels, the whole miserable lot of them, they're eatin' jewels and just crappin' out whole treasure chests! But no need to fret about it, because me and you in the end, we'll get to eat cake! Trust me, girl, we don't stand down and we *will* get to eat cake."

"But we'll chew up the Dictator first," replied Jennifer. "We'll chew him up and spit him out, and then we'll eat cake."

A BRAIN OF WORMY CHEESE

Flat on his back the Dictator lay motionless beneath a gold satin sheet that was tucked under his chin and which ran the length of this body. So profoundly still did he lie, in fact, that his chest did not discernably move with his breathing. Indeed, for sheer inertia, he could have rivaled any given corpse on a slab at the city morgue. However, the Dictator was not quite moribund, but merely stretched out slumbering. And how sweetly he slept, his head on a plump goose-down pillow, his body sunk in a bed abundantly soft and ample, while to heighten the grandeur of his repose there was at each corner of the bed a chunky post of ornately carved mahogany that towered upward, its every detail polished to perfection. No less impressive was the headboard that rose high above the Dictator's head, a massive piece of wood with dark rich grains where, dead center, was a large depiction of the Dictator's very own coat of arms, a grand bit heraldry, to be sure, its every nuance intricately whittled. To behold this emblem of royal ego was to confront a broad shield inlaid with three bold chevrons one atop the other, under which a two-headed vulture grasped a human skull in its talons, while standing atop the shield, unmistakably, stood a dodo bird perched in rampant pride, its beak conveying a long pole from which a pennant waved, the inscription on the pennant boasting the Dictator's motto: *Mea Fuckupicus Magnificus.*

Yet despite all the notable particulars of this bed, there was yet another feature put in place by the Dictator himself, a modification quite all his own. Indeed, anyone who dared to peek beneath the gold satin sheet on which the Dictator lay would find a form-fitted barrier of thick neoprene that hermetically sealed the mattress and box spring, a modification whose purpose was to allow the Dictator to frolic in freewheeling piss parties, orchestrated orgies during which hot urine was jetting and squirting right there in the royal bedroom as the Dictator flailed about, peering out through plastic goggles at the entangled limbs of the women with whom he frolicked, this while the high-end bedding supporting it all remained completely dry.

How often these "baptisms of ire" (as they were known among insiders) occurred was not exactly clear, but as more and more details leaked out there was talk about the Dictator's peculiar penchant. People were catching on, and all of it was verified by reliable sources who noted that in order to carry out the Dictator's hot and pungent whiz bangs he would procure call girls from a very exclusive international escort service that ensured these girls would submit to the Dictator's every whim, which meant, of course, not only getting drenched in the sordid splish-splash of golden showers, but also following the Dictator's orders to squat over his head and "Piss like your lives depend on it!" The repeated effect of this practice, while certainly providing great pleasure for the Dictator, also went a long way toward explaining the peculiar color of his hair, especially when considering the high pH levels that exist in urinary enzymes.

For the record, however, on the previous night there had been no piss party, but this should not suggest that the Dictator was lying in drydock exactly, for overnight a slimy excrescence had been seeping constantly from his pores. By morning, as always, a thick residue of slime had congealed, hardened and tenaciously taken hold of his entire body, so that the man found himself bound fast to his sheets, encased in a sticky goo that had soaked through his monogramed pajamas and bound his arms tight to his chest. Slime had also dribbled from his nose and banked off his lips like veins of melting wax before gumming up in the corners of his mouth. It was such a tough and icky substance that it had even fused the Dictator's lips shut, requiring that he now mew irascibly to get attention.

Summoned by the Dictator's mewing, two young black women from Burundi now enter the room walking on their knees. Dressed in strict accordance with the Dictator's demeaning whims, each woman wears a coconut-shell brassiere and a grass skirt of yellow raffia, their heads downcast as they approach. The scarred and callused feet of the women are bare, and about their necks dangle strings of plastic beads. Yet the most humiliating adornment lies atop each woman's head, where tied in her hair is the leg bone from a bucket of Kentucky Fried Chicken on which the Dictator has personally gnawed. Impassively accepting these slights and insults, the two women now continue shuffling along on their knees as best they can until, when only a few feet from the Dictator's bed, they raise their coppery arms overhead and begin a series of languid and visually poetic salaams, after which their voices break out in unison, delivering a clear and deferential greeting: "Oh, Great Bwana, we who are about to clean the slime salute you."

At this, the Dictator jiggles his body and gives a peevish grunt. The women snap into action. Lithe and supple, and with a strength that belies their exceedingly thin arms, they work in perfect tandem, flipping the gross tonnage of the Dictator out of his sheets with a forceful maneuver, his body tearing free from the sticky satin with a rip like muffled Velcro. With everything happening too quickly for him to comprehend, the Dictator finds that he has been bounced off the bed and is now grasped in midair and leveraged into an upright position, propped up by the women until he can stabilize himself and stand unassisted.

Next, after peeling, pulling and vigorously wrestling the Dictator out of his pajamas, the two women get to work. They assess the thick buildup of slime on the man who now stands before them. They then drop to their knees and reach under the bed to pull forth a heavy box filled with seashells. Sorting through this box, each woman grabs a seashell and beings to scrape the slime from the Dictator's body. With long, even strokes, the shells glide steadily over the pudgy flesh, curving around the man's neck and shoulders, liberating his armpits and moving ever lower to the nether regions. Throughout the process, gobs of slime accrue in the seashells, slime that, by the way, possesses a distinct orange hue and hints at high concentrations of Sunset Yellow FCF, a dubious but essential ingredient typically found in Cheetos. This fact, however, is neither here nor there with the women from Burundi. They continue with their scrupulous and at times delicate scraping, and when the seashells are laden with slime they toss them into a green plastic biohazard bag before obtaining new shells.

After the most obvious layer of slime has been removed from the Dictator, the women next turn him in the direction of the royal bath. This provokes a scowl and harsh snuffling sound. Perhaps the Dictator is displeased. Perhaps he has judged the efforts to clean the slime from his body not up to par. Who knows? All that can be said is that the Dictator now begins to walk, thrusting a stiff and cumbersome leg out in front of him, his foot landing heavily on the floor as his other foot rises behind him, swinging forward to surpass the foot in front, the Dictator bowling himself along in a lumbering waddle.

As he crosses the room, harrumphing as he goes, the Dictator appears distracted, in a fog, or even, as some people say, not all there. To be sure, the man cannot quite sort out his thoughts. Although he wants his morning coffee, he finds himself seized at the same time by an impulse to launch missiles at North Korea, a prospect that fills him with delight, causing a barrage of devastating explosions to play out in his mind. These mental pictures, however, soon give way to an altogether different vision, one even more vivid and realistic, namely that of a large four-armed Gumby who happens to be strangling Pancho Villa. Make no mistake, the Dictator actually sees this altercation as if it were taking place before his very eyes. He watches as Pancho Villa kicks the four-armed Gumby in the crotch. He gets excited as the four-armed Gumby throws Pancho Villa to the ground. He watches with more and more fascination, waiting to see how this fight will conclude, but so tumultuous is the backlog of onrushing balderdash coursing through his head that Pancho Villa and the four-armed Gumby find themselves swept away by it, leaving the Dictator staring off into space, stammering and glassy-eyed, and in a state very much akin to being punchdrunk.

Meanwhile, the women from Burundi follow the Dictator from several paces back. Each is a model of self-effacing reserve and discretion, yet given the size of the hulking man who now walks naked before them, their eyes cannot help but grow wide, staring at his big ugly ass and the wads of fat that hula from side to side with each step. It is not a pleasant sight, but before long the Dictator is at last standing within the white-tiled walls of a huge walk-in shower stall. So cavernous is this area that every little sound echoes. Anxious, impatient and testy, the Dictator looks daggers at the women, who now hustle as fast as they can, one of them wheeling forth a huge gas-powered 3,100 psi pressure washer that they now prepare for use. As one of the women takes steps to make sure the exhaust fumes are vented through an available duct, the other pulls the start-up cord. Instantly a loud, unrelenting *VROOM* pierces the air, chattering like a machine-gun doubling down on its own noise due to the prevailing echo. Amid this deafening racket, the Dictator turns down the corners of his mouth and turns up his nose, bracing himself. Holding a long steel nozzle that is connected by a hose to the pressure washer, one of the women now takes aim, blasting away, firing at the Dictator with a narrow stream of water so concentrated and powerful that it burns into him like a laser. Crusty patches of slime that resisted the scraping of the seashells now quickly disintegrate and fall away. In other places the stubborn cling of the slime simply gets vaporized. Succumbing to the precise and powerful pounding of the water, the Dictator raises his arms and widens his stance, waiting for every last bit of slime to be pummeled out of existence, waiting to be squeaky clean once again.

When the job is finally completed and the power washer gets turned off, the Dictator stands dripping wet. Still somewhat groggy, he looks absently around and finds he must take a moment to collect his thoughts. Then he snaps his fingers at the women and both of them instantly respond, retrieving from a towel warmer two large plush towels of dreamy soft cotton. Very thoroughly, they begin patting the Dictator dry, taking special care to make sure that the flamboyant initials monogrammed on the towels make no contact with the Dictator's skin, as whenever this has happened it has caused a slight chafing that greatly angers the Dictator. Thus, the women dry the Dictator with great care. They pat and dab, they caress and gently swab, absorbing every last bit of moisture until all is gone and the Dictator, at long last, curtly dismisses them, awaiting the final obeisance which must be paid. Falling to their knees, the women bow forward in a parting salaam, but as they do their coconut-shell brassieres drop down and the Dictator cranes his neck, trying to see just how much of their breasts are exposed.

Only too glad to be taking their leave of the Dictator, the women quickly exit the royal bath and continue across the royal bedroom, their grass skirts swishing. One of them, however, unexpectedly stops, turning her gaze toward a far corner of the bedroom where a large terrarium sits atop a cast iron stand. Through the glass of this terrarium, the woman can see countless scorpions scurrying about. Moving this way and that over a landscape of sand and rock and paper shavings, the scorpions work their claws and kink their tails upward as they prey upon dead and lethargic mealworms. Yet what is most unusual about this miniature waste land is that littered about it are a dozen or more Green Cards which the Dictator has placed there for "safekeeping." In fact, two of the Green Cards belong to the women from Burundi, who have known strife and hunger, death and despair, but have never known anything quite like the brute anger of an excessively privileged man, that being the Dictator.

THE EXCELLENCY SUITE

On legs waterlogged by lethargy and general sloth, the Dictator lumbers ponderously through the corridors of his royal confines. He is on his way to the Excellency Suite, for therein lies the Dictator's office, his nucleus of power, where the Exalted One holds court with his minions while sitting up on a dais, ensconced on a red velvet throne. Here amid the garish ostentation of the Excellency Suite, the Dictator reigns in all his glory, the walls surrounding him cluttered with snooty family portraits, while priceless gewgaws and gauche set pieces crowd the entire room, including one particular item of which the Dictator is particularly fond—two golf clubs of solid gold that hang crisscrossed like swords on a large plaque that bears the Dictator's initials inlaid with sparkling rhinestones.

Upon entering the Excellency Suite, the Dictator looks about suspiciously. His little pig eyes are simmering with malice, though the eyes soften a bit as his gaze settles on a large chalkware statue of himself, virtually life size. Hand-painted in crisp jewel tones by a renowned Russian miniaturist, the statue looks out over the room with bold condescension. Quite taken by this replica of himself, the Dictator admires it with smug complacency. Next, speaking in tones that are disturbingly intimate, he actually talks to the statue, saying: "We're going to make so much money, tons of money, me and you, you'll see, so much money, unbelievable amounts of money, money like you've never seen before, I know, I'm rich, if people want to know about money, the money, it will be rolling in, I guarantee it, lots of it, lots of money."

Although the Dictator continues on in this vein for quite a while, the chalkware likeness makes no reply and simply stares back at the man. The Dictator, however, is in no way bothered by this reticence. In fact, he actually welcomes it, wishing everyone could so readily accept his infallibility, his certitude, his blanket statements, instead of pestering him with questions and pressing him for details and, worst of all, holding him accountable to facts.

Having at last taken a seat behind his large, spacious desk, the Dictator now considers his agenda for the day, the first order of business being, in fact, a top-priority meeting with Luigi, his tailor. Normally a meeting with Luigi would have offered the Dictator great pleasure, for Luigi, through the most exquisite measurements, the deftest cuts and the most nimble tucks of material was able to perform a sartorial sleight of hand that took a fat lunk like the Dictator and, by means of a new and stylish Brioni suit, transform the man into a reasonably symmetrical human being, the end result being, as Luigi put it—an Adonis! And the Dictator could not have agreed more, even if he did think an Adonis was a sleek Italian sports car. Indeed, with each new suit that Luigi delivered, the Dictator gloated. He would put the suit on and go stand before a full-length mirror where, in all his self-important splendor, he would beam over the fact that he had gone from being fat to simply being big. Fat was bad. Big was good. Big was imposing. Big meant he was formidable and tough. Big meant he could intimidate other people. So, needless to say, Luigi had done his job superlatively, and the Dictator was eminently pleased.

Until now.

Now Luigi had a problem. The wads of fat hanging off the Dictator's carcass were getting bigger and bigger, and they were getting the better of Luigi. As the rings and moguls of adipose tissue continued to grow, Luigi, in order to conceal these unsightly blobs, was forced to forgo the stylish flair he so cherished and give the Dictator's blazers a broader and more general sweep, allowing the material in front to fan out uninhibited while letting the material in back simply drape down in a smock effect, for this was the only way to stop the Dictator's fat ass from pushing open the center back vent. These efforts, however, for all their good intentions, did not prove successful. Indeed, Luigi's latest design, far from making the Dictator look like a stylish alpha male, made him look more like a sausage trapped between two gullwing doors, which sent the Dictator into a trembling rage. He yelled at Luigi. He insulted Luigi. He sarcastically mocked Luigi's Italian accent and broken English, and he gave Luigi an ultimatum—return in three days with a suit of clothes that fits properly or else!

Now three days had passed and Luigi was here. On entering the Excellency suite, Luigi was met by a look of stern repugnance. Sitting behind his desk, the Dictator glowered at Luigi, his jowls puffing out as if with sacs of venom, his anger rising at the mere sight of this man who had dared to tailor such an inferior suit, a suit that was so far beneath the Dictator's lofty station that it constituted an effrontery of the highest order, being, as it were, a virtual slap in the face to the Dictator. And so the Dictator was on his guard, seeing red, in no mood for trifles, while Luigi, for his part, greeted the Dictator warmly, saying, "Good morning, Your Excellency," the tailor continuing to make small talk with a few harmless pleasantries. The Dictator, however, seeing that Luigi had arrived empty handed, wasted no time in biting off the head of this otherwise soft-spoken man from a small village north of Rome, bellowing at the top of his lungs as he demanded to the see the newly tailored suit that was, at least to the Dictator's mind, his God-given due.

Clearing his throat, Luigi, despite the Dictator's anger, maintained his composure, smiling a weak but sympathetic smile as he apologized for not having the suit. He explained that it was his greatest pride to make people look fashionable, to give them every stylistic advantage, but the fact remained, he stated most earnestly, that he could not produce the optical illusions necessary to make a Gargantua like the Dictator look like a Slim Jim—no, this he could not do—because, sad to say, there was no suit of clothes on Earth that could accomplish such a feat. On the other hand, Luigi tactfully suggested, if the Dictator would perhaps consider going on a diet and not eat so many hamburgers, so much pizza, so much ice cream, so much Kentucky Fried Chicken . . .

Alas, however, even before Luigi could finish his sentence, he noticed a disturbing change come over the Dictator. Indeed, the orange Creamsicle complexion typical of the Dictator was beginning to set itself ablaze, igniting the man's whole face with a hue of red-hot lava. In addition, his chin was growing bigger, doubling in size, while his cheeks billowed out like balloons. Even the Dictator's nose grew bigger and bigger, the pores expanding in a high-definition *peau d'orange* that was frightening. Incredulous at what he saw, Luigi took a few steps backward and continued to watch as the Dictator's whole head began to swell, the occipital plate of his skull leveraging upward and heaving against the flesh of his scalp as if it were under some immense pressure that could not be contained. Luigi wondered if the man's head would explode. He watched as the Dictator's lips pulled back in a menacing sneer, the lips twitching uncontrollably as the Dictator began to cough and hack, gripped by a guttural spasm that racked his whole body, for in his rage the Dictator had swallowed his tongue and was now desperately trying to spew it forth—which he finally did by means of a harsh and violent hack that sent his tongue immediately wagging in a gushing, garbled screed:

"You fucking filthy wop! Crooked sham! Trying to pawn off your hideous shit on me! It's crap! Garbage! Crap! A clown wouldn't wear the shit you've got the nerve to call clothes! Coming around here! With garbage! The rags of some loser immigrant! Hideous! Worthless! Total garbage! You're good for nothing! Nothing! Hear me! You're a stupid joker who just got off the boat! A foreigner! Trying to sell clothes! It's disgusting! Cheap rags! A charity wouldn't take them! They'd go in the trash! Sickening! Clothes for paupers! Paupers! Trying to pass off this shit! You'll get arrested! This is America! No joker just walks in here and does whatever he pleases! You good-for-nothing piece of shit! You're dirt! Stupid! Couldn't sew a napkin together! You'll get sued! Worthless! You're worthless! Get out of here! Drag yourself off to some soup kitchen! You're fired! Damn shyster! Worse than a Jew! You're fired! Fired! Fired! And you're not getting paid!"

Luigi sighs in dismay. With his arms hanging complacently at his sides, he now stands erect and nimbly bows to the Dictator, saying, merely, "As you wish, Sire," after which he shuffles backward, his head remaining bowed until he has backed himself completely out of the Excellency Suite, closing the door behind him. As he walks away, Luigi now gives a low whistle of relief and then voices his feelings aloud, regardless of whether or not anyone can hear him, "*Mama mia*! Theze unfortunate Americanos. Why they no elect some nize person to be leader? Why they elect *stronzo—maiale fascista*? They be in the big trouble, theze Americanos, they going to learn zee hard way."

IDIOTS

Back in the Excellency Suite, the Dictator sits with his fists clenched atop his desk, still stewing about Luigi, galled at the nerve of the man to be peddling chintzy garbage that didn't fit. An insult! That's what it was. It ought to have been clear right from the start that the guy was trouble, the Dictator surmised, especially as the man was just a shade too brown. That was the clincher. These brownish people were always trying to have it both ways. They couldn't be trusted. Not that he had anything against Italians per se, the Dictator reminded himself. He knew Italians. He liked Italians. But some of them could be a little brown. It might just be a healthy tan, somebody might say, but then again, the Dictator pondered, you couldn't know for sure. You had to be on your guard with brownish types—wetbacks, Puerto Ricans, Arabs. In some ways they were worse than blacks. Black people were at least above board. You could see that they were black. But these brown people were like chameleons. They got browner around their own kind and then whiter around white people, when they wanted something. They could pass themselves off as something they weren't. They could infiltrate the government. They were dangerous, sly, murderers and rapists, that's what they were. Even Luigi probably had a rap sheet a mile long. Tighter security, that's what was needed, the Dictator decided. There was something suspicious going on with all these undesirables. They were after something. They were plotting, lurking in the shadows, out to stir up trouble. The filthy parasites! Something had to be done about them, the Dictator reminded himself. Something needed to be done now! He needed to talk to Wizard Breitfahrt. Where was Wizard Breitfahrt? He'd know what to do about these brownish degenerates.

"Where is Wizard Breitfahrt!" the Dictator suddenly bellowed, jabbing a button on the intercom to page his secretary two doors down. "Get me Wizard Breitfahrt! Find him! Get him in here!"

Flustered and impatient, the Dictator now sits twiddling his thumbs, his eyes shifting back and forth across the top of his desk, on which there is nothing but a long irregular zigzag of red and white Lego blocks snapped together in a continuous wall several inches high. The wall is a prototype of that which the Dictator plans to build along the entire length of the Rio Grande, a big wall, a massive wall, a wall that will once and for all keep out the murderers and rapists that have been spilling over the Mexican border and pillaging the countryside. However, as of yet not one shovelful of dirt has been broken to build this much-vaunted wall, and so the Dictator must content himself with building a token wall from a heap of little blocks, a jumbled pile of which sits on his desk, ready to be used. Very carefully, the Dictator now selects one of these little blocks, a white one, which he eyes with satisfaction, fingering the smooth plastic as if it were a talisman. Next, he moves this block to a far end of the wall where he aligns its holes over the raised pips of some other blocks, pressing the block down until it snaps into place. Hearing this sound triggers a bizarre smile in the Dictator. He begins to fawn over the various angles and abutments of the Lego wall. He tilts his head to get a more inspired view, allowing his gaze to roam the wall's entire length as he envisions little men with rifles and machine guns standing atop it, men with piercing eyes who scan the borderland beyond for anything that moves, anything that dares to make its way up from that stinking cesspit called Mexico. Curiously, one of the little men that the Dictator envisions suddenly comes to life, transfiguring himself from a kind of fluid inkblot into an actual little man who paces back and forth energetically along the top of the Lego wall. Then the little man jumps in the air, standing rigidly at attention, saluting the Dictator with a quivering arm.

The demeanor of the Dictator brightens at this proud display of loyalty and subservience. Aglow with satisfaction, he gets up from his desk and is just about to return the salute when something catches his ear—a discordant cacophony, a strident combination of kazoos and clashing cymbals, coupled with the noise of belligerent voices that grow louder and louder until they have gathered just outside the Dictator's door. This hive of nasty chatter and unruly griping is, the Dictator realizes, the entourage of Wizard Breitfahrt, a motley crew of men no more than three feet high who now throw tantrums outside the door, punching it and kicking it, squealing petulantly like stuck pigs. But before the Dictator can give the command for this passel of halfwits to enter the room, the door suddenly flies open on a blast of malodorous air that nearly bangs the door off its hinges. Stomping into the room in the wake of this ill wind arrive two dozen or more stunted little men who grimace with hatred. They hale from far and sundry, these specimens. One little man from Slag Heap, West Virginia, clouds the air with coal dust every time he moves. Another, who festers with anger, is covered in cobwebs from an Alabama outhouse, his four remaining teeth working diligently to mince up a plug of tobacco—work-work, chaw-chaw—after which the ruminant spits a brown stream of juice onto the floor, saying: "No nigguhz! We dun don't want no nigguhz!" Hearing this, a cross-eyed chicken plucker from Kentucky grins idiotically and clashes two cymbals together. CLASH! "And no Jews either!" squawks a pot-bellied man wearing camouflage clothes and a plastic stormtrooper's helmet. "Yeh, no fuckin' kikes!" shouts still another as the cross-eyed chicken plucker snorts and whinnies and clashes his cymbals together yet again. CLASH! "Dat's right," sputters a man named Jedediah Cogtooth, who sports a confederate flag tattooed across his forehead. "Dis here America!" declares Jedediah. "We duh best! We gonna get dem Mooslims, too! We gonna drown 'em in pig's blood! The Dictator promised we gonna drown 'em in pig's blood!" At this, everyone cheers and the kazoos erupt in rabid feistiness, the cymbals clashing over and over as the little men all hop up and down, their arms reaching overhead as they bat about an enormous bubble of translucent shit that has been floating above their heads the whole time.

Standing within this bubble, wobbling about and trying to keep his balance, is Wizard Breitfahrt. Although somewhat obscured by the mucilaginous texture of the shit bubble which encases him, one can nevertheless see the dark hair that hangs Hitleresque over Wizard Breitfahrt's forehead. One can also see scabs of vomit dried in the stubble of his chin, not to mention a sebaceous treacle akin to rendered animal fat that dribbles from one corner of his mouth. The paunchy Wizard Breitfahrt now looks down knowingly at his cadre of little lickspittles as they leap in the air and swat at the bubble, driving it in one direction, then another, although where it actually goes is really of no consequence so long as they keep the shit bubble airborne. Pleased by these antics, Wizard Breitfahrt opens his mouth and releases a sour-brash emanation whose toxicity would kill a man were it not contained by the membrane of the shit bubble. Nevertheless, traces of this deadly halitosis permeate to the outside world, stinging the eyes of the little men and making their nostrils twitch. Yet the little pissants are undaunted by such discomfiture. In fact, nothing excites them more than to be goaded into a state of irritation, hostility and sneering disdain, especially at the hands of Wizard Breitfahrt, who has made it his speciality to pump up these hollow men.

The Dictator, having had enough of this commotion, gruffly clears his throat, a signal to all present that it is time to adulate the Dictator himself, to defer to his petty braggadocio, to revere his pretense of contemplation and deep thought, which he puts on full display as he walks toward the Aryan oracle in the shit bubble, the Dictator doing his best to appear solemn and profound, as would befit any man whose wont it is to consult the all-knowing Wizard Breitfahrt, though in the Dictator's case, rather than appearing like a man who is savvy, sharp and in control, he looks more like a dazed mope who can't remember what day of the week it is. Nevertheless, he faces the shit bubble with a show of great confidence, raising his arms in a gesture of grand entreaty, while the question on his lips, he believes, is so incredibly crafty that it is bound to impress the wily Wizard Breitfahrt: "You, Aryan oracle," barks the Dictator, "I seek an answer. I seek your great wisdom, such incredible wisdom, so much great wisdom, wisdom like nobody else has anywhere, and so I ask you, how brown is too brown?"

"BROWN!!!" yells Wizard Breitfahrt, his reply roaring forth in a gush of vomit chock full of bile, hair balls, bezoars and blood clots, not to mention the greasy offscourings of numerous cheap diners, all of it unleashed with a force that sends it bouncing off the membrane of the shit bubble, the vomit breaking apart, splintered off into orts and gobs and wriggling streamers that ricochet every which way in the near zero-gravity conditions within the bubble. Eventually, however, the speed of these trajectories begins to slow down, slower, slower, until what ensues is an eerie snow-globe effect, one in which Wizard Breitfahrt stands surrounded by a morass of floating odds and ends, everything from dead cockroaches and bits of fecal impaction to the soggy guts of road kill, which Wizard Breitfahrt routinely ingests at breakfast.

The Dictator, stunned by Wizard Breitfahrt's vehement answer, stands taken aback, his wits scrambled, a blank stare on his face as his lips purse and purse again, as if he were attempting physically to dredge up an apt word or two with which to impress Wizard Breitfahrt. At a total loss, however, the Dictator is left with no recourse but to repeat the single word Wizard Breitfahrt himself has stated, though the repetition of this word, it must be noted, is meant clearly to show a kind of decisive affirmation, as if the Dictator had been testing Wizard Breitfahrt all along and was now taking it upon himself to sanction Wizard Breitfahrt's answer. "Yes! Brown!" repeats the Dictator with gusto, satisfied and relieved that he has executed such a fine rhetorical parry. Indeed, so satisfied is the Dictator that he is now emboldened enough to pose another question. "And tell me, Aryan oracle, my worthless tailor, Luigi, that worthless huckster, is he too brown?"

"Look at a penny," suggests Wizard Breitfahrt, his tone sickly sweet, "and behold Abraham Lincoln, he who freed the slaves, is *he* too brown?"

This comeback absolutely floors the Dictator. He doesn't know what to make of it. He starts to stammer, then shuts his trap, while the little men beneath the shit bubble grow antsy and agitated. They begin to snarl and kick the floor. "It's a left-wing conspiracy!" yells a bloke in faded blue overalls. "Dem damn liberals is sellin' out the white folk!" proclaims somebody else. "Dat's how dey do it," chimes in a third voice, "sneaky like rats, dey is, makin' Lincoln a nigguh." As the little men further expound, they gnash their teeth and swing their fists, while continuing to reach up and tap their hands against Wizard Breitfahrt's shit bubble, ensuring that it bobs about above them.

The Dictator, for his part, finds that the spongy conduits of his brain have difficulty processing what Wizard Breitfahrt has said, and yet the little men—whom the Dictator watches indignantly—seem to have grasped the implications of Wizard Breitfahrt's comment quite readily. This observation rankles the Dictator. To think that he, the Dictator, that he who is so rich, that he who has so much money, that he could possibly be upstaged by a bunch of little hick runts no taller than his thigh sets his teeth on edge.

"I'll close down the U.S. Mint!" bellows the Dictator, his eyes bulging in a bloodshot rage. "No more brown Lincoln! It's fake news! The fakest news ever! Fake! Fake news! The mint is closing! By executive order!"

On hearing this, all the little men in Wizard Breitfahrt's fan club stop short, all turning to look at the Dictator—then they erupt in fits of jubilation. They jump up and down and shout with glee. One of them falls to the floor and rolls about, jiggling with joy. "No more stinkin' Lincoln!" yells a pipsqueak in a straw hat. "No more nigguhz!" blurts out a man from the Ozarks conceived by two first cousins. As cymbals clash and kazoos pierce the air, the man from the Ozarks begins to dance a spastic version of the "Cotton-Eyed Joe," the fervor among the little men intensifying until a man from Tennessee goes so far as to run full tilt across the room and butt his head into the wall, fracturing his skull and knocking himself out cold. They can't contain themselves, this peanut gallery, and so heated is their racism that the hot air filling the room sends Wizard Breitfahrt's shit bubble floating up to the ceiling on its own accord.

Noticing this spectacular ascendency, the little men, one by one, stop what they're doing to gaze upward at Wizard Breitfahrt. Their mouths drop open and they stand overcome by a kind of deranged rapture, starry-eyed and beside themselves with awe as they bear witness to what can be only called, to their minds, a miracle. Wizard Breitfahrt, meanwhile, although his face is obscured by the opaque and hazy grains of the shit bubble, looks down upon them, nodding his approval with the kind of sanctimonious authority typically reserved for popes. As he speaks, Wizard Breitfahrt's words sound tinny and have little to no resonance, and yet they are heard very clearly by the people below, very clearly, indeed: "Make America *white* again!" exhorts Wizard Breitfahrt, "Make America *white* again!" Hearing this, the little men in the entourage start to applaud and to cheer and to vigorously hump each other, while the Dictator, believing once again that all is right with the world, stands very still, an imbecilic smirk frozen on his face.

RHONDA REDWING

Meanwhile, a young Mohawk woman named Rhonda Redwing sits in a coffee shop located in Seneca Falls, New York. With a cup of black coffee and a half-eaten omelet before her, she reads an article in the morning paper that happens, just by chance, to be about Wizard Breitfahrt. With disgust and dismay, Rhonda Redwing reads about how Wizard Breitfahrt is the poster boy for American bigotry and how he has been in devious cahoots with the Dictator, both of them crafting a racist agenda that underlies their domestic policies. She also reads how Wizard Breitfahrt and the Dictator regularly conduct little prototype versions of the Wannsee Conference, in which they discuss with relish how to disenfranchise black people, intimidate Muslims, demonize Hispanics, and bully women for good measure, all of it a dry run for more severe and violent tactics that are waiting in the wings. This article is so repugnant to Rhonda Redwing that as she brushes back her hair from her eyes she must force herself to continue reading, balking as the article concludes with a quote by Wizard Breitfahrt: "By any means necessary, we're going to reclaim this great nation. We're going to solidify power. We're going to be the only agenda in town and we're going to make America white again!"

"*White* again?" Rhonda Redwing asks herself with sudden pique. Then she takes a deep breath and reflects on what it's like to be a second-class citizen in her own homeland, an invisible outlier whose people were either relegated to central casting roles in dumb westerns or made a cultural spoof for the benefit of what the white man thinks he understands. Thinking back to hundreds of years ago, she can barely fathom the attrition suffered when a genocide of germs first washed ashore and 90 percent of her people died agonizing deaths, the real pestilence, as the Dictator would have called it, not having come across the Rio Grande in caravans, but across the Atlantic in ships from Europe. The remnants of her ancestors who survived this European pox lived on only to find themselves outnumbered and outgunned, beaten back again and again until they lost their land, their way of life and their dignity. At the end of a gun barrel, they bore witness to the dying of their dreams until, in the end, her tribal kinsmen were backed into the miserable wastes of the reservation, the Federal government humoring them now and then as if they were animals in cages.

Every treaty along the way had been little more than a con job. Every good intention, like Thomas Jefferson wanting all the land west of the Mississippi to remain sovereign Indian territory, was just lip service and another lie. And now, thought Rhonda Redwing, all that treachery and deception had come home to roost, for the biggest conman and liar of them all had gripped the reins of power and was firmly in charge—the Dictator, who looked out at a nation of sheep and found that he had more than enough wool to pull over their eyes, who promised them the moon while dismantling their freedoms and sacred rights, who launched blitzkriegs of patriotic propaganda while imposing martial law one decree at a time. With the stranglehold of tyranny growing tighter and tighter, Rhonda Redwing could only wonder as to why this nation of dullards had not yet taken a stand against the man who was destroying them.

Then again, she wondered as well if she could even be bothered to care. It was the white man, after all, who had laid waste to her people. He had crossed the ocean and rode roughshod over the land, bringing his disease, his guns, his Bibles, thinking he was finding freedom for the hordes and hordes of people that followed him when all he had to show for it now was a king more demented than George III, a power-drunk fool scraped from the bottom of a filthy barrel. How ironic, thought Rhonda Redwing, that two hundred years of democracy had been crowned by a depraved despot, with his racist henchman having the gall to claim they would make America white again. "*White* again?" Rhonda Redwing muttered once more with a snicker. "Who are these people anyway?"

CHAMBER #9

The darkness for McPherson was a kind of self-contained deprivation zone. It made him uneasy to have his head cloaked in a hood of dense black material. It heightened his sense of vulnerability, naturally, as did the two men who sat next to him, one on either side. Together, all three of these men occupied the back seat of a large black Mercedes-Benz, its windows tinted to the deepest possible depth. Although McPherson could not see the men who flanked him, he recalled them as classic boilerplate agents—very fit, astute, self-composed, each wearing an identical pair of Rēvo sunglasses. They had accosted him as he walked home from a favorite Greek restaurant after having had a hearty meal of lamb leftiko. With deadpan authority, one of these agents had stepped out onto the sidewalk and blocked McPherson's way, informing him that he was wanted in Chamber #9. Turning down the corners of his mouth, McPherson shrugged his shoulders and was then directed toward a waiting Mercedes-Benz. Sliding into the backseat, he soon found himself sandwiched between the aforesaid agents, who, after yanking closed the doors of the car, quickly pulled a black hood over McPherson's head, making a perfunctory apology as they did this, noting it was all in the name of standard procedure. Yet there was nothing standard when it came to Chamber #9, this McPherson knew very well.

As the Mercedes veered and turned, McPherson could feel his body shift one way, then another. At times he would pitch forward when the driver hit the brakes, only to recoil back softly against the seat when the braking ended. McPherson knew, of course, that this little joyride was all for show, being a way to obliterate any sense of direction on his part. For that matter, he might have spent the last forty minutes going around and around in one big circle, barring a few variations. It was impossible to say. All McPherson knew was that at long last the Mercedes finally did slow down and turn off the road, proceeding very slowly until it drew near to the loud rumbling sound of a garage door opening automatically. When the rumbling stopped, the Mercedes eased forward, gaining just enough clearance so that the door could close, dropping shut with a metallic clank.

Next, a moment passed in which no one in the car said or did anything. Then a strong hydraulic hum began to reverberate through the vehicle, causing McPherson to experience a subtle tug at his insides, making him realize that the car was perched on a moveable platform that was now dropping downward. The descent continued for some time, but once the desired level had been reached everything grew still. All movement had stopped. Then, very cautiously, the driver accelerated forward a short distance and cut the engine. At this point, the agents chaperoning McPherson escorted him from the car. McPherson realized at once that everything he heard possessed a slight echo, while his nose breathed in a dank coolness. He was in a subterranean hollow of some sort. Guided along by the agents, he was made to walk directly ahead for several steps and then stop, where he waited until the unmistakable sound of an elevator door gliding open could be heard.

Next, with an agent on each side of him, McPherson was ushered into this elevator and another descent began, at which point the dark hood over his head was yanked off. Glancing around, McPherson took a deep breath and noticed that the agents who accompanied him were still wearing their sunglasses. He honestly could not fathom why anyone associated with Chamber #9 would want to see him. His hiatus from political subterfuge and intrigue was already quite long, so long, in fact, that McPherson rightly believed his days as an operative were over, his status being something on the order of dormant, if not defunct. Indeed, to his own mind, he was retired. He was no spring chicken. His hair was more than a little gray. He had drifted away from all the hurly-burly of the espionage world, all that dirty dealing. He had instead become an avid practitioner of Tai Chi, and he had begun to read extensively about primitive man back during the Würm glaciation, Cro-Magnons and Neanderthals. His life, in short, had gradually transitioned onto a different plane. He was even learning how to play the saxophone and could perform an admirable rendition of "La Vie en Rose." So it can be said that McPherson's best days, at least as an intelligence operative, were behind him. And yet those were the days, it must be said, when McPherson would hew to his task with relish, helping to wangle information caches out of compromised hands, acting to undermine incipient regimes, sowing discord among the endless legions of scoundrels rearing their heads. It was tedious work mostly, but it benefitted both from McPherson's analytical skills and his innate paranoia. In short, he found his work ennobling and had taken pride in his accomplishments. All this, however, was years ago. McPherson was so far out of the loop that the advances in technology alone had made him obsolete. He had no cause to stay abreast of technology and had actually not stayed abreast of anything at all. Furthermore, the government which had previously provided him a viable context in which to operate had since been steamrolled into a chaotic mess, a totalitarian soap opera in which a demented dictator was laying everything to wrack and ruin, gutting key institutions and selling out the nation's safeguards, the ship of state foundering in a vicious whirlpool of its making that was sucking it down.

Considering this scenario, McPherson found it highly unlikely that anyone would want to enlist the services of an over-the-hill operative like himself. He was a relic from another place and time, and so he puzzled over why he was brought to Chamber #9, which, for the record, did not so much signify an actual place (there were various Chamber #9s around the world), but rather a highly secret and exclusive channel of communication.

When the elevator stopped and the door opened, one of the agents nodded at McPherson, indicating he should step out, which he did, while the agents remained inside. Once the elevator door had closed, McPherson was left alone in a cavern of grimy brick, dimly lit by an old kerosene smudge pot burning on the floor, the likes of which McPherson had not seen since he was a boy pedaling his bicycle one night on a rural New Hampshire road. Now he watched as the flame from the smudge pot flickered, its smell apparent, its dancing light illuminating a black metal door in front of him. Rapping his knuckles on the door, McPherson then reached for a silver doorknob and turned it, making his way inside.

What greeted McPherson on entering was a haze of diffuse blue light from a source overhead, its glow soft and limited, enabling McPherson to see the faint silhouette of an upholstered chair directly in front of him and another chair at a desk facing it from several feet away. Straining his eyes, he tried to discern if anyone was sitting in the chair that faced him, but could not be sure, the darkness being too shadowy and impenetrable.

"Take a seat, Mr. McPherson," urged a somber voice.

Obliging, McPherson did as he was told. Then he waited, discreetly cleared his throat and watched as a faint glow began to appear, gradually growing brighter, causing his range of visibility to expand, as if someone were turning up a dimmer switch, until a partially visible man could be seen sitting directly before him. Although this man still remained rather deep in the shadows,

McPherson noted that his head was mostly bald, that his remaining hair appeared gray, and that the surface of the desk at which he sat was so polished it gleamed with a murky reflection. The man wore a button-down shirt that was probably white while his hands were out of sight, perhaps folded in his lap. To read his expression was impossible. He might have been serious, weary, bored. What appeared to be bags under his eyes were accentuated by the shadows, and when he spoke his bottom row of teeth was faintly visible, teeth that were even as a straightedge. Who is this guy, wondered McPherson, noticing a dark stain near one of the man's shirt pockets, a stain which, for some reason, McPherson supposed might be gravy.

"Your record of past service is admirable," said the man.

"Thank you."

"Not much activity of late, however," the man additionally pointed out.

"Not for many years," said McPherson, clearing his throat.

"So you're saying you've not had any contacts with anyone from your past involvements for a long time?"

"It's fair to say, yes," McPherson corroborated.

"Are you a loner, Mr. McPherson?"

"I think of myself," paused McPherson, "as a private person."

"Rightly so," said the man. "Tell me," he continued after a moment, "have you done any reading on the Russian Revolution?"

"Yes, some."

"What about on the French Revolution?"

"Yes, some, one very good book actually."

"As far as fascists like Franco and Mussolini go, you do, of course, have a general understanding of these people, I trust?"

"General enough, I would think," McPherson replied.

"Do you believe you could cite certain qualities they shared, things they had in common?"

"To a degree, perhaps."

"Would you agree we're better off to have such fascists nipped in the bud?"

McPherson deliberated and suddenly felt very warm. "I couldn't say in all cases. Variables of historical context might come into play, but generally I'm not partial to fascism in any form."

"Of course," said the man dryly. "But you are familiar with the term *Los Desapacidos*?"

"Yes . . . " said McPherson slowly, hesitating, his voice trailing off.

"Do you believe in the occult, Mr. McPherson?" the man suddenly asked, his voice rising with an almost chipper note.

McPherson, not sure if he had heard correctly, looked at his interlocuter in astonishment. "I beg your pardon?"

"The occult. Supernatural effects, necromancy, spells, conjuring, that sort of thing, do you believe in it?"

"To be honest," admitted McPherson, at a loss, "it's never been a matter of consideration for me."

"So there's nothing in your past then that would predispose you to consider such things?"

McPherson drew a blank, shook his head and answered no, stating that he never had such predispositions, while the man across from him leaned forward a bit, his eyes narrowing. When he again spoke, the man's line of questioning had taken a different tack, his tone of voice suggesting wry satisfaction: "Are you aware of what's going on in the streets of late, the sporadic unrest that keeps cropping up?"

"It's hard to ignore it."

"Across the country various groups and factions have organized, mobilized, taking the nation's leadership to task, getting more and more restive. What do you think motivates these people, their objective, if you will?"

McPherson watched as the man now lifted his hands from under the desk and rested his elbows on its surface, meshing his fingers slowly together. "Although the particulars may vary," McPherson began, "I'd say the baseline objective of these people is to ensure the survival of those rights and principles on which the nation was founded."

"How so?" the man asked, his voice low but decidedly crisp.

"It's clear," McPherson swallowed and then continued, "that they've been exerting political pressure, contradicting the state propaganda, organizing demonstrations. There have been very calculated instances of obstruction, even intimidation, along with very tenacious legal maneuvering."

The man behind the desk did not react, but watched McPherson intently before he spoke. "All of it being a type of recourse with which you are very familiar, wouldn't you say?"

"Not exclusively," McPherson dodged.

"Do you think," the man asked, appearing very grim, "that a person in this country, a citizen or, say, a foreign national, could be made to disappear at the hands of the government?"

McPherson balked. "Possible?"

"No, no, let me rephrase that—probable, rather, do you think it's probable that a person could disappear at the hands of the government?"

"Our government?" asked McPherson, gesturing to himself.

"The prevailing government," said the man with an edge in his voice.

"I . . . "

"Let me make something clear, Mr. McPherson," the man interrupted, his hand rising up as if to deliver a karate chop. "Just so we have an understanding, be aware that there's no need to equivocate. You can be as forthright as you wish. No need to be worried about treading lightly. Say what's on your mind. The details of this conversation are entirely off the record. But just to clear the air and get things out in the open, firstly, people are disappearing, just as they would in a Third-World regime run by a two-bit overlord, and secondly, be aware from here on in that you occupy a rogue chamber, Mr. McPherson."

A jolt of alarm made McPherson stiffen. Suddenly he had to recalculate his entire conversation with this man. Everything was instantly skewed to a new and incomprehensible angle. McPherson tried to rehash everything that had transpired, going over in his mind anything he might have said that could impact his standing with this man. The implications of what he had just been told were mindboggling. A rogue chamber was a sign of staggering fallout, and he had now been thrust right into the midst of it, caught completely off guard and having no idea what was coming next.

"You have a reputation, Mr. McPherson," the man began anew, "of being a divergent thinker. I've looked over your 201 very carefully. You have a knack for coming at situations in a unique way. To the chagrin of stodgy, by-the-book people, you have eschewed the typical way of doing things at times, devising an altogether new means to accomplish your end. People don't like that, Mr. McPherson, it makes them uneasy. In this business, there's always the question of what people like yourself will do next, the unpredictability factor, though no one can quibble with your results. Pat yourself on the back, Mr. McPherson, you've earned much admiration over the years, if somewhat begrudgingly."

"That's probably a fair assessment."

"As I said, you see things differently," the man continued with something telling in his voice, "you construe things from a vantage point which others likely will not have. Consequently, you have delivered results that might not otherwise have been obtained."

"I've always done my best."

"There's no question," acknowledged the man, and then his voiced turned very sharp, as if whetted on a barber's strop. "Have you ever killed anyone, Mr. McPherson?"

43

McPherson felt his jaw tighten. "I don't believe there's any documentation to support that."

Leaning back in his chair, the man studied McPherson, his brow knitting just a notch, the corners of his mouth edging back. "Well said, Mr. McPherson. I believe we're on the same page," the man ventured. "As you know, when an adversary, a foe, someone who compromises our national security is murdered, the ensuing mess can have horrible consequences, a great many geopolitical repercussions, even retribution. It can be quite counterproductive. That's why we react only in self-defense, isn't it Mr. McPherson?"

"It's a policy I've always abided by."

"There's no question. Your years of service, different countries, different situations, they all speak to that fact, even your time in Bulgaria. Yet a curious thing happened there, in Sofia, I believe. I'm sure you're aware of it. A very problematical person suddenly ceased to exist. Our surveillance on him was tight, he was a threat to our people in the field, he had become the beneficiary of some highly classified information. We had considered bribing him, buying him off, but we couldn't kill him, that's not really an option, as you know, and yet a very different result altogether materialized, for the man simply vanished into thin air. It was as if some curious sleight of hand had intervened—Abracadabra! Suddenly he was gone. No evidence of foul play, no bothersome forensics, no witnesses, no trace, so that no one was left with anything to go on but a big black hole of ambiguity. Where did this man go? What happened to him? I don't think we're talking about a self-defense reflex at work here, I don't think so, not when it comes to a corpse disappearing. One would have to be exceptionally resourceful, highly meticulous, very premeditative to pull that kind of thing off. I guess we'll never really know what happened to that fellow. But in the end it was all one and the same," sighed the man, "our national security reaped a clear benefit by his disappearance, as did that of our allies, almost invariably."

"I would think so," agreed McPherson, blandly.

"Speaking of allies," the man continued, "I remember a time when trusted and dependable allies were invaluable complements to our nation's survival, a hedge against myriad threats. That was back during a time when the word reciprocity was not too big to get one's head around, not as it is now, with a total dimwit at large in our leadership, a man abundantly surrounded by other dimwits. I believe you know just how troubling these times are, Mr. McPherson, I need not belabor it. There's a lethal threat undermining the nation, a threat as lethal as it is ugly, sapping our vitality. We grow weak and vulnerable. We have become ripe for contagion, the signs of which appear in the guise of Neo-Nazis, white supremacists, religious Luddites, and various other forms of idiocy that have found a breeding ground in the scourge that hangs over the land, not to mention those people of the over-weaned leisure class who seek a diversion from the ennui of their gated communities and now occupy critical government posts that they know nothing about. The nation is growing feeble, Mr. McPherson, weighed down by incompetence and discord. We have become a sick nation, direly sick, and we need to restore ourselves. But a traditional means of recovery does not seem an option, not with the specific threat we face. It is too inveterate, this threat, too inured, too glutted with reserves of money and power. Perhaps some new approach is needed, a different but perhaps promising solution. Perhaps what is needed is someone who thinks out of the box, a divergent thinker like yourself, so to say, someone who would be able to facilitate such a solution."

McPherson sat stone-faced and wary, and then hung fire: "I'm not sure exactly what you're getting at."

"What I'm getting at is that we will not wait around to see what happens, we will not merely hope for the best and go merrily on our way. We are compelled to resolve our problem, to neutralize it, to do whatever it takes."

"What I think you're advocating," replied McPherson, his words catching in his throat, "what I think you're leading up to, is that we're talking about somebody doing a wet job on you know who."

"That's one way to put it."

"It's impossible, it's crazy, nobody can pull such a thing off, and why bring it up with me?"

"Relax, Mr. McPherson," encouraged the man, adopting a warm and conciliatory air, "no one is talking about anything incriminating, not at all. Your fingerprints don't go anywhere near this thing. Remember, we're trying something new, thinking out of the box, as I've said. All that you're required to do is set things in motion, to oversee things, and keep your fingers crossed."

"But what? What am I setting in motion?"

"Let's call it spooky action from a distance."

"That's a physics term," McPherson pointed out, totally bewildered.

"Correct, it's the notion that matter or particles can be directly influenced void of physical contact. It may technically be physics, but it might just as well pertain to some ancient grimoire, no?"

"I'm not following you."

"You were born and raised in New Hampshire, Mr. McPherson."

"Yes."

"The motto on the New Hampshire license plate is 'Live Free or Die.'"

"It is."

"I've often wondered if the inverse phrasing of that motto might be 'Kill or Live in Chains.'"

"I've never considered it," said McPherson, feeling numb.

"Not that I would have expected you to, Mr. McPherson, but consider this," said the man with an air of finality. "There's a fellow named Norman Modrak. He's a curious sort of person. You owe it to yourself to look him up. He knows about spooky action. You'll receive a brief profile of the man. Don't prejudge him. I suggest you meet with him and hear him out."

"Is he an agent?"

"Not by any means. He has a formal background in anthropology, but he's something of an oddity, an eccentric, a man very familiar with witchcraft, demonology, theurgy. You get the picture, don't you?"

McPherson was dumbfounded.

"Remember, Mr. McPherson," the man continued in a consoling tone, "we're thinking out of the box. When KGB agent Nikolai Khokhlov defected from Russia back in the 1950s, he made it clear the Russian government was very interested in parapsychology. They had serious studies underway in this regard. Metaphysical phenomena were no joke to the Russians and no joke to Khokhlov. He advocated that the United States undertake their own inquiries into such matters, which upset the Russians greatly. They tried to kill Khokhlov in Frankfurt in 1957. Fortunately they failed."

"And so along the way we ended up with our own psychic investigations," interrupted McPherson, "StarGate and other research. I'm generally aware of it, but . . ."

"But what?"

"But has any of it really worked?"

"None of it has been successful to my knowledge."

"Then why pursue this? Why should I make contact with some supernatural charlatan?"

"Careful, Mr. McPherson," the man replied with some impatience, "let me illustrate as clearly as I can what this is all about. Nina Kulagina was a Russian woman from a Red Army tank regiment. She was also a psychic who through sheer mental exertion was able to stop a frog's heart from beating. In the same manner she was able to drive up the heart rate of a human being to a dangerously high level. Do you see where I'm going with this? We should not be too hasty in ruling out options that could provide a potential boon for us. We cannot presume that we've exhausted all avenues of potential, however much of a long shot they seem. Success can be very elusive in any endeavor, and in some cases it may never actually materialize, but there are times when trying is obligatory, in spite of the odds."

"So you want me to contact this Norman Modrak and do what exactly?"

"Find out how he can best help us. Come, Mr. McPherson," the man added, "don't look so beleaguered. I believe there's something to this Norman Modrak that will give us an edge, or otherwise you wouldn't be here."

"But why would he be inclined to help?"

"I suggest you proceed tactfully with this man. These days, people are playing it safe, they're not forthcoming. With regard to Modrak, there are legions of crazed and hypocritical evangelicals and other religious nuts out there who are lining up behind a ruthless dictator and doing it in the name of Jesus Christ. They've been empowered by a madman, as have many others, and they have no tolerance for someone like Modrak with all his New Age ideas and paganism and what have you. People like Modrak are targets, scapegoats for fanatics. He had a rather bad experience in this regard, so he may be inclined to lie low. Don't scare him off, Mr. McPherson, bring him into the fold. Make your own assessment and take it from there. Something tells me he'll sympathize with our cause. We are providing you with a profile of Norman Modrak, and once you read it I think you'll agree that Modrak will likely prove himself a fellow compatriot."

"And what is the cause, exactly?"

"No need to play dumb, Mr. McPherson, you understand the cause better than anyone."

At a loss for words, McPherson stared in befuddlement as the man behind the desk now began to dwindle back into the shadows, the light around the man fading away, a growing darkness falling over him, creeping into the hollows of his eyes and filling the cleft of his chin until his entire face was gradually drawn deeper into nothingness. When the room was in complete darkness, he heard the man's voice one last time. "And by the way," the man added flatly, "good luck with your saxophone playing."

SAL RONGO SPEAKS

Freddy's Bar, Brooklyn, NY

I don't know what to make of anything anymore, Willie, but give me another beer and I'll tell you the way it all got started was I was just minding my own business at the kitchen table cracking open some walnuts and this woman of mine suddenly lays into me like right out of the blue, telling me to *please*, if it's not too much trouble, to *please* fold the hand towels when I'm done wiping my hands in the bathroom because what she wants is to have them nice and folded all the time like we're living in the Waldorf–Astoria or something, if you can fancy that, but me, I'm a practical guy and say it's unsanitary to have damp towels folded up like that because they'll get musty and that you want to spread them out so they'll dry because it's healthier that way, like any doctor will tell you, but the woman, she can't listen to reason, and so all she can say is could I *please* do as she says for once, and I'm like, come on, spare me, because I really can't be bothered with this nonsense when the next thing I know she's harping on how I don't make enough fucking money and maybe I should try getting off my ass now and then and try to get a better job, that's how it is with her, she's going on the warpath with all this tommyrot and I haven't done nothing, Willie, I'm just sitting there cracking walnuts and looking at the newspaper, but she's got it in for me, the woman smells blood, she's just not going to let things lie and before I know it she starts laying into me about how when I get up in the middle of the night to take a piss I never put on my bedroom slippers and so when I'm walking down the hallway to the bathroom I'm tracking up all this cat hair on my socks and then dragging it back into bed with me, because I sleep in my socks, you see, because the woman makes me sleep in my fucking socks on account of my toenail fungus, which she don't want no part of, no way, no how, and so I can't get into bed unless I've got a pair of socks on my feet, because there's no way in hell she wants to catch any of that fungus, and so I got the socks on because of her and so now I'm getting shit from her for wearing what she wants me to wear, the socks! Which I don't really want to wear, Willie, but they're on my fucking feet and so how am I supposed to help it if cat hair gets on them because I don't even think of putting on my bedroom slippers in the middle of the night when I'm all groggy and have to take a piss, I can't be bothered, and anyway the cat itself is her fucking cat to begin with, this big friggin' cat that's like a wooly mammoth and doesn't do nothing but loll around all day and shed hair, and so here's the woman throwing up all this shit in my face about me dragging cat hair into the bed from which is what is her cat and she's the one making me wear the goddamn socks! And so I've had enough, Willie, being that a man can only take so much injustice and so I say to the woman, hold on a minute, like what is it— tarantulas, centipedes, black widow spiders, what is it exactly? To which she scowls at me and asks what in fucking God's name am I talking about? To which I say, the *bug*, the *bug*, that's what I'm talking about, what exactly is the *bug* up your ass? I put it to her, just like that, but on hearing this she blows a fuse and the next thing I know a fucking tea kettle is flying through the air right at my head so that I have to duck so as to not get clobbered, and that's when I say the hell with this shit and go in the other room to watch TV.

Well wouldn't you know it, Willie, I close the door and turn on the TV and all of a sudden here's this news guy talking all about these Civil War statues down South that people are saying should be torn down because they commemorate racists, which no one can deny, I mean, it's a no brainer, because what these Johnny Rebs were fighting for was to keep people in chains so they could have Ol' Black Joe to boss around and do all the work while a bunch of Southern weenies just sat on their asses and drank moonshine and then maybe go screw some slave girl if it struck their fancy, because that was the deal, and what civilized person is going to stand for that kind of bullshit, so it all had to get duked out in a war and the Johnny Rebs got their asses kicked, I mean, they *lost* the friggin' Civil War, and so what don't they get about that? And who the hell goes and puts up a statue of some loser? It's crazy, I mean, are we going to go put up a statue of Wendell Willkie because he lost the election to FDR? We going to put up a statue of General Custer because the Indians kicked the shit out of him? Christ, the next thing you know we'll be putting up statues of the damn stinking Giants because they're the worst team in the whole NFL and couldn't win a fucking game if their lives depended on it. So it all makes no sense, and these jokers down South must have cooties in their hair that have eaten down into their brains for them to be clinging to a bunch of loser statues and belly-aching about a war they lost a hundred and fifty years ago. I mean, take General Pickett at Gettysburg, the guy was an asshole, he leads a charge of thousands of guys across a big open field in broad daylight straight into the guns of these Union soldiers who are just waiting on the other side of that field, hunkered down, rifles cocked and at the ready, while Pickett all the while knows the Union soldiers are there, but he don't give a shit, he just gives the order to charge anyway, and all these redneck boneheads that he's leading jump up and do like they're told, hooting and hollering and giving Rebel yells like they all escaped from a loony bin, while the Union guys can't believe their eyes and just wait for these nitwits to come into range before they start blasting the hell out of them, cutting these chumps down until it turns into a complete slaughter, and this is the kind of crap we're going to glorify with statues? Dumb assholes who think they're entitled to own other human beings? I'm no bleeding heart, Willie, but watching this news report got under my skin, it really did, it pissed me off to hear about these clowns down there in the Land of Cotton whining about their dumb-ass statues, but—that's when like a light goes on in my head and I think of my brother, yeh, you met him, he used to come in here kind of regular for a while, Tony Rongo, a skinny guy with a pointy little beard, he looks like the Devil, but smart, I'm telling you, he just sailed through NYU and got his degree like it was nothing. He's the one who inherited all the brains, not me, but what occurs to me, like flashes through my mind, is that Tony lives down there in the South, in Memphis, he took a job at FedEx where he's a systems analyst or something and makes really good money, you know, but anyway I went to visit him maybe a year or so back just to shoot the breeze and catch up on things, see how he's doing, and I recall one day as we're driving along the Mississippi River we turn into this park to stretch our legs a bit and enjoy the weather, and as we're walking along I see this statue of Jefferson Davis, who was like the president of the whole Confederacy, yep, there he is, up on a big pedestal with his arm sticking out like he's going to tell everybody everything they need to know. But I don't think nothing about that statue ever again, it just went in and out of my mind—until this latest brouhaha about all these Civil War statues, and that's when that light goes on in my head because what it means, Willie, is that I'm going to call in a dare on my brother, Tony, I'm going to spell it out for him, you see, on account of it's a game we play, where like if he dares me to do something and I do it and get away with it, then the next time round it's my turn to have a say and put a dare to him, that's how it works, we been doing this since we were kids, with the first dare I took being to blow a fart in church, for which the old man almost twisted my ear off while Tony was buckled over in the pew in stitches, chewing on his prayer book trying not to laugh. But anyway, the way it is now is that it's my turn to call Tony out on the latest dare, because I did the one previous, I did, which was to show up at a job interview with my clothes on backwards, for which Tony helped me get all ready for, like by zipping up my pants, but with the zipper being like over my ass, you see, and then he buttoned up my shirt and even tied a necktie on me that was hanging down my back, it was totally crazy, but I did the dare and went on the job interview and Tony was in stitches all over again because he got to see these two security guards drag me out the building and throw me into the street, and so you see, even though that was years ago the dare game still goes on. So it was maybe a week or so ago I called Tony and told him at long last I was proposing a dare, and what I do is I remind him of that statue of Jefferson Davis that's out there in that park down in Memphis, and he's listening real close and hearing me out and says, yeh, so what, what about that statue? And I tell him what I'm daring him to do, which is to go to a hardware store and get some buckets of tar, like real gooey tar, like what people seal their driveways with, that kind of stuff, and then I tell him he needs to buy a few pillows, but they've got to be feather pillows, full of real feathers because my dare is to go out late at night and tar and feather that fucking Jefferson Davis statue from head to toe, really nail the bastard and give all those Dixie-whistling dumbbells down there a royal heart attack, that's what I'm telling him, and I can tell Tony's chewing on it, I can tell he's thinking this is a real ballsy dare and that if he pulls it off he'll be like the cat's pajamas because how many people can say they tarred and feathered Jefferson Davis? Ha! It's the dare of a lifetime and Tony says to me to let him think about it, pointing out that the statue is pretty damn high, that it's on a big pedestal, and that he'd have to figure out how to get up on it and hoist the tar up and all of that, and I'm like, sure, sure, Tony, there's no rush, but I know sure as shit the wheels are spinning in his head and he's figuring out how to pull it off, and so we say goodbye and that's that, and I go about my business, but I know if Tony does decide to take me up on this thing he probably won't tell me anyway, that's his style, he'll just creep out of the shadows one night on the sly and have everything planned so he can get to work, and damn, Willie, that's exactly what he did! And God knows it's impossible to say how he pulled it off, but he kind of lassoed a noose around the statue's neck and with the end of the rope he connected himself to this harness he was wearing to hoist himself up, and he had these other ropes on like little pullies that he used to pull up one by one these containers of tar, and when he was done using them he pulled up a sack of feathers, doing it all sneaky and sly and quiet with nobody the wiser. So imagine that, in the wee hours when nobody's around, here's my brother Tony basting that whole statue in tar, smothering it from head to toe, all this glop dripping off it and then he douses it with tons of feathers. God I wish I could have been there, Willie, because that damn statue ended up looking just like the fucking joke that it is, I saw pictures of it on the Internet, while Tony gets away scot free and never even bothers to tell me that he did the deed, because the way I find out is through a news report about how this flake of an Attorney General we've got down there in Washington happened to hear about poor Jefferson Davis and got himself into a major snit, bitching and moaning with a big public statement on the matter that the news outlets all picked up on and ran with, and so the next thing I know is it's all right there in front of me on TV, the Attorney General looking all put out and peeved and reading the riot act about how nobody's going to tolerate this kind of desecration of our hallowed monuments like what happened in Memphis, and how the perpetrators will be brought to justice because our nation's heritage will not be defiled and all this other crap, as if the jerk didn't realize that slavery itself had already defiled our precious heritage, and all the while I'm thinking, buddy, you're a sad-ass lackey for the Dictator, but you're never going to catch up with Tony Rongo, he'll play you like a tin whistle, and I got to say, Willie, this was one dare that just went clear over the top, and that brother of mine he just acts cool as a cucumber, like it's all in a day's work, and good for him, I mean, it's not every day you get to tweak the Attorney General's nose and give him what he's got coming to him, and so here's to the Rongo brothers, a little toast, Willie, go ahead and top off my glass and have one on me!

HORNSWOGGLE HALL

B ehind the tall oak doors of Hornswoggle Hall sits the Dictator. Trapped in a television trance, the Dictator stares glassy-eyed at a rectangular screen rife with the bleat of voices and the endless jump of images. The Dictator has been completely subsumed into this visual vortex, his eyeballs hopscotching about helplessly in their sockets as he stares into a hodgepodge of ever-shifting cuts and close-ups, angles and live feeds, all of which bore into his brain with a spinning whorl that leaves his gray matter teased out into neurofibrillary bolls wispy as cotton candy. Cerebral craters such as these, of course, do not enhance in any way the Dictator's capacity for logic, analysis, deduction or any other higher order of mental functioning, but instead serve only to heighten the herky-jerky ramblings of a scatterbrain, his chronic outbursts so disturbing they have fostered broad speculation that the Dictator's mind is going. Thus, as he continues to stare at the television before him, it is not surprising to see his mouth drop open in the manner of a halfwit, saliva pooling behind his lower lip before overflowing in a glistening thread that stretches downward onto his chin.

Frowzy and bedraggled, the Dictator sits with his shoulders stooped, hunched over in a voluminous bathrobe which he clutches tightly. Given his tousled hair and slack jaw, not to mention the glazed and blankly staring eyes, he can easily pass for a benumbed psychotic sitting in a ward at Bellevue, but lest anyone contend that he is too far gone, let it be noted that once a cable news program gets underway the Dictator exhibits signs of life. Not only do his eyes begin to flicker, but the corners of his mouth also start to twitch, his brow weakly attempting to furrow. Little by little, the fog which has shrouded his mind slowly begins to lift, which enables the Dictator to detect certain words spoken on the television. These words, in fact, he vaguely construes as pertaining to himself, words that are something on the order of bungler, clown, idiot and despot—words that go whipping through his ear canals before sparking the neurons in his temporal lobe, the result of which is that the Dictator gives a snort of irritation, his lips quivering as he struggles to purse them, trying to form the word *who*. And who, indeed, can be making such scurrilous remarks on national TV? The Dictator must find out, and dazed though he may be, he strives to shake off his torpor and grow cognizant again, his effort assisted, in fact, by the television itself, which continues to pepper his ears with demeaning comments—*the man's a numbskull . . . he couldn't run a lemonade stand, much less a nation . . . a total wingding . . . the jerk paid millions of dollars for a fake Renoir, some wheeler-dealer . . . you know, he's a nincompoop . . .*

Tuning in more and more to these outrageous statements, the Dictator grits his teeth, his anger bubbling up as he hisses. Clearly his efforts to regain consciousness are fueled by rage and retribution, his thoughts barrelling through his brain until, of their own accord, they manage to break out into a region of relative clarity, one in which the Dictator's eyes are once again able to focus, allowing him at last to see the man on the TV who spouts such detestable lies, who throws such brazen stones, who spews such unpatriotic venom, a man who, as it turns out, is none other than the Dictator's former Chief of Staff, Prince Penis.

"You fucking dick!" roars the Dictator, at which point he jumps to his feet, his arms flailing to keep his balance, for he is none too steady on his pins, this harrumphing galoot. "You fucking asshole!"

he further bellows, glaring at the television while Prince Penis continues unmolested with his interview . . . *without his money, he's nothing but a sordid piece of white trash . . .* These latest words cause the Dictator to grab his own hair and yank his head to and fro, launching into a tirade of such high-decibel anger that people now come running.

First on the scene to assist the Dictator is the esteemed General Au-Pair. The general is a snappy military man who knows what he is about, a man with a "can-do" attitude, a man of unflinching loyalty, and yet however peppy and self-assured this fellow may be, he is undermined by his curious attire, namely a long red tailcoat befitting a circus ringmaster, a garment that, while stunning in itself, is also perfectly matched with a pair of high, black boots, boots so high and stiff, however, that they chafe the general's knees. Nevertheless, to see the general decked out in such showy regalia is quite a sight, leaving no doubt that this fellow commands, if nothing else, attention, and rightly so, for when it comes to appeasing, persuading, indulging and generally kissing the Dictator's ass, General Au-Pair is the guy for the job.

Seeing that the Dictator is fast heading into a full-blown shit-fit, the general adeptly springs into action. In an effort to calm the Dictator's volcanic fury, he begins to hop about in a sprightly dance, his boots tapping double time while he jabs his fingers into his mouth and pulls his lips awry, producing a goofy face meant to humor the Dictator. Indifferent to these antics, however, the Dictator fulminates with even greater ferocity, his face flushed with fiery rage as he bellows: "Sue that bastard, Prince Penis! He broke the oath of allegiance! Sue him! Sue the rotten piece of shit!" Then, as if fending off an array of phantasmagorical beings that he alone can see, the Dictator begins swinging his arms violently about, thrashing at the air and spinning around abruptly, first one way, then another, as if foes of every kind were closing in on him.

General Au-Pair watches as the Dictator throws wild punches in the air and then flips over the TV. The general also notes the extent to which rage and bitterness have distorted the Dictator's features. The situation has clearly become troublesome, but the general is a man true to his calling, a man of action, a man who grasps the situation and responds, first by stomping his feet and then leaping high into the air, giving a banshee holler as he does so while his arms fly above his head, remaining there as he lands on legs that now stretch out impressively fore and aft on the floor, the man having performed a full frontal split that would be the envy of even the best high school cheerleader. Still holding his arms aloft, the general smiles broadly, flashing the shit-eaten grin of a true brownnoser. Then, from under each cuff of his red topcoat pops a red, white and blue pinwheel, pinwheels that turn slowly at first but then begin to spin briskly, powered by small lithium batteries. Waving these pinwheels all about, the general now gets to his feet and begins a robust cheer: "Great again! Great again! Yes, we are so great again! Great again! Great again! Our nation is so great again! RAH! RAH! RAH! RAH! Two, four, six, eight, who do we appreciate? DICTATOR! DICTATOR! DICTATOR!"

When General Au-Pair's cheer is over, he gazes at the Dictator with sunny and upbeat resolve, as if to win the Dictator back to his senses through sheer, ingratiating nicety. But to no avail. The Dictator yells at the general to take his pinwheels and blow them out his ass.

Uh-oh.

This is serious.

Recognizing the gravity of the situation, the general wastes no time in reaching into his tailcoat and pulling out a walkie-talkie, into which he barks a stark command: "Code Red! Code Red! Pussy Grabber Brigade needed in Hornswoggle Hall! Code Red! Code Red! Pussy Grabber Brigade needed on the double!"

As he awaits critical backup, General Au-Pair makes an attempt to calm the Dictator down. He urges the Dictator to breathe deeply. He commends the Dictator on the vast array of totalitarian decrees he has imposed. He reminds the Dictator that the nation would be lost and at sea without him. He extolls how the Dictator's leadership has embodied the majesty of Alexander the Great, has exemplified the courage of Caesar, has dispensed the wisdom of Solomon. As he praises the Dictator's countless virtues, General Au-Pair places one foot behind the other and leans forward in a low bow, spooling out his wrist in a lavish flourish, lauding the Dictator profusely, declaring him a God among men, a messiah of the masses, a man who towers above all others in the exalted pantheon of politics. Utterly in earnest, the general even heaps praise on the size of the Dictator's hands, boasting how truly blessed every man, woman and child is to be entrusted to such big, beautiful and bona fide hands. Then, dropping to his knees, the general venerates the very ground the Dictator walks on, prostrating himself, kissing the carpet beneath the Dictator's feet, tasting the fibers of broadloom as they brush against his lips, this while the Dictator, dumbbell that he is, quiets down and actually eats up all this bullshit. However, the hiatus in the Dictator's raving is short lived, for although the Dictator has thrown his television to the floor, it continues to broadcast, and in the silence that ensues once General Au-Pair has concluded his paean, the following news report can be heard.

"We go now to Cleveland, Ohio, where thousands of people have gathered at Fort Huntington Park holding pikestaffs on which they have stuck life-size replicas of the Dictator's head. The crowd has been growing in size since late afternoon and at any minute will begin marching for a rally in front of the county courthouse. The mood is one of visible outrage in response to the recent abduction and murder of a student from Cleveland State University who had been advocating for the preservation of First Amendment rights.

This is a very tense situation, and as the crowd in Fort Huntington Park grows so does the police presence. As our live footage shows, this is a very turbulent gathering, with the marchers growing more confrontational, their chants growing louder in these past few minutes."

The Dictator freezes in his tracks as he hears this report, while the aforementioned chants begin ringing in his ears—"He has no heart! He has no soul! This fascist pig, his head must roll!" Fuming for a moment, the Dictator lets loose a blood-curdling shriek, a cry so unhinged it causes General Au-Pair to stick his fingers in his ears, the general looking dismal, for his efforts to assuage the Dictator have failed. Once again in the throes of a maniacal rage, the Dictator gnashes his teeth as rivulets of foam run down his chin. Picking up a vase, he smashes it into pieces. He then moves on to his next target, a lampshade that he grabs and chews on, tearing it asunder with his teeth before crushing it in a bear hug. As if possessed by demons, the dumb lummox fills the room with a guttural wail, continuing his rampage with frenzied zeal, flipping over a table, throwing a brass horse into the wall, knocking a marble bust of Socrates off a pedestal, the clash and clatter of his destruction reaching a full crescendo until he stops, catches his breath and heaves a Chippendale chair high into the air where it lands amid the loops and filigrees of an ornate chandelier, the chair hanging there tenuously, swaying to and fro amid the tinkling of myriad crystals.

Seeing that the Dictator has popped a major gasket, General Au-Pair again does his best to distract the madman, first by producing three colorful balls that he furiously juggles while singing several refrains from "I'm Just Wild about Harry," an offkey overture that for some reason mystifies the Dictator, but only briefly, causing the general to segue into his second act, hustling himself into a one-man line dance as he loudly sings the lyrics of a song called

"Chattahoochee," the general being at wits' end and greatly relieved when the Pussy Grabber Brigade at last bursts into the room.

This Pussy Grabber Brigade consists of eight tall and muscular men wearing matching white pants and shirts along with white soft-soled shoes. Quickly arranging themselves in a loose circle around the Dictator, the men begin to exhibit deft and extravagant movements that are reminiscent of ballet. In the midst of these serene and enticing movements, one member of the Pussy Grabber Brigade produces a red velvet pouch with a braided gold drawstring. Reaching into this pouch, he pulls out a handful of pale blue tablets that he attempts to toss into the Dictator's mouth, an endeavor that continues as another brigade member readies a last resort, a 15-gauge hypodermic needle whose payload is a syringe full of Haldol.

"Keep him calm! Keep him calm!" urges General Au-Pair, on tenterhooks as he crouches like a panther, his red tailcoat and high black boots a stunning foil to the men in starched white who continue to stretch and weave about, performing their arcane hoodoo.

However, to gain sway over the Dictator is no mean task, for a crazed and entitled buffoon such as he does not readily countenance mere mortals, especially those who dare insinuate themselves on his behalf, no more than he would countenance the cadres of resistance fighters and agitators taking aim at his nepotism, his cronyism, his deceit and his gleeful trashing of inalienable rights. To the Dictator's mind, the discontented riffraff who oppose him are part of that larger scourge that includes black people, Mexicans, liberals, Muslims, people who read books and faithful husbands, all of them comprising a cloud of disgusting flyspecks that obstructs the Dictator's privileged view of the world, a dark cloud, indeed, a repulsive cloud of people who are of no consequence and never will be, a despicable horde made all the more despicable for their pathetic lack of money.

In no mood to tamp down his fury or see even a glimmer of reason, the Dictator, like a Sumo wrestler, now jumps into a broad squat, his feet thudding on the floor, his jaws quivering as he clenches his fists with white-knuckled rage, his face flushed lobster red while his blood pressure skyrockets. As for those in the Pussy Grabber Brigade, they aren't going down without a fight. They can see that the Dictator has flipped his lid, that he's going to pieces, that his eyes gleam with wild paranoia. They realize that this is one demented buckaroo they've got on their hands, watching as the Dictator crouches down into a tight ball, glancing furtively every which way, audibly sucking in a deep breath and then screaming at the top of his lungs, demanding he be given his tinfoil hat, insisting that the liberal news media is assaulting his mind with secret brain beams transmitted to his head through the wall sockets.

"Relax, Your Excellency, relax," responds a member of the Pussy Grabber Brigade. "Everything is fine. Everything is under control, Your Excellency. There's no need to worry. Just take a look at that man over there. He's got something special for you, Your Excellency, just look what he's got for you."

Pointing his finger, the brigade member indicates in which direction the Dictator should turn, but the Dictator, shifty-eyed and hesitant, suspects a trick and will not comply. Stuck in a funk, he gets lost in the muddle of his thoughts, unsure of what to do until, after much encouragement, he finally does turn his head—by miniscule degrees—witnessing a sight that brings a smirk of great pleasure to his lips.

Greeting the Dictator's eyes is another starched white member of the Pussy Grabber Brigade, but what sets this man apart from his peers is that he holds a long fishing pole of flexible graphite, a pole from which dangles, by means of a thin vinyl cord, an unbelievably lifelike representation of a woman's vagina, a pussy made from phenomenally soft and supple CyberSkin. Indeed, the pussy in question is altogether uncanny in terms of its resemblance to the real thing, having actually been molded from the real-life genitalia of one of the nation's hottest porn stars, Lucy Lustgarden. With pussies being one of the Dictator's favorite things to grab, it is not surprising that he is wholly captivated by the pussy dangling before him, the Dictator ogling it to the point of absolute fixation. Growing lightheaded, even woozy, he gazes at the blushing folds of the labia and the little chickpea of the clitoris. With his mouth dropping open, he mumbles incoherently and begins to drool, his hands reaching upward eagerly, his fingers opening and closing. Clearly he wants to grab the pussy, but is thwarted by the man with the fishing pole, who keeps Lucy Lustgarden's private parts just beyond the Dictator's reach, moving the pole from side to side while the Dictator follows it as if hypnotized, riveted to this tantalizing piece of snatch as if nothing else in the whole world mattered.

To everyone's relief, the efforts of the Pussy Grabber Brigade seem to be paying off. The mere presence of the CyberSkin pussy holds the Dictator in check. He is decompressing. He is stabilizing. He shows signs that soon he will be capable of being re-directed. General Au-Pair, in fact, jumps in the air and clicks his heels together, so relieved is this lackey that the Dictator is once again on the road to being manageable. But danger still lurks. As per protocol, if the Dictator shows he can compose himself and demonstrate a capacity for self-control, he is always allowed to finally and actually grab the pussy that he so desires, being allowed to squeeze it so that the plastic squeaker embedded inside it will respond. To permit this indulgence is a matter of bargaining in good faith, so to say, a matter of positive reinforcement, though there have been times when the effect of such reinforcement has been too positive, when grabbing the pussy has sent the Dictator into such delirious raptures that he has completely broken down all over again, which is exactly what is about to happen.

So then, with everyone satisfied that the Dictator has been drawn into a state of modest equilibrium, the Pussy Grabber Brigade consents to give him his due, and the man with the graphite fishing pole begins to lower—very slowly—the striking facsimile of Lucy Lustgarden's provocative pussy. As the pussy draws ever nearer to the Dictator's grasp, the Dictator begins to pant, even wheeze as if in respiratory distress, his hands shaking as they reach overhead, his fingers twitching in anticipation, this while the other members of the Pussy Grabber Brigade, in an attempt to keep the Dictator pacified, create a soothing background susurrus by repeating the word pussy over and over—*pussy, pussy, pussy, pussy, pussy*—the goal of their dulcet tones being to gently calm the Dictator, everyone watching as he gets ready to take in hand the pretty pudendum dangling above him—when suddenly he leaps up and grabs it, fiercely, like a starving man thrown a hock of meat, the Dictator now throttling his prize in a crude display of selfish possession, hugging the pussy to his chest as he squeezes it and squeezes it and squeezes it, activating the squeaker within, the Dictator giggling maniacally as he squeezes it more and more.

Squeak-SQUEEEAK!

Squeak-SQUEEEAK!

Squeak-SQUEEEAK!

Almost immediately it is obvious that the Dictator is once again flirting with all-out madness. The dazed and far-off look in his eyes says as much, as does the over-zealous way in which he clutches and squeezes the fake pussy—*Squeak-SQUEEEAK! Squeak-SQUEEEAK!* The more he squeezes it, in fact, the more this high-rolling pussy grabber wants to squeeze it. There is no question that the man's bizarre and rabid urge to grope this fleshy squeeze toy is consuming every last shred of his wits. Indeed, to the trained eye of General Au-Pair, the Dictator is careening toward a la-la land of complete insanity. Something must be done right away, the general realizes, some urgent action must be taken, and yet he knows that to pry the pussy from the Dictator's hands by force will result in grave and savage violence, likely sending the Dictator into convulsions of distress from which he may not recover. Thus, the general has no choice but to concede that the Dictator's one and only hope now lies with his marital sidekick, Primo Bimbo. And so, with great martial muster, the general reaches into his red tailcoat and again pulls out his walkie-talkie, brusquely giving the order to commence operation Bimbo Bombshell, his last resort.

With bated breath, everyone in the room now awaits Primo Bimbo. General Au-Pair has plopped himself down into a plump leather armchair, biting his lower lip as he clasps his hands together. The Pussy Grabber Brigade, meanwhile, continues their soft, mantra-like repetition of the word pussy, still attempting to temper the Dictator's trembling over-excitement—while the Dictator, himself, for his part, remains oblivious, his hands working fiendishly as he kneads his prize pussy as if it were a lump of dough.

Squeak-SQUEEEAK!

Squeak-SQUEEEAK!

Beyond Hornswoggle Hall, news of the Dictator's plight is now travelling fast. Among his inner circle, a flurry of tweets and texts, calls and shouts all go zipping through an exclusive grapevine. To be sure, it is not every day that one gets to see one of the biggest idiots alive reduced to a state of even greater idiocy, and so even before Primo Bimbo arrives a whole vaudeville act of mooching parasites comes prancing into Hornswoggle Hall, all of them rubber-necking for a curious look at His Excellency, all of them eager to show their heartfelt concern and deep worry. First among these toadies is Lucre Munchkin, Secretary of Greed, who stands wrapped head to toe in large sheets of newly printed $100,000 bills. Totally encased, the man has essentially been transformed into a green paper cylinder, his head perched atop it like that on a Pez dispenser, except that the treats popping from his jaws are confections of the most extreme flattery:

"*Sieg Heil*, Mein Excellency! You will be well soon enough. Your affliction will pass, and then we shall line our pockets. Remember that by forgetting history we are committed to repeat it, creating even greater atrocities, especially in the name of greed, Mein Excellency. Money! So I must tell you that I have forfeited every shred of decency and principle I might ever have possessed in order to serve in your glorious reign of wealth and riches. You will get well, Mein Excellency, trust me, you will recover from this little setback, and then together, together, you and I, we will gouge the poor, drain the middle class, deprive the ill and handicapped, and, yes, brainwash the youth until we have a nation of *dummkopf-jugend*, stripling ninnies who grovel to embrace your lies and do your bidding—just like the fools in Alabama and Kansas and other jerkwater places, where people would rather listen to empty rhetoric than face hard facts, where people would gladly cut off their noses to spite their pathetic faces rather than denounce their great Dictator. And they do this no matter how badly we bleed them dry, no matter how badly we sell them out. And why? They are dumb, Mein Excellency, we want them dumb! We want to sell them out, and we will sell them out, you and I both, and anyone who tries to stop us, any of those reprehensible men of principle who cannot be bought, I will send them to the gallows! To the gallows! Every last one! How better to achieve loyalty than to utterly contrive it? And by doing this, we will be the masters, Mein Excellency, the whole population will be putty in our hands, so think how we will exploit everyone, think what it will mean for our genetically superior monied class. Why it will mean more money! More money all around, Mein Excellency! More control, Mein Excellency! The membership dues at your Golden Putter Golf Club will go up and up and up. Million-dollar membership fees, Mein Excellency! The rich will get so much richer. We will put into place the new Reich of Feudalism, with you as its vanguard and I your humble servant. My signature that appears on these bills I am wrapped in is printed in ink, but the spirit of that signature is writ in blood! Blood, Mein Excellency! Blood and money—and soil too if it is prime real estate—these are the cornerstones of the new Reich of Feudalism. And so the hour is at hand, you must get well, Mein Excellency. You must pull through. You will lead us forth to crush the petty notions of truth, justice, liberty and equality. Yes, we will crush them, for in you alone is manifested the bright and glowing beacon of our greatness, and through your paramount leadership we will obtain the key to great and unabashed criminal wealth, wealth for the exemplary chosen few, like you, like me, like all those who will pay a million dollars to be members of the Golden Putter Golf Club. We will be rolling in money, Mein Excellency, and in turn we will graciously endow the poor slobs of this nation with the sacred privilege of servitude, strife, destitution and despair. Don't forget, Mein Excellency, *arbeit macht frei*! *Sieg Heil*, Mein Excellency, *Sieg Heil*!"

Squeak-SQUEEEAK!

Squeak-SQUEEEAK!

By now a large crowd has gathered around the Dictator, a restless assemblage of advisors, ambassadors, *aides-de-camp* and corporate donors, their ranks swelling with committee heads, CEOs, billionaire confidantes as well as on-call burger flippers and fascist oinkers from the Dictator's rallies. All have joined the fray, all of them shouting and clamoring as they muscle Secretary Munchkin out of the way, knocking him to the ground, the green cylinder of $100,000 bills now rolling on the floor where it gets trampled underfoot by everyone pushing nearer to the Dictator, Secretary Munchkin cursing a blue streak as everyone else cries out loudly, bidding up their stakes for an audience with His Idiocy.

It's a harum-scarum scene here in Hornswoggle Hall, but before matters get even more out of hand one of the large oak doors leading into the room swings open, and then, cool and haughty, in steps a man of very regal bearing. Wearing black tights and a blue tunic tied with a flaming red sash, this man pauses and looks grimly at the people before him. Next, while standing very erect, he raises a long brass trumpet to his lips. A small banner displaying the Dictator's coat of arms hangs down from this trumpet, and as the man blows into it the room fills with clear and rousing notes, notes of such force that they command complete attention. Instantly, all the peevish chatter and scuffling that surround the Dictator stop. The Dictator himself stops squeezing Lucy Lustgarden's pussy, and in the somber and reverent silence that follows all eyes turn to the man with the long trumpet, while behind him Primo Bimbo suddenly appears, walking into the room on a pair of gleaming titanium stilts.

Primo Bimbo, in fact, has arrived straight from a naked photo shoot in which she has been salaciously intertwining with supermodel Fifi Sweatlick, the two women bearing buns and boobs galore like the good tarts that they are while frolicking in lewd abandon in, around and on top of a sparkling new cherry red Lamborghini convertible. Now, however, duty has called and Primo Bimbo must stand by her man, providing in this case, vital succor.

Perched high on her titanium stilts, Primo Bimbo makes a dramatic entrance into the room, her gait steady, though somewhat halting on account of the exaggerated stride of the stilts. Feasting their eyes upon her, everyone present at once fawns over the woman and her death mask of hermetic makeup. They see the sunken dustbowl of her cheeks and wonder at her eyes, empty and dim and lost behind eyelashes that open and shut languorously, like two Venus flytraps overdone with mascara. Yes, this is Primo Bimbo and none other, her hair expertly cut and layered, teased and flipped, adhering to its roots by an exotic alchemy of conditioners, sprays, lotions and oils, thousands of dollars worth, actually. Her attire, however, at least on this occasion, is rather modest, for in the rush to get to Hornswoggle Hall she has quickly donned a black silk kimono, quite simple in and of itself, yet tailormade and sporting cuffs trimmed with fur from one of the few remaining red wolves left on the planet, a wolf gleefully shot and killed by the Dictator's own heir apparent.

Of course, it is under this kimono where things begin to get interesting. Although Primo Bimbo has neglected to put on a bra for expediency's sake, the French crotchless panties that she wears have been deliberately chosen, being necessary for the task that is forthcoming. And while these crotchless panties have also facilitated an occasional quickie with Brutus, Primo Bimbo's muscular bodyguard, and at times have allowed for spontaneous nookie with her private sous chef, Marcel, one should not pass judgement on Primo Bimbo, especially given that the Dictator has, for a long time now, been ignoring his conjugal duties, the man seeming to have permanently slipped into Mr. Softee mode.

Running up to Primo Bimbo, General Au-Pair delivers a clipped but courteous greeting before gallantly sweeping out his arm, extending it in the direction of the Dictator. As if magically controlled by this gesture, the crowd around the Dictator immediately parts down the middle, creating a clear aisle through which Primo Bimbo can walk. Indeed, one of her titanium stilts is already swinging forward, the other following in a fluid gleam of metal, each stilt landing with a light thud as Primo Bimbo struts boldly on. Her expression, as everyone can see, is cold and distant, that of a woman bound by her sacred obligation to protect the deep pockets of her sugar daddy, a woman who knows what's in it for her, a woman who knows that the role she must play is very much like adopting a pose, no different than any pose she might strike as a supermodel, an art in which she has had much practice, this stylish and moneygrubbing poseur.

Dutybound then, Primo Bimbo draws nearer to the Dictator one step at a time, her stilts moving with all the precision of a spider walking on its web. Aloof and disaffected, Primo Bimbo can't be bothered to even glance at the Dictator. She would rather ignore this sorry-looking man who sits coddling a fake pussy, but in the end it is she who must provide the "ablution" that will revive him. Thus, to get into position, she now begins to pivot, her strides having a more lateral swing to them as she attempts to straddle the Dictator's head, closing in on him, then backing up, then closing in again, adjusting her alignment a few degrees at a time until at last the Dictator's head lies directly below her crotch.

As she looks down at her dearly betrothed, Primo Bimbo now asks a question: "You want for I to piss on your head like dirty little Russian *devotchka*, darling?"

"Ug-ug! Hubba-hubba!" blurts out the Dictator, becoming more attuned to reality simply on hearing this enticing proposition.

"You want maybe to be my pretty little chamber pot, huh, darling?" she continues.

"Ug! Oooooo-wheeee!" cries the Dictator.

"Say it, darling, say you want to be my pretty little chamber pot. Then I piss on your head."

"Ah . . . Ah . . . I . . ."

"If you no say what I want, then all the golden showers go down the drain."

"No-no!"

"Yes, darling, you must say it. Say what I want to hear."

The Dictator, shaking violently in anticipation of the delights that Primo Bimbo promises, struggles to form the words demanded of him, but all that comes out are the sounds a blithering idiot: "Ahrgo-bluh-bleh-plish-plochot!"

"If you no say it properly, darling, then I guess I go piss on Brutus, my bodyguard."

"Noooooooo!"

"Then say it, darling, say what I want to hear, what we all want to hear, say it! Say it or I go piss on Brutus! Big, muscular Brutus!"

"I . . . I . . . I'm your . . . p-p-p-pretty . . . I'm your . . . pretty little chamber pot!"

"Darling!"

Relaxing her sphincter urethrae muscle, Primo Bimbo now unleashes a long, hot whizz of urine directly onto the Dictator's head, his eyes blinking away hot trickles, his hair plastered down flat and dripping, so that in no time at all he appears to have just been submerged on a ducking stool. Yet more to the point, in very short order he is much more himself again, looking about meanly and ready to attack anyone who might serve as a handy scapegoat for his rage. Coupled with his familiar fury, there is also a detectable and perverted air of satisfaction, something that prompts a sigh of relief from General Au-Pair.

Hubba-hubba.

NORMAN MODRAK

A s McPherson walked along the street to Norman Modrak's house, he glanced up to see the moon scumbled by clouds quickly gliding by, riding high on a wind that mussed his hair and made him feel young again, for as he listened to the wind rushing through the trees he recalled how as a young boy he had climbed to the top of a tall birch during a windstorm, holding fast to the branches as they swayed and tossed him to and fro, pretending he was far out on a sailing ship, high in the crow's nest with white sails billowing all around him, the pitch and roll of the ocean taking him far away.

Aware that such reveries were becoming more common of late, McPherson began to wonder why. He wondered why he was indulging in thoughts from a carefree and happier time and if such thoughts were symptomatic, if they provided a kind of solace in light of the fact that the nation's leader was a reckless bonehead who milled about fingering the codes to an arsenal of nuclear weapons as if he were fondling a lucky rabbit's foot. This was but one of the many sinister shadows the Dictator had cast across the land. Another such shadow concerned the fact that although the Dictator was born too late for duty at Auschwitz, it was clear he derived a sadistic pleasure from persecuting disadvantaged human beings, the horrible consequences of which he construed as righteous and just, providing him a metric by which to gauge his chronically challenged manhood.

That more and more people grew uneasy and disgusted in the wake of such lunacy was understandable. The Dictator was nuts, after all, an imbecile given to such warped and nefarious behavior that it was not surprising to find a faction within his own government that was now determined to put him to bed with a shovel, a task that fell, at least for the moment, to McPherson.

On at last reaching the residence of Norman Modrak, McPherson looked up to see an old Four Square house that had known better days. One of the upper story shutters had dropped to the ground and a gutter which had torn away from a corner of the house was sagging. On the ground floor, a few lights were on. Leading up to the house were an array of moss-laden slates that caused McPherson to momentarily lose his footing, but as he climbed the steps to the front door what caught his attention was his own shadow weirdly flung this way and that due to an overhead light on a chain swinging in the wind.

After glancing at his watch to make sure he was on time, McPherson looked for a doorbell. Not finding one, he gave the door before him three solid raps. As he waited, the house seemed unduly quiet and the hour even later than it was, but before long the door swung open and Norman Modrak appeared. He was a tall rail of a man wearing flimsy black trousers and a black turtleneck, over which a shapeless tweed jacket stood out mainly for looking like it had been slept in. Inviting McPherson to enter, Modrak gave his visitor a courteous nod and then moved back a step into the vestibule. He had a head of loose brown curls that were turning silver, while his face, which seemed more worn by weather than age, was long and ruddy. As the two men shook hands, McPherson took note of Modrak's eyes, which were a soft blue topaz.

Also catching McPherson's eye was the oriental rug beneath his feet, whose intricate patterns of red and gold, although faded, were impressive nonetheless.   Taking McPherson's jacket, Norman

Modrak hung it on a large hall tree of dark oak. It was with more than a little surprise that McPherson noticed a stuffed crow sitting atop the hall tree. The crow, wary even in death, seemed to possess a vigilance more finely tuned than anything a man could muster, and while McPherson considered such a decoration strange, he was all the more stunned when the crow suddenly flapped its wings and flew forth over his head, gliding off into another room.

"That crow's alive," McPherson couldn't help exclaiming.

"And a very agreeable companion," put in Modrak.

Norman Modrak then led McPherson down the hallway and turned to the right, opening a glass-knobbed door that led into a cluttered study. On one wall a brick fireplace glowed with fading embers, the room having a smoky smell on account of the chimney flue needing to be closed because of the wind. Over the fireplace hung an old engraving of two bare beech trees, its paper yellowed and wavy behind the glass, while flanking the print on each side was an iron sconce depicting a roaring lion's head, each sconce having two flaring arms that held thick stubs of white candles. Across the top of the fireplace mantel were several hardcover books with antiquated bindings. Some of the books stood upright between bookends while others lay flat atop one another, while along all four walls of the room there were hundreds more books packed to overflowing, stacked on shelves that reached right to the top of a high plaster ceiling spidered with cracks. Notably, on one of the shelves, there was an obvious gap among the books where several bottles of old Port and Madeira stood, and in a far corner of the room, under a window whose dark green drape was drawn, a mahogany desk stood so awash with papers, notebooks, correspondence and scattered documents that it appeared to have been shipwrecked and left where it lay.

At Norman Modrak's request, McPherson took a seat in a plush armchair before the fireplace, with Modrak settling into a similar-looking chair, the angle of each man's chair such that he could ponder the glowing embers on the hearth while easily engaging the other face to face. To McPherson's mind, the whole scenario had a peculiar and inexplicable gravity about it, something he could not quite put his finger on, and which was further driven home by Norman Modrak's crow, which now flew into the room and bounced several times on the floor with its wings extended.

"Any trouble finding the place?" asked Modrak, breaking the ice.

"No, none at all, it's a very quaint little town. I did some walking through it, admiring all the old homes."

"Yes, like stepping into a bygone era," acknowledged Modrak with apparent satisfaction. "I feel very much at home here. But as to your visit, on the phone you talked of using my services, of working toward some mutual end. I must say I'm curious as to what you had in mind."

"I was advised to see you," McPherson began, but then found himself distracted by the crow, which now flew up to perch atop the fireplace mantle, the crow's glinting eye meeting McPherson's. "I was advised," McPherson began again, shrugging off the crow and telling himself to get on with it, "that you might be of some assistance."

"I'm at your service," said Norman Modrak affably enough, cocking his head in a manner not unlike the crow's.

"To begin with," stated McPherson, trying not to sound too forward, "I learned that, if I understand it correctly, you were taken to court for putting a curse on somebody."

"That's true," answered Norman Modrak with a smile, "but of course there's no physical evidence with a curse."

"Did it work, the curse?"

"Are you from the press, by any chance?" asked Norman Modrak, taking McPherson's measure very closely.

"No, not at all, but I'm interested in your expertise, what you do and whether it's psychic or more rightly in the realm of magic."

"I see."

"And as a starting point," McPherson added, "I was interested in that court case."

"Then let me explain. I was taken to court, you're correct, but no curse was involved on my part. The judge threw the whole thing out."

"But there must have been some basis, some grounds for the whole thing to have escalated to a court of law."

"No basis at all," countered Norman Modrak with an almost whimsical air. "Look, there was a case out in Oklahoma where the principal of a high school suspended a girl for fifteen days because he came to the conclusion she had put a curse on a teacher. The teacher became quite ill and had to be hospitalized. The girl ended up being ostracized by her classmates. The hysteria, the sensationalism of it all, got out of control. It was a little microcosm of Salem all over again. The girl's parents started a lawsuit against the school district seeking damages, while the school lawyer was so utterly dumbfounded by the whole thing he couldn't even comment. It's true the girl had been reading some books on Wicca, which she had checked out from the school library, but what is more to the point is that people have a dogged persistence in believing what they want to believe, whether it's believing that they have been cursed by a witch or that someone *is* a witch."

"I don't understand," said McPherson. "You sound like you're dismissing all this, but this is what you're known for. There are references to you online. You're cited in different articles. There are all kinds of links on the Internet. You concern yourself with the supernatural, the black arts, sorcery, white magic, too. It's no secret. You have a reputation for it, and it's all in the public domain, as I'm sure you know."

"I'm not dismissing anything unless it needs to be dismissed," clarified Modrak. "I'm sure you're aware there's a whole cottage industry that's cropped up around the occult these days, but the heart of the matter does not concern drawing pentagrams on the floor or lighting black candles or putting on a monk's cowl and chanting incantations. It doesn't work that way, and that girl in Oklahoma is certainly no witch, even if people think she is, even if *she* thinks she is. All these gothic predilections, a lot of people buy into it, and let's face it, it might be exciting to fancy oneself a witch, but none of it adds up to very much. However," said Norman Modrak, his voice lowering, "there have been things connected to some other realm that I've been forced to acknowledge, and people, for the sake of open-mindedness, should be allowed to follow their inclinations, including that girl in Oklahoma. Questing after life's mysteries and possibilities is more important than being rocked to sleep with pat answers. One must live in a state of uncertainty and possibility, that's what fires the quest to enlighten oneself, that's how we expand ourselves."

"But if you're acknowledging something," pointed out McPherson, "aren't you quantifying it as fact?"

"Absolutely."

"So what you're saying," pressed McPherson, his eyebrows going up, "is that you do have a basis for believing in the occult."

Norman Modrak leaned back in his chair and put his hands behind his head. "Yes," he answered with a certain finality, "though I don't really like the word occult."

"What is your basis for believing?"

Biting his lower lip, Norman Modrak studied McPherson before concluding, "You're not my usual clientele, you know. I can tell you don't believe one whit in any of this. That's okay, however."

McPherson made as if to protest, but Norman Modrak waved him off: "No need to explain yourself, but it's a chilly night and I tend toward a glass of Port on a chilly night. Would you care to join me?"

Thinking it politic to accept, McPherson did so, and in short order Norman Modrak place before him a glass brimming with ruby Port, an action which prompted the crow atop the mantle to suddenly swoop down, landing directly beside the glass, its head tilting to and fro as it eyed the Port from one angle, then another.

"Shoo!" commanded Modrak, adding, "He's got something of the magpie in him, I believe, a curious fellow, and very dignified."

McPherson watched as the crow's wings now fanned out and the bird lifted off into the air with such graceful ease it appeared to levitate, rising up again to its perch on the mantel.

"It may interest you to know," said Norman Modrak, sipping his Port and pursing his lips with satisfaction, "that I majored in anthropology, even went on to get an advanced degree. While studying at the University of Pennsylvania, I volunteered to do field work up in Ontario one summer. There's an old longhouse up that way, and as soon as I entered it I got this feeling, a feeling that chilled me to the bone. I mean I really got it, and I realized that as impressive as some structures are—Westminster Abbey, Santa Maria del Fiore, Notre-Dame—all of which I've seen, these structures are testaments to man, to his ingenuity, his aptitudes, his grandiosity, perhaps. Oh, they purport to be testaments to God, but they're not. But that longhouse," said Norman Modrak, wagging his finger, "inside it there was something bigger, deeper, more all-encompassing. I felt it in some nether region beneath my heart, maybe my soul. But what really took me for a loop was that my colleagues and I had an opportunity that summer to meet an Indian shaman, a Mohawk, I believe, and within the walls of that longhouse one evening, with a drum and a rattle, that shaman beat out a rhythm and worked himself up into a deep, quivering trance. I'd never seen anything like it. He took himself to the brink of death. We were all mesmerized watching this man, and if there is such a thing as being able to feel an aura as opposed to seeing it, then that's what happened. I felt this man's aura pass right through me, a stream of raw energy that was in possession of us all, daunting and as real as I'm sitting here."

"But isn't your experience highly subjective?" asked McPherson, watching Modrak's every move.

"One could say that, but even though the people around me were of a scientific bent, as was I back then, we all felt it, all of us."

McPherson pondered a moment. "But how does this energy, providing I buy into what you're saying, how does it square with the supernatural?"

"Now that," confided Norman Modrak, looking like the cat who ate the canary, "is why you had to be there. This shaman, whatever kind of medium he was, was tapping into energy that could be uplifting beyond belief or decidedly deadly, it's a matter of directing it. That's what shamans do."

"So what you're getting at," said McPherson, trying to work matters out in his mind as he spoke, "is that certain people, through some power, some ability, are capable of harnessing this energy, whatever it is, which in turn leads to—what? A spell or incantation, some means to an end?"

"You're half right," complimented Modrak, edging forward in his chair. "You're right about the energy, but there are no spells, there are no incantations. Such things might act as an inducement, and certain rituals might get you started on your way, but the key is purity of purpose in a mind of such clear penetration it can accommodate the necessary energy. Spells and words are actually handicaps. The key to directing this energy is to purge language from the mind altogether, to get rid of it. Clementine of Alexandria believed that words were too trifling for beseeching the gods. In other words, to tap into that realm of the other worldly one needs to get on a different plane. It's not the plane of language. It's a plane beyond us, the plane a shaman goes to by means of a trance."

"I'm not sure I follow you," said McPherson, sipping his Port.

"You'd follow me better," suggested Norman Modrak, "if you told me exactly why you're here. What is this mutual concern that you mentioned on the phone?"

Nodding, McPherson put down his Port glass and decided to cut to the chase: "If possible, if there's any efficacy behind it, I need to put a curse on someone."

Hearing this, Norman Modrak's eyes grew wide. Then he stroked his chin, apparently giving the matter some thought. "What puzzles me is that you don't believe in any of this and yet you seek my services."

"Let's just say that you came highly recommended."

"By whom?"

"I can't say," McPherson hesitated, feeling a bit foolish, "meaning that I really don't know. This person chose to remain anonymous."

Staring in disbelief, Norman Modrak took a while to reply. "I'm not used to such high intrigue, but clarify matters. You want a curse put on someone, correct?"

"Yes."

"And the outcome of this curse, what might it be? Illness? Financial ruin? A marriage falling apart? Maybe no more than someone's hair falling out? People can get colorful with their requests when it comes to curses. You must have something in mind."

"Death."

Modrak suddenly looked hard at McPherson and slowly reached for his Port glass, nursing a long sip. "Are you on the level?" he asked.

"Can it be done?"

"Death is a tall order."

"But is it possible?"

"That depends on who's executing the curse."

"But I thought it would be you," said McPherson, taken by surprise.

"Let me explain," cautioned Norman Modrak. "Among those of us who take these matters seriously, to curse someone to death is an issue of stark moral and personal concern. I've never had anyone request that someone die. No doubt that's because believers understand the import of it. Were I to perform such a curse, it would mean metaphysical blood on my hands, which I might be seriously conflicted about. But alas, I don't really perform any curses, at least not anymore. I function more in the way of a procurer for the job, and that's not exactly a small thing, if you get what I'm saying."

"I think I do, but I would emphasize that my request involves a matter of moral concern, a moral imperative, most decidedly."

"That's the other issue I wanted to address," said Norman Modrak, "because if this is a matter of blood sport, vengeance, settling a score, monetary gain, I can't be part of anything like that. But not knowing the details, not knowing your intent, I'm left hanging. You need to come clean and tell me who the object of this curse is."

"The most powerful man in the world," said McPherson, "and one of the biggest idiots."

Norman Modrak's features froze as he sat there. Dwelling on what McPherson had told him, his eyes became fixed, his voice now muted and soft. "Is this," he at last began, "the mutual end you referred to on the phone when we spoke?"

"It is."

"And you believed you could count on me?"

"I did."

"How so?"

"I know for a fact you haven't been exempt from threats and intimidation. You and many others like you," stated McPherson, "are targets of the current regime. A couple months back you organized a gathering of witches to come together in public expressly to put a curse on the Dictator. Something called a binding curse, if I'm correct, something meant to curb the man and hold him in check. It was a bold and defiant act. Not the kind of thing that goes unnoticed by a totalitarian regime. As you and your group were off in a field that night forming a circle and conducting your rites, a sniper opened fire. People were wounded. One person was killed. Cars were vandalized as well, and if the police reports are correct, your own car had its tires slashed and the windshield shattered."

"That's correct," said Norman Modrak, giving McPherson a long and studied look, "There was a sniper at large that night and we were fired on with several rounds. The woman next to me was shot through the neck. You don't forget those last gasps of someone choking on their own blood, you don't forget that ever, not even amid all the screams and pandemonium going on. One might say it defines the battle lines very clearly."

"To say the least, what happened is profoundly regrettable," said McPherson, "but it happened because you and your companions are different, because you don't conform, because your beliefs are out of line with what the state says you should believe. You don't have the benefit of the state's imprimatur and furthermore you don't want it—and that makes you dangerous, you refuse to abide, and yet you're well aware of the stakes. Some monsters devour their enemies, but the worst monsters belittle, dehumanize and justify eliminating those that they devour. It's a way to usurp moral authority for immoral ends. That's what happened with *Malleus Maleficarum*, as I'm sure you're aware."

"I'm very much aware," said Modrak, looking impressed, "and you're very well informed. Not everyone knows about *Malleus Maleficarum*."

"Then I'm not telling you anything new when I say that the Dictator and his party hacks have written their own *Malleus Maleficarum*. They've damned a lot of people to torture and death— all sorts of refugees, scientists, people of color, Muslims, liberals, any woman who wants to be seen as something more than an overt sex object. The list goes on and on, and I think you'd agree it certainly includes witches and Wiccans or anyone else with beliefs along pagan lines."

"You make your point," said Modrak. "It is, indeed, a tragic juncture that we've arrived at. In Europe, over the course of three centuries, 100,000 people were accused of witchcraft, almost all of them women, half of whom were found guilty and murdered, usually by burning at the stake. The *Malleus Maleficarum* was instrumental in sealing these women's fate. When corruption and depravity work their way up to the top of the hierarchical pyramid, life below that pinnacle becomes very, very cheap, regardless of whether or not the top of that pyramid is Vatican City or the White House."

"I absolutely agree," said McPherson, "and I'll add that the incident of a psychotic sniper attests to this fact. Given how the Dictator's henchmen operate, I tend to see your smashed windshield as your own personal *Kristallnacht*. If the trends of the Dictator's regime hold true, the next time round it will be your head that they're smashing, not your windshield."

"Obviously," stated Modrak, raising an eyebrow, "the Dictator has great appeal among the nation's warped and pathological minds. He and his stormtroopers have an irresistible desire to persecute others."

"Can I assume then," pursued McPherson, "that we're coming at this from the same angle."

"That's a given."

"No moral conflict about it then?"

"No," clarified Modrak, "rather a moral imperative, as you earlier suggested."

"Then how do we proceed with my request?"

"To begin with," commenced Modrak after taking a long sip of his Port, "it should come as no surprise that your request is hardly a novel one, you are hardly alone in your intentions. I know that in certain quarters there are curses being put on the Dictator which are taking a sinister turn. Some witches are delving into the black arts, verging on what might be called Satanism, seeking to bring about very severe consequences. I know a few of these practitioners and all I can say is that there's something very strange afoot, an agitation in the air. But while I'd never rule it out, I doubt these witches could pass muster with the kind of curse you desire."

"Then who? Who can do it?" asked McPherson. "I didn't think it was this complicated."

"It's tricky," explained Modrak. "You need the right person to make this happen. A really genuine witch isn't out there suckling imps or stirring cauldrons. In fact, that exceedingly rare person who might be a witch is more likely than not not even aware she is one. She likely doesn't understand herself, doesn't sense her place in the world. Modern life doesn't afford a witch or a shaman the leeway necessary for what's inside them to come to the fore. Not anymore. The capacities of such people either get stifled or break out in aberrant ways, but every now and then someone joins a coven or happens to come along who has a capability inside them that is truly alive."

As McPherson listened, the crow glided down onto the floor where it hopped about and then tilted its head, seeming to scrutinize the arabesques in the rug before fluttering off into another room. "And do you know such a person?"

"Perhaps . . . perhaps," repeated Norman Modrak, deliberating as he spoke. "To bring this about, to unleash what's needed to impact such a high-profile individual as you describe, you need a brainstorm of energy and a very lurid vision, a trance frenzy that channels everything a person's got, everything into this one single thing, someone, ideally, for whom it would be absolutely unbearable *not* to perform this curse."

"A witch, a shaman, who?"

"Not a shaman," considered Modrak, staring at the floor and shaking his head. "No, in this case we want a woman, a witch, most definitely, because of the male-female polarity factor and how it will enhance the necessary energy current. And given the scale of this thing, we also want a virgin witch."

"A virgin witch," McPherson repeated, dumbfounded.

"Someone like I have already described," insisted Modrak, "someone who hasn't really realized her abilities, someone not quite sure of them, a budding witch. Yes," Norman Modrak reflected, "that's important, someone who can summon up pure intent in a way that is absolute and unhindered, someone hardy enough to endure the physical demands of it, committing her whole being to the task, that's what we want. My instinct tells me to avoid anyone who thinks they might know how to go about this, anyone who thinks of employing taglocks or *voces mysticae* or any of that stuff. We don't want that. We want someone who doesn't think about it at all, someone who just does it, unbridled energy, that's what we're after. To bring about someone's demise, our witch must go on a kamikaze mission of the soul."

"Do you have someone in mind?" asked McPherson, a bit taken aback by the growing fervor with which Norman Modrak spoke.

"I have contacts, people in various covens and such. I'm regularly in touch with them. I visit these covens as a guest speaker and give presentations, so I get around a bit. Off the top of my head, I can't name a specific person who might perform this curse, but I do recall an incident that may point the way. I have a certain contact. She's a high priestess in the Coven of the Golden Moon, which is an affiliate under the Covenant of the Goddess, which means that ethically she can't directly involve herself with the kind of curse we plan on carrying out, it goes against the coven's moral tenets, but she can assist in this initial stage," said Modrak, knocking back the last of his Port before getting to his feet and pacing about. "This high priestess told me about a young woman who sought membership in her coven. One never knows about such people's motivations to do this. For some women, a coven is a female equivalent of a boys' club, there's something exclusive, a comradery. Misfits, outcasts, those seeking a sense of place, they might gravitate toward a coven. It's a self-discovery endeavor. For others it's female companionship on a level that's both arcane and intimate, even quasi-sexual. All sorts of motivations come into play, as you might imagine, and they don't necessarily detract from people's earnest interest in witchcraft. But very few if any of these people are true witches. That's why the high priestess of the Golden Moon comes to mind. She told me not all that long ago of a young initiate, a moody lost soul of a girl who had an impulse to learn about witchcraft. The girl really couldn't articulate anything about her motives, which is actually a good thing. Even before meeting her, the high priestess had had a premonition about this girl, something that foretold her arrival. Immediately upon seeing her, my high priestess friend was greatly intrigued and got talking to her. She claimed the girl had an inner turbulence, an inner fire, a heightened awareness that seemed to come from some inner void, which convinced the high priestess that the young woman was a solitaire, a rogue witch trying to find herself, still not awakened to what she is, someone treading on that dividing line between this world and other mysteries, someone in touch. The bottom line is that the high priestess was drawn to this person, she's very hypersensitive that way. It takes a keen awareness to detect a witch, especially a latent one, and this young girl was someone who stood out, the real deal. The high priestess wanted me to meet her as this was a rare occurrence, but the young girl stopped coming to the meetings. She drifted away as people do. I never did get to meet her."

"Do we know her name?"

"I know for sure my high priestess friend would not have forgotten it."

"So what's the next step?"

"I'm leaving that up to you. I'm completely on board," assured Modrak, "but this is your initiative."

McPherson turned his neck to one side as if he had to work out a crick. Then, holding his glass of Port up to the light, he admired its ruby color before drinking the last of it down. "When we find her, what happens then?"

"We must endear the task to her, try to persuade her, but first she might need to be convinced of her own inherent ability. Some people are in denial. But if she's receptive, if we can solicit her interest and gain her confidence, she may commit to the undertaking. It's a roll of the dice. I would suggest that initially we let the high priestess discuss the matter with her. She's very good at putting people at ease."

"It's all sounding ludicrous," blurted out McPherson, suddenly appearing downcast.

"What do you mean? This is what you wanted," reminded Modrak.

"Yes, but to approach somebody out of the clear blue because we think she's a witch, she'll call the police on us, this girl, and with good reason. This is the height of absurdity, a curse getting cast on someone, a curse, like I'm in some medieval melodrama, and having it cast by a witch who doesn't know she's a witch until somebody convinces her that she is. It's all going too far."

"I see your point," said Norman Modrak, "but it was you who sought me out for this."

"God knows I did," said McPherson, shaking his head.

"And what we're doing is not the height of absurdity," added Modrak, becoming more and more vehement as he spoke, "but possibly the antidote to a stratospheric absurdity that has taken up residence in the highest office in the land. Everybody knows this. It's like having Charles Manson running the nation. One really cannot get any more absurd. So where does that leave us? In my opinion, it's like we're fighting a disease, a terrible cancer. It's an aggressive cancer and so time is of the essence, and in such a situation it's only natural that people will resort to nonconventional treatments, an experimental drug or even, perhaps, a witch doctor, a medicine man, a *curandera*. So it's best to think of our endeavor as a kind of experimental cure. Maybe it will work, maybe not. All I know is you made your case and now I'm making mine."

Before he could reply, McPherson noticed the crow flutter over to the top of Norman Modrak's desk, perching there, stretching out its wings before shaking itself, after which it began pacing back and forth, stopping eventually to examine a marble bust of William Shakespeare, to which it gave a single peck.

"Does that crow have a name?" asked McPherson after a few moments of silence.

"Marcus Corvus."

"Do you get along with him?" asked McPherson, genuinely interested.

"He's a fellow Earthling," said Modrak agreeably, turning up the palms of his hands as if to indicate such things were self-explanatory.

Both men watched as the crow, still atop the desk, stretched out its wings once more and grew still, the yellow ring of its eye alive with a planetary brightness.

Norman Modrak, after observing McPherson closely, once more affirmed his commitment, "I am willing to go forward with this, as I believe I made clear earlier. Simply say the word and the game's afoot."

"Going forward is the only way to go," said McPherson, his voice sounding distant as, inexplicably preoccupied, he continued to stare at the crow. Then, at last turning to Modrak, he calmly added: "I think we should proceed as soon as possible."

"Very well. There's no point in delaying," said Modrak, looking pleased. "It's simply a matter of getting in touch with the high priestess. I'll get as much information as I can, our witch's name and anything else I can learn about her. I'll ask the high priestess to intercede on our behalf, not that I'd divulge our specific purpose, but use her to break the ice, pave the way, seeing as she and our witch already know each other. The high priestess has exceptional insights, she'll get a bead on this budding witch of ours. Once I have more information, I'll be in touch, naturally. We'll know better how to proceed at that point."

"Pass on her name," suggested McPherson, "and I can get the lowdown on her as well. It's what I do, that sort of thing, kind of stock in trade."

"That's interesting," said Modrak, reflecting for a moment. "There are so many plots these days, and all of them thickening. For now, I'll let you know what I find out. Leave this end of it to me."

"Agreed," said McPherson, and then, as an afterthought, he wondered if Norman Modrak charged for his services and asked if any payment was required.

Norman Modrak gave a slight cough and scratched the bridge of his nose. "On my honor," he said warmly, "I do appreciate the offer, it's well intended, I'm sure, but certain issues in this world simply can't be reduced to one of money."

"It's a gentleman's agreement then," concluded McPherson, and the two men now got to their feet and shook hands, rehashing their plans once more as Norman Modrak led his guest out of the library and to the front door. Stepping out into a chill wind, McPherson zipped up his jacket and noticed again the porch light above him swinging on its chain. As he listened to the rush of the trees, his ear also caught the sound of Norman Modrak's crow, which from somewhere back inside the house cawed three times as the door creaked closed.

KISS-ASS A GO-GO

Anything goes at the Kiss-Ass A Go-Go. Sitting on his throne holding a scepter topped by a golden dollar sign, the Dictator smugly looks out at a feeding frenzy of ingratiating leeches mobbing him with smarmy compliments and glowing rounds of praise. The jostling crowd is verging on a melee as they shove each other out of the way and claw up each other's backs. Desperate to catch the Dictator's eye and win his favor, a posh investment banker loudly proclaims the Dictator to be the Incarnate Second Coming, at which the Dictator smiles, while a white-collar racketeer weary of his private island and numerous slush funds begs to be made ambassador to Brazil, an honor for which he profusely kisses the Dictator's shoes, only to get yanked out of the way by a competing rabble of suck-ups, all of them scrambling and throwing punches, doing everything they can in the way of fawning and finagling, anything so long as they can get a bigger slice of the taxpayer's pie— a juicy pork pie stuffed with superfluous defense contracts, corporates subsidies and tax loopholes to coddle the rich, all of which constitute a lavish windfall that requires no oversight and needs no legislation, but is simply decreed by the Dictator on the spot, this instant gratification fueling everyone's fervor, their determination to wring greater and greater spoils for themselves so rabid that they now slug it out in a massive brawl, for they know a plum opportunity when they see one, these fellows, and what could be more plum than handouts bought and paid for by the average American Joe? Indeed, be it waste, fraud, bogus wars or kickbacks, just stick the average American Joe with the tab because he's the gift that keeps on giving, forever and a day.

And no one, of course, knows this better than the lampreys who attend this gala of shady deals and dirty money, among them the Dictator's very own kith and kin, Daughter Ditzy Doll Eyes and her hubby, Squire Kushitush, esteemed personages who act as key advisors to the Dictator, who huddle with him on serious matters of state, who bask in his idiocy and who sometimes (giggle-giggle) even sit on his throne when he's not around. And why not? It's all about empowerment, which no one knows better than these two icons of nepotism. With her great affluence and "Daddy's" influence her trump card, Daughter Ditzy Doll Eyes waltzes through her business dealings with a blank check that certifies success at any cost, while Squire Kushitush has all his life graced those high circles in which the monied class moves and important contacts are made. A dandy of the most prestigious sort, Squire Kushitush is a strangely hypothermic man, cool and blank as custard, as if he had inherited the pale skin of a longtime jailbird, a man with that putrefied look of death warmed over.

Indeed, Squire Kushitush has all the makings of an elegant ghoul, and yet he is at heart a milksop. In fact, the sight of the contentious row playing out before him makes the knees of Squire Kushitush knock together nervously, the knocking knees triggering a loud borborygmus that goes roiling through his guts. Such a delicate and hollow-boned popinjay as Squire Kushitush cannot, in fact, endure very well the turbulence he sees playing out before him, men clashing tooth and nail as they battle desperately for political appointments and special favors, men who comprise a maelstrom of shifting allegiances, who casually undercut their partners and who break their own promises. The sight of this backstabbing imbroglio does, indeed, leave Squire Kushitush appalled. The squire prefers to fight his battles by proxy, through well-paid lawyers skilled in the art of fine print, wordy clauses and contractual sleights of hand, all of which make for a discreet and gentlemanly way of screwing somebody over—not the brute lambasting to which he now bears witness. In fact, the stress of having to watch such a donnybrook causes Squire Kushitush to stiffen with fear, his abdominal muscles tensing, which prompts him to cut a small, involuntary fart. Small though it may be, this little fart nearly bowls Squire Kushitush over. He must flail his arms in order to keep himself from falling, realizing that he has not only farted, but has also shit himself.

In the case of Squire Kushitush, however, to have shit himself merely means that a Styrofoam peanut has popped out his ass. Yes, this cadaverous man is a tried and true lightweight, a human scarecrow without even shit in his bowels to act as ballast. Yet Daughter Ditzy Doll Eyes has in the past come to hubby's aid on this account by enlisting the services of a Chinese seamstress who, although earning only three cents an hour, has meticulously stitched long lengths of heavy drapery beads into all the blazers, ties and slacks that the squire wears, this as a means to weigh the man down and to keep him from toppling over should a breeze or sudden downdraft come his way.

With a rubbery, eel-like arm, Squire Kushitush now reaches behind him and puts his hand down the back of his pants, feeling around for the lately expulsed Styrofoam peanut. At last, with a little squeeze, he gets hold of it, his milk-white fingers holding it up to the light. Yet this moment of inspection does not last long, for out of nowhere charges in Lucifer Deadzone, a wily lobbyist for such corporate stalwarts as Black Horse Pesticides, Cobalt Bombardier and Toxic Sludge Fertilizer, Inc. Mercilessly tackling Squire Kushitush, Lucifer Deadzone now grabs the peanut for himself while yelling out that he bids $200,000 for the item. Then, holding the peanut triumphantly overhead, he begins to stomp his feet in an orderly rhythm that has him moving like a deranged marionette.

Soon enough, however, this little performance ends, for at this moment Congressman Jackalope Katpiss from Upstate New York leaps on the back of Lucifer Deadzone, tightly locking his arms around the man's neck as he bites his ear, for Congressman Katpiss cannot countenance the fact that someone else has taken possession of the peanut, that someone else might win favor with the Dictator's Royal Family. No way. No how. In fact, to ensure he get dibs on this honor, the congressman now ups the ante and bids $250,000 for the Styrofoam peanut, proclaiming his bid loudly to the room, his voice marked by such distinct clarity that it leaves many who are listening stunned because Congressman Katpiss is renowned for constantly talking out of both sides of his mouth, the polarization between the left and right sides of his oral cavity having produced nothing over the years but a spate of gibberish not uncommon among men who lack the guts of a personal conviction, men who forever want to have it both ways.

Try as he might to wrest the Styrofoam peanut from Lucifer Deadzone's hands, however, Congressman Katpiss finds himself hurled to the floor by a bit of expert jiu jitsu on the part of Lucifer Deadzone, who now breaks free and runs away, the peanut tight in his fist as all sorts of other whackos eager to ingratiate themselves start chasing after the fleet-footed Lucifer, all of them ready to pay exorbitant sums for the peanut that has popped from Squire Kushitush's ass, a peanut that is sure to become a sacred peanut, a relic to be preserved, a testimony to family greatness, a peanut which represents Squire Kushitush's peerless and profound ability to (supposedly) execute trade deals renowned for their huge domestic benefit and economic wizardry, to (miraculously) alleviate hunger and poverty for over 45 million Americans, and to (preposterously) establish a blissful and everlasting peace throughout the endlessly warring and strife-ridden nations of the Middle East—because if anyone can do it Squire Kushitush can! And lest there be doubters among you, take heed that the Styrofoam peanut acts as a profound symbol, a holy talisman, a potent manifestation of exactly the kind of stuff from which Squire Kushitush is made, this peanut being both the hallowed advent of his essence and a boon borne directly from the anal vault from whence there also sprang his head! Amen!

With a horde of sycophants now giving chase to Lucifer Deadzone, a kind of high-speed follow-the-leader game has been set in motion, its course twisting and turning around the room, growing longer and more tortuous, suggesting a snake wriggling all about. As this "snake" brushes past the newly appointed ambassador to Brazil, however, the man bursts into flame and is immediately turned into a heap of smoldering ash. Yet this in no way hinders the human snake, which sinuously twists and turns, now going one way, then another, the easy flow of its long body alive and enticing from end to end, the men comprising it all moving as one. To enhance this effect, they place their hands on the hips of the man in front, creating a unified conga line. As they do this their bodies begin to release an oily discharge which on contact with the air starts to congeal and whiten, and as the unabated flow of this discharge increases it forms layer upon layer of an ever-thickening exudate, a pliable sheath that grows tough in its depths while remaining exquisitely supple. Beneath the murky whiteness of this incipient snakeskin, the men who comprise the snake's body soon disappear, having been reduced and compacted into small remnants of shadow that have jelled together in a single slithering mass. Meanwhile, Lucifer Deadzone, at the head of this snake, finds himself transfiguring into various pieces of cartilage and connective tissue, his eyes shrinking into fixed and beady points, his jaws opening wide to make way for two menacing fangs.

Without question, the snake is now a fully-formed reptile, slithering over the floor with enough stealth to make the creature barely noticeable, a ghost snake passing by inconspicuously like a shadow and largely ignored, even as it raises its head and looks across the room, holding deathly still as it draws a bead on the famous media mogul, Murdoch Muttongun. Sizing the man up, the snake watches as Murdoch Muttongun pops exotic finger food down his throat, a whole tray of delicious dainties that have been presented to him by a small robot constructed in the likeness of a 1930s cartoon version of Little Black Sambo. "Thank you, boy," says Murdoch Muttongun to the robot, while the robot responds as programmed, saying, "Yessuh, Massuh." Hearing this, Mr. Muttongun laughs heartily, as the snake, meanwhile, eases its head down gracefully to the floor and wriggles rapidly toward the media mogul, its body giving off a suffocating jungle scent that makes everyone in the room drowsy.

As it slithers on its way, the snake happens to pass Congressman Prickbrain Widowspeak, who sips a whiskey and ginger ale and gives a lesson in semantics to one of his aides, explaining that when he says he's going to reform Social Security he really means he's going to *gut* Social Security, and when he says he's going to revamp Medicare he's really going to *defund* Medicare. With a delicate flick of its tail, the snake touches the senator ever so slightly and jolts him up off the floor, having administered an electric shock so great that the man shudders and contorts in midair, his eyes bugging as he drops dead. Slithering on, the snake next takes refuge under a long table upon which multitiered fountains flow with vintage wines bubbling and sparkling, all for the taking in rows of fine crystal glasses. From beneath this table, the snake spots a well-heeled fellow wearing black Testoni shoes, and zeroing in on these shoes the snake quickly coils around them before racing up the man's body, looping around the man's legs and torso in a tight spiral that holds him fast. Caught in the snake's crushing grip, the man feels his guts squeezed to bursting, his face wrenching with pain as he breaks out in a cold sweat and turns purple—just as his heart explodes. As the man stiffens and dies, the snake relaxes its hold and leisurely weaves back down his body, leaving the man standing there perfectly upright, balanced like a ten pin even though he's dead.

Now streaming across the floor in a smooth flow of muscle and pellucid flesh, the snake leaves no doubt that it is still bearing down on Murdoch Muttongun, watching as the man gives Little Black Sambo inane and pointless commands over and over simply to hear the robot say: "Yessuh, Massuh . . . Yessuh, Massuh . . . Yessuh, Massuh . . ." Over and over again, these base and shameful words cause Murdoch Muttongun to chuckle, for the robot serves to epitomize Murdoch Muttongun's quest to find men who can be completely and utterly manipulated—the classic dupe, the easy mark, the sucker born every minute—in other words, men so lacking in any capacity to think for themselves that they are only too glad to roll on their backs and have their bellies scratched by the blowhards on Murdoch Muttongun's very own news channel, a third-rate schlock house known nationally as Vulpine News Network, where any given pixel puss who can look sage and serious gets to go on the air and spout whole slop buckets full of bullshit. In fact, if truth be told, the employees on the set and in the newsroom at Vulpine News have found the workplace so overflowing with rank excrement that they've taken to wearing Wellington boots to keep their socks and trousers dry.

Still chuckling at Little Black Sambo, Murdoch Muttongun has in the meantime remained oblivious to the powerful snake that is wending its way toward him. Soon enough, however, a waft of air laden with the scent of corpse flowers passes over him and Murdoch Muttongun recoils, becoming sick to his stomach, his face turning ashen green. Nearly passing out, he must close his eyes in order to stop the room from spinning—only to find that when he opens them there is a large snake at his feet, circling around and around him, as if delineating a bull's eye at which he is the center. Frightened by this serpent, Murdoch Muttongun looks down at the reptile with fatal fascination. As if trapped by an invisible forcefield, he does not dare jump over the snake, but stands there helpless, the air around him growing hot and stifling, his lungs wilting while a terrible fever now takes hold. Shivering uncontrollably, the man cannot stop his teeth from chattering, teeth that begin snapping together with such violence they get pulverized in his mouth, sending a fine spray of chips and shards flying forth, bony particles that transform into diamond-like flecks as they fall, the area around Murdoch Muttongun's feet becoming littered with luminous fairy dust.

As Murdoch Muttongun continues to convulse, his Adam's apple begins to pump vigorously, each upward thrust filling his mouth with a mealy foam riddled with blood clots, his cheeks filling out until mouthfuls of bloody fluid spill from his lips, staining his shirt. Racked by nausea and stomach cramps, the media mogul finds there is also a growing bulge in the middle of his abdomen, for his navel is swelling like a giant boil, bright red and tender, a whey-colored oil oozing out from the wormy twists of his umbilicus. Although this fluid smells of sickly sweet decay, a more rank and sulphurous discharge is running down the man's legs, for as the snake circles around and around Murdoch Muttongun he has completely lost control of his bowels. In addition, welts and blisters now pop out on his face, and with his lips shriveling up into a black eschar, Murdoch Muttongun at last knows that he's done for. Taking his head in his hands, he despairs to find that pieces of his scalp are sloughing off in his fingers, and so, alas, looking like shit on the ass of the Grim Reaper, Murdoch Muttongun breathes his final breath and topples to the floor, lying there flat on his back.

Having watched the unfortunate ordeal of Murdoch Muttongun, Little Black Sambo now walks up to the man and bends down beside him, scooping up some of the glittering fairy dust that has sheared off his chattering teeth. Tossing this dust into the blank and staring eyes of the man, Little Black Sambo waits to see if there is some reaction, some hint of life. But to no avail. The man is stone cold kaput, Murdoch Muttongun's rosy tenure in the beanery of billionaires having at last fizzled out, prompting Little Black Sambo to pass a final verdict, uttering words that he has never, under any circumstances, been programmed to say: "Mistah Muttongun—he dead."

Picking up on these words and having watched in dread as the brutal attacks of the snake have unfolded, Squire Kushitush now takes umbrage at what he has seen. He finds it inconceivable that Fate would be so bold as to subject him to such cruel and unsettling horrors, horrors that have awakened in him a startling apprehension—that there are seeds of insidious self-destruction sprouting up within the very milieu in which he has for so long been happily prancing about. And yet, such a portent cannot be, concludes Squire Kushitush, it simply cannot be. Fate must be lying down on the job, he tells himself, for is Fate not aware that he, Squire Kushitush, has been honored since birth as a Knight Servitor of the Plush Carpet? And does Fate not see how his lucrative marriage to Daughter Ditzy Doll Eyes further exempts him from all the ugly trials and tribulations of those accursed commoners? And can Fate really be so oblivious as to how he has obsequiously endeared himself to the Dictator, who has praised him and favored him not only with the most lavish perks, but also bestowed on him titles so lofty and influential that the entire regime beams with pride at the mere mention of his name? Does Fate not see these things? Does Fate not know that he is special and that the school of hard knocks is one from which he has been given a pass?

Rue the day! For in Squire Kushitush's world, he is a man of preordained and exemplary standing, a man whose personal destiny has been brightened by big, big bucks, a man whose primrose path has been made incontrovertible by the sublime configuration of the stars. That he is, in truth, a useless shithead never dawns on the fellow, for by being the cosmic beneficiary of jet-setting thrills and highfalutin luxuries he has no time for self-reflection. Rather, he is convinced that simply by having it all he is fulfilling one of the highest orders of being, living atop the very pinnacle of humanity, a place so exclusively reserved and blessed that it cannot, he believes, ever be contradicted or taken to task or undermined in any way.

And yet something, as they say, is rotten in Denmark, with Squire Kushitush growing more and more ill at ease as he watches the pandemonium around him continue. Indeed, the abominable snake, which goes on killing with deadly efficiency, keeps growing larger, having just strangulated and swallowed whole the Dictator's very own spiritual advisor, the Reverend Dingus Bull, a man well-known and revered, founder and sole preacher at the Church of the Divine Dolt, a rickety hovel of fire sale clapboard slapped together on the main drag of Boogerville, Kentucky, where Reverend Bull's fiery sermons of repent and remorse would ring out loudly among the rafters, accompanied by the sobs and sighs and general boohooing of his purblind congregation, a collection of various idiots who, for years, have had no clue that their "Man of God," the impeccable Reverend Bull, in spite of all his devotional tears and hand-wringing petitions to the Lord Jesus, has actually been racking up a long rap sheet of charges most notable for money laundering, mail order fraud, sex with a minor, embezzlement, vandalism and various other untoward crimes, the latest of which include supplying black market flamethrowers to the Ku Klux Klan and selling contraband bazookas to the National Rifle Association.

Of course, given the fact that he has now been devoured by a large snake, it is obvious that Reverend Bull will not be showing up at his arraignment, the man having been reduced to a lumpy mass deep within the snake's body, his limbs still twitching even as his flesh disintegrates amid powerful gastric juices, the energetic motility of the snake's digestive tract breaking the reverend down bit by bit, reducing him to a pulpy chunk of shit.

As an eye witness to this carnivorous attack, Squire Kushitush trembles and blanches, his bloodless face turning, as the phrase goes, an even whiter shade of pale. Jangled and perturbed, this delicate creampuff with his jellyfish fingers has seen enough, and having no desire to become fodder for a huge, malicious reptile, he now decides to vamoose. Thus, turning around slowly, he clenches his fingers together and draws his arms tight to his body, hunching his shoulders high up to his head as if physically trying to shrink himself from view. With teeth tensely gritted, he now begins to tiptoe discreetly out of the room, his eyes shifting about in search of his bride, Daughter Ditzy Doll Eyes, who is blithely ignoring the carnage going on about her as she insists on showing a Saudi Prince the red, white and blue straight jacket she has designed especially for "Daddy," eagerly producing this item while pointing out its sturdy attributes and stylish features, noting how it is just the thing for when "Daddy" goes bonkers and turns into a vicious and apoplectic psychopath. And yet, the interests of this giddy entrepreneuress go well beyond restraining "Daddy," for her keen business eye tells her that the recent up-swell in patriotic nutcases goose-stepping behind her father will send sales of the straight jacket skyrocketing.

Crooking a finger at Daughter Ditzy Doll Eyes, Squire Kushitush invites her to join him in his escape, but he never waits to see if she follows, the squire slinking along his jittery way, tiptoeing toward the door, leaving behind a free for all of men cavorting about with the unmistakable sashay of great wealth and little else. As if caught in a firestorm of paparazzi flashbulbs, these men blink wildly at each other in a frantic face-to-face light show of their own vanity, for it is they who broker the power, who buy the influence, who secretly cut the deals. Whether getting chummy on the green at the Dictator's Golden Putter Golf Club or conferring in low tones at some millionaire's retreat, they keep it among themselves, these men. And now, dizzy with greed as they jockey for illegal shortcuts and greater and greater favors, they step blindly on the bodies of those who have fallen, stumbling and staggering, their footing lost as the enormous snake slithers along, causing the floor to shift and buckle with tectonic grumblings, the walls cracking, the creak of steel beams growing louder as a fine dust falls from the ceiling.

Inspired to do something manly in the face of this disruption, the Saudi prince who had been accosted by Daughter Ditzy Doll Eyes now steps toward the snake and draws a gleaming scimitar from a bejeweled scabbard worn dashingly at his side. Wielding this scimitar in a challenging display, the prince confronts the snake, which whips back its head and with lightning speed flashes two bright fangs that shoot streams of burning venom straight into the prince's eyes, his head all at once bursting into flame, his scorched hair and flesh filling the air with plumes of acrid black smoke that catch the attention of Texas oilman Big Bo Slickers, who strides right up to the prince on big bow-legs, admiring his burning skull as he takes out an Arturo Fuente cigar, which he lights on the prince's head. Puffing away with uncommon satisfaction for a moment, Big Bo Slickers at last says, "Fuck them solar panels, Prince, and fuck them electric cars, too. Allah or no Allah, you need to stop being a human drapery rod for all those fancy robes you're wearing and get the fucking mirages out of your eyes—because we got to get down to business! Because oil is on its last legs! So we gotta rip apart every last shred of this here fucking planet in order to get every last drop of oil out there, because down where I come from in Hind Tit, Texas, that's what we all call mining the black gold, and gold means money!"

With the Kiss-Ass A-Go-Go extravaganza having turned into a shambles, the Dictator sits livid on his throne, his face a shiny puddle of flushed capillaries, his little pig eyes sweeping back and forth across the room as he watches this gathering of moochers turn into a rout, every last one of them running willy-nilly, the floor beneath their feet heaving as chunks of plaster fall from the ceiling. From a large crack in the wall, there now flows a river of locusts taking flight in a blinding swarm, their shrill buzz unbearable as men try to swat them away. The snake, meanwhile, keeps chalking up victims, its milky color having changed to an oily iridescence that leaves a wet trail along the floor, its great size more daunting than ever as its tail whips to and fro, knocking men off their feet with one fell swoop before it snaps back the other way, demolishing chairs and tables or whatever else lies in its path. That the entire gathering has become the stuff of nightmares is obvious even to a dunce like the Dictator, who watches with mounting anger and disquiet, his urge to lash out and yell held in check by the sheer overtness of things which, he tells himself, cannot really be happening, though the incomprehensible gist of it all is made even more apparent by a large white horse that has appeared at the far end of the room, its nostrils flaring, wet and vibrant, its rider a decomposing goblin in a weathered musketeer hat, his threadbare cravat smudged and dirty.

With his lips ravaged by decay, the horseman's grin is a jagged exposure of rotten teeth and black gums, the sallow skin of his face taut and wizened, while his eye sockets are dark holes ringed with crusty bits of flesh. Clasped in the crooked bones of his fingers are the horse's reins, to which the rider gives a delicate flick, the white horse responding with a solemn nod before clopping forward several steps before stopping, the horse and rider implacable, displaying such rigid composure that they rile the Dictator, who grows even more agitated when the horseman calmly lifts up one of his arms, on which he wears a goatskin gauntlet, his gesture providing a perch for a falcon that now slings itself out of nowhere, careening around the room and grazing the Dictator's head, leaving a bloody welt before it wheels off in a dazzling bolt of speed toward the horseman, where its powerful wings open to slow itself, the falcon hovering lower and lower until its talons clutch the horseman's arm.

Now conjoined in a triumvirate of man, beast and bird, all three of these entities stare at the Dictator with unflinching self-possession. The Dictator fidgets on his throne. Not knowing what to do or say, he grows exasperated, unable to shake the thought that the horseman and his companions have something in store for him. Flummoxed by his inability to come to terms by what he sees, the Dictator glowers, his anger intensifying to such a keen level that his only recourse is to jab a glowing red button that sticks up from the arm of his throne, a button which signals to his staff that the Dictator demands a can of Coca-Cola. Responding pronto to this demand is none other than Little Black Sambo, who soon appears with the beverage in hand, approaching the Dictator as if nothing could please him more than to attend to his all-powerful Lord and Liege, though in spite of his obvious deference, Little Black Sambo suddenly hurls the can of Coke square into the Dictator's face, the incorrigible robot now dropping to one knee and throwing out his arms as he raucously sings, "Mammy! My little Mammy!"

EL GITANO BAR & GRILL

I n the backroom of El Gitano Bar & Grill sit Amber Lamphere, Glass-Eyed Johnny, Jennifer Golembeski and Professor Peter Rasmussen. Disparate as their backgrounds are, they are all members of Action Underground, a network of altruists, safe house keepers and rapid-response drivers with vans and souped up cars who transport persecuted people on the run from the Ice Man. These persecuted people go about their lives tense with fear and apprehension, always on guard, always aware that at any moment the Ice Man might train his crosshairs directly on them, but with the help of Action Underground these undone and struggling people have created various escape routes, the templates of which they have learned by heart, be they hunted down at work, at home or at the house of a friend or family member, and for each escape route a default plan has usually been put in place as well. So sophisticated have these measures to elude the Ice Man become that highly polished bait-and-switch techniques are now common.

These evasion tactics will at times employ a human decoy who will distract and effectively lead the Ice Man astray, going to great lengths to string him along while his actual quarry has vanished, having gone underground to the sanctuary of a safe house. Rapid-response drivers also execute their own ruse, racing their vehicles over long and circuitous routes while knowing full well that the Ice Man is in hot pursuit, believing himself to be chasing a cargo of undocumented immigrant workers. When at last closing in and bringing one of these suspected vehicles to a stop, however, what the Ice Man finds is that the occupants of the vehicle are nothing more than inflatable love dolls dressed in ponchos and colorful serapes— like Central Americans! While the real quarry has flown the coop. That these poor and disparaged people have escaped deeply upsets the Ice Man, which usually results in the rapid-response driver getting punched in the head.

Yet for all the painstaking efforts to protect people from the Ice Man, the best laid plans do sometimes go awry, as is the case tonight with Rosa Cortinas, who knows that nothing better heralds the coming of the Ice Man than the hurry of jackboots thumping up a flight of stairs, the sound of which sends her grabbing her jacket and hopping out the window of her apartment, then charging down the fire escape without looking back. With her feet moving faster and faster on the metal steps, she reaches the bottom in a panic, her heart pounding as she darts around the back of the building. After quickly running across a parking lot, she hops up on a curb and races across a short field before leaping down into a ditch and then clambering up a steep embankment on the other side. Here she goes bounding over a line of railroad tracks before disappearing into an expanse of weeds and brambles and scrubby little trees, pressing on until she reaches a cyclone fence that borders the grounds of a paperboard factory. At this point, hidden behind some bushes, an opening has already been cut through this fence, a passage through which Rosa Cortinas now wriggles on her hands and knees, breathing fast, the dark ringlets of her hair stuck to her temples with cold sweat, her world having been flipped into a topsy-turvy nightmare.

Finally taking cover in an overgrown patch of dense brush, Rosa huddles herself tightly together, listening, trying to determine if anyone is on her trail. Hearing nothing but her own breathing, she now opens a clamshell phone and begins texting a distress signal to

Action Underground, letting them know what has happened and where she has taken cover. Within minutes she has a reply urging her to go to a prearranged place of rendezvous with which she is already familiar, El Gitano Bar & Grill. Relieved at having made contact with the good people at Action Underground, she replies that she will go to the appointed meeting place, but indicates she'll remain in hiding until after dark. "OK. Be careful. We'll be waiting," reads a final text from Action Underground, after which Rosa Cortinas takes a deep breath and tries to compose herself, feeling a pang in her chest as if something inside her has collapsed, which she thinks might be "hope" itself, the hope to better herself and improve her life, the hope that she could prevail over the strife and poverty that left her father a broken man back in Mexico, a man worn down by the cruel shame that try as he might he could not feed his family. In the end, the last dignified thing he could do was place his hand on his daughter's shoulder and say, "Go north, Rosa, go north," his eyes closed as he said this to capture his tears.

As she continues to wait in her hiding spot, Rosa Cortinas shudders with fear, knowing that the Ice Man is out there with submachine guns and attack dogs straining at their leashes. As evening settles in and the sky darkens, a damp chill takes hold of her and she zips up the jacket she has been instructed to take with her should she ever need to go on the run, for safe within the jacket's inner pocket is some money, a couple of protein PowerBars, and a list of helpful phone numbers, including that of a pro bono lawyer known to waive his legal fees for victims of the Ice Man. None of this, however, is any consolation for Rosa. She knows that by now her apartment has been ransacked and that her personal belongings have been confiscated, supposing as well that the crumpled family photograph taken at her *quinceañera* and which she cherished so deeply has probably been thrown in the trash. She also thinks about the small pots of cilantro, parsley and chives that grew on a table by a sunny window and how they wouldn't be watered and would wither and die, and she thinks too about what will happen to her today, tomorrow, and the day after that—the horrible unknown, but this she really cannot fathom and so she thinks instead about her job gluing gaskets into metal housings for a manufacturer of industrial lighting fixtures, and how when she got this job she was the happiest person in the world and wanted to dance. Now, however, she is devastated by guilt because in the morning when it's time to punch the clock she won't be there and the work that was hers to do won't get done and Brad, her supervisor, will be disappointed and puzzled, never understanding why someone who worked so hard and did such a good job just stopped coming to work. Such thoughts make Rosa Cortinas sick to her stomach, but she takes modest comfort thinking about Jennifer Golembeski, that intense and single-minded girl with the purple dye in her hair who works in the warehouse and actually befriended her, for Jennifer is one of those good people who accepted her and who wanted to help, a person for whom it does not matter if somebody is poor and down on their luck and lost in the world, and that is why Jennifer had joined Action Underground, because as Rosa once heard her say, "I'd rather help an honest fugitive from Mexico than listen to the lying creeps that are selling out the nation."

At long last, once Rosa Cortinas can see that night had fully settled in, she crawls from her hiding place and carefully creeps across the grounds of the paperboard factory. Sticking to the shadows, she works her way from one patch of shadow to another, sometimes taking cover behind a tree. Eventually she finds herself approaching the main gate which, after making sure the coast is clear, she quickly walks through without looking back, turning right on the road that stretches out in front of her. As she picks up her pace, she clings to the farthest edge of the road's shoulder, hoping the shadows there will give her some cover. Cringing with fear at the headlights of each passing car, she can feel a lump rise in her throat, dreading that any minute the Ice Man or his cohorts—the KKK, the Neo-Nazis—might close in on her, in which case she will be arrested and beaten, and then deported or, even worse, sent to Circulo del Diablo in the Arizona desert.

At Circulo del Diablo, it is well known that people are not allowed to eat any food unless they drop to all fours and lower their heads into dog bowls full of corn mush. Some people are even denied food and water altogether, starving for days on end until they gasp in agony, their throats parched and their innards broiling as they slowly die from dehydration. At Circulo del Diablo, it is understood that one's survival largely depends upon the whims of a stoop-shouldered and vicious old man called Loco Joe, who proudly brags that he runs Circulo del Diablo "just like a concentration camp." On his nightly rounds, in fact, Loco Joe walks vigilantly among the tents and barracks of his desert compound, searching eagerly for someone to inflict pain upon, followed by several guards in black hoods who wheel along a huge brazier filled with hot glowing coals. Nestled within these coals is a cattle brand whose end has been forged to look like a sombrero, and once Loco Joe selects a victim, he lifts this branding iron from the coals, pausing to admire the red-hot sombrero. Growing excited, he grins, the toad-like bore holes of his nose widening until, all at once, he thrusts the branding iron forward, landing it on the cheek of an inmate, pressing it hard, gleeful at the sound of sizzling flesh as he watches his victim scream and writhe, held fast by the hooded guards as Loco Joe continues to press the branding iron into his victim's cheek, harder, harder, a feverish gleam in his eye.

Although disfiguring someone's face would typically suggest a depraved and disturbing level of sadism, nothing of the sort applies to Loco Joe. In fact, far from being vilified, this man has been singled out by the Dictator as a star-spangled hero. The Dictator cannot praise Loco Joe enough, pontificating on the debt of gratitude that

Americans owe this man for protecting them from the untold legions of murderers and rapists arriving from Mexico. The Dictator even goes so far as to champion Loco Joe as the gold standard of patriotism, extolling the man as the very best, the most fantastic, the most tremendously incredible example of patriotism there ever was. Despite the Dictator's affinity for thugs and slimeballs, however, no amount of bombast can hide the fact that Loco Joe's "patriotism" is nothing more than the vile result of a twisted mind, that of a man eager to fall in line with the same idiots who gave their blessing to slavery, eugenics, lynch mobs, Japanese internment camps, and a host of other fine American legacies for which they will have bragging rights in hell.

As for Rosa Cortinas, all she wanted to do was pledge her allegiance to a flag that allowed her to work hard and feed herself and sleep soundly at night without worry. This, however, would not be the case. Sometime after leaving the grounds of the paperboard factory, as she was heading out to meet with Action Underground, the fate of Rosa Cortinas took a grim turn in that the young woman simply vanished. As the night wore on, as the minutes ticked by, she never appeared at El Gitano Bar & Grill, causing deep concern among the members of Action Underground, who after some talk agreed that Jennifer Golembeski and Professor Rasmussen should head out to search for her, leaving Glass-Eyed Johnny and Amber Lamphere behind in case she showed up. The search that night, however, yielded nothing. No hospital emergency room had admitted Rosa, no record of arrest had been filed in her name, and no one answered her cellphone when it was called. Dismayed and frustrated, Jennifer insisted on trying to retrace the steps that Rosa likely would have taken upon leaving the paperboard factory, but to no avail. No sign of her could be found. No inquiry turned up anyone who had seen her or thought they had seen her, and as Jennifer searched up and down the streets that night, as she peered into the shadows, an icy chill ran down her spine, for the shadows had become so fixed and pervasive that it seemed anyone caught in their depths would cease to exist.

When Jennifer and Professor Rasmussen at last return to El Gitano, it is obvious from their faces that their search has been in vain. Jennifer is somber and withdrawn and the professor baffled, stating more than once, "This ought not to have happened." No one else says a word. No one dares contemplate the fate of Rosa Cortinas. The sound of Glass-Eyed Johnny's Dos Equis foaming in his glass as he pours it is magnified by the silence, as is the tinkle of ice cubes in Jennifer's gin and tonic as she raises her glass. Professor Rasmussen stares into his zinfandel with his elbows on the table.

"Something went wrong tonight," Professor Rasmussen at last mutters, prompting a look of annoyance from Jennifer, who takes a slug of gin, pulling an ice cube into her mouth as she does so and shuffling it around with her tongue before spitting it back into the glass. Sighing at this uncouth behavior, Professor Rasmussen says no more and once again everyone is silent, knocking back their drinks until Jennifer detects something moving in the corner of her eye.

It is not only Jennifer, however, who catches sight of this apparent motion, for some vague object, some diaphanous thing, has gone fleeting by the periphery of everyone else's vision as well, causing heads to turn. But whatever it is that this group has seen, it has retreated out of sight and disappeared—only to immediately reappear, however, in the tail of the eye once again, causing heads to turn, first to one side, then the other, heads turning to and fro as everyone tries to get a glimpse of whatever it is that skirts about them. It is Glass-Eyed Johnny, perhaps because he only has one eye, who first draws a more definite bead on the object, detecting a thin wisp of smoke which he manages to hold steady in his gaze, watching as it elongates upward in a slow swirl, hanging in midair, its presence more and more definite until it is seen by everyone else at the table as well, everyone staring at a shapeless apparition that grows before their eyes, a tangle of misty veils weaving sinuously about and which, in the end, does not so much take shape, but lifts like a fog, revealing the presence of man who now stands fully materialized before them, his level of clarity disturbing in that there is no doubt that he is actually there.

For many, it would be obvious that the man standing before them is the ghost of Saint Max, his hand holding a smoldering pipe on which he puffs, while from behind a pair of black-framed eyeglasses he looks about the room. Most striking, however, is the glowing halo of tie-dyed colors that crowns his head. Looking calm and wise and at peace with himself, Saint Max now gives a nod to the table, his eyes bright and benign as he begins to speak. *She won't be coming back, I'm sorry to say* . . . he informs everyone, *She's on my side now* . . . And then, with his dark eyebrows rising, he adds, *The kids, they got it right, you know* . . . *We really should have listened to them, but it's too late now* . . . *too late now* . . . And with that, Saint Max looks complacently about and gives another nod, at which point he begins to fade away, every detail of the man softening, growing nebulous, becoming more and more transparent as he disperses into nothingness, every one at the table straining to see what is at last no longer there—when out of this nothingness a small spark suddenly jumps out and makes contact with Jennifer, the others watching in astonishment as she reacts with a jolt, a blast of voltage simultaneously flooding through the wall sockets, giving the jukebox a power surge that makes it jump to life, its lights blinking and brightening as the pounding strains of "Street Fightin' Man" begin.

"There's something happening here," says Glass-Eyed Johnny, anxiously looking around and touching his brow as if he had a headache.

"I'll say," agrees Amber, gripping the edge of the table until her knuckles turn white.

"But . . . but . . . what is happening?" Professor Rasmussen manages to say, his mouth hanging open as a sheen of perspiration appears on his upper lip.

"Oh, come on, don't you guys know?" asks Jennifer, her voice low and quavering. "It all came clear to me in a flash."

"Jen, look, you're shaking," observes Amber, gently resting a hand on her friend's arm. "You're shaking bad. Try to calm down."

"Are you okay, Jennifer?" asks Glass-Eyed Johnny, turning his one good eye upon her with concern.

Stretching out her arms, Jennifer now places her hands flat on the table to keep them from trembling. With a certain degree of difficulty, she manages to swallow and then takes several deep and audible breaths, her eyes closing briefly, then darting open, flashing left and right as she lurches forward. "The point of no return!" she blurts out. "That's what's happening, that's why we're here—you! And you! And you!" she barks, her finger jabbing clockwise around the table. "We're here because we wanted to fight the good fight and now Rosa is dead! We're here because we don't want no privileged snot of a Dictator with all his millions blowing smoke up our noses or our asses or wherever else while him and his cronies and his lickspittle kids who don't know shit from Shinola about anything scoot around and line their pockets at our expense and then don't do nothin' for nobody, telling you one thing and then doing another with all that fancy hogwash they're foisting on us like we're saps, like we're all part of the Dictator's song and dance, a con man, a two-bit hustler, and the poor dopes that bought into all his malarky and wait for their petty lives to get better just can't see through it— they've been shafted, dicked up the ass, they swallowed a whole line of shit like it's candied rose petals falling into their mouths from heaven, but it's a bunch of smelly tripe so rotten that not even a sewer rat would touch it, and that's what's going down, because the Dictator got an itchy trigger finger and he's cuttin' loose on his own people with goons and Nazi assholes, because you don't mess with the Dictator, you don't disagree, and you don't call him out on all the dumb-ass shit he spews that would insult even a halfwit, because we're all supposed to sit back and wave our little American flags that really should have fifty little fucking bananas on them instead of stars because we're going the way of the biggest, half-assed banana republic you ever saw, but people cheer at the Dictator's pep rallies like they're a bunch of little Mary Janes back in high school—Rah-Rah-Rah! Ain't we great! America this! America that! Bullshit! More and more people are falling through the cracks every day and nobody can go a day without getting his back up over all the crap and lies and empty bluster getting rammed down our throats, and so now there's a crackdown on anyone who's not a lockstep pantywaist living the Dictator's lie and giving in to his power grab while anyone who don't fit in with his hotshot ideas about what we're all supposed to be gets squashed, and people like Rosa Cortinas get routed out and driven underground and now maybe killed just for doing what the Dictator never did not once in his life, which is an honest day's work, while we go out and bust our humps and have less and less to show for it and then on top of that get lied to our faces by a lowdown scumbag trying to pass himself off as Mr. Salt of the Earth, Mr. Working Man, Mr. Man of the People, all of it phony bullshit, because the fucking weenie with his buffed fingernails never did a hard day's work, never broke a sweat not one day in his life unless it's because some Russian spy is threatening to rat him out about all his dirty business deals and money laundering and piss parties with whores, because the Dictator is out for no one but himself and his power brokers, while the rest of us get left holding the bag and get tossed out with the trash, and so that's how it is and that's how it hits me, and I'm getting goose bumps all over my body telling me something is wrong, really big-time wrong, real bad-bull wrong, and my flesh is creeping, telling me that something's going to happen, and it's coming down so hard it's like history repeating itself and I'm in the hot seat because it's like shadows reaching out for me from whatever it is we're repeating and they're grabbing me and shaking me and telling me to get off my ass—because the whole country's going down one big, stinkin' gully hole and believe me there's not one person left who has the ever-loving fucking guts to admit it and so what I'm saying is just that!"

Stunned into silence, Jennifer's companions sit staring at her, not moving, when just then Don Alvadoro, the owner of El Gitano Bar & Grill, steps forward from a backroom and approaches, his heels growing louder on the old oak floor as everyone turns to look at him. With his white shirt impeccably pressed and a crimson neckerchief knotted smoothly around his neck, Don Alvadoro possesses a poised and rugged dignity, that of a man who has kept calm while weathering many a trying storm.

"Pardon my interruption," says Don Alvadoro, "but I have a message for Señor Rasmussen."

EL GITANO BAR AND GRILL—AND BEYOND

O n hearing that someone has delivered a message for him, Professor Rasmussen looks up in surprise, at once suspicious and ill at ease. "No one should know that I'm here, Don Alvadoro," remarks the professor. "This is touchy business we're involved with. Are you sure this message is for me."

"Señor, here at El Gitano, you know you can count on us for the utmost discretion," reassures Don Alvadoro. "We too have concerns during these troubling times, but the message I bring is most certainly for you."

"What is it?"

"It is strange, Señor Rasmussen."

"Strange? In what way?"

"The man conveying this message, he was unusual," explains Don Alvadoro. "I was back in my office working at my desk when a pounding started at the back door. Why someone would be there pounding on a door that no one uses I could not figure out, but the knocking continued and so I had to get up to see what was going on. I expected to find a lost drunkard, perhaps, and tell him to be on his way. But," Don Alvadoro hesitates, "this was not the case."

"Go on."

"Professor Rasmussen, Señor, when I opened the door I saw a man in a crudely cut smock. It was made of a coarse, heavy material and splattered with dirt and mud. His face I could not see because it was wrapped in filthy rags. I could only see his eyes, only just barely in the darkness of the alley. There was something odd about this man. I hoped he would simply go on his way, but he stood there, and then put a question to me, asking whether I might be Don Alvadoro. I told him that I was, and that's when he said he had a message for you."

Hanging on Don Alvadoro's every word, Professor Rasmussen's initial concern is now giving way to a greater apprehension. "Did this man give you a name?"

"I asked him that very question and he said his name was Jack Goodfellow," replies Don Alvadoro, gauging the professor's reaction.

"I know of no such person."

"Are you sure?" interjects Amber.

"I know of no one by that name."

"Let's hear what the message was," encourages Glass-Eyed Johnny.

"Yes," agrees the professor, "what was the message?"

"Señor, his very words, what he said to tell you was, 'She's the girl.' Nothing more than that. It was all he said."

"*What?*"

"I know, it is crazy, Señor," apologizes Don Alvadoro, "but I heard him say it clearly enough. The rags around his face had muffled his voice. I wanted to be sure I had heard him correctly and asked that he repeat himself. Señor, this man was determined. He took a step forward, and although he was hunched over and slightly unsteady on his feet, there was no mistaking he was a powerful man, it was something I could see, and as he leaned toward me his words could not have been more clear, Señor. He said it again, 'She's the girl.'"

"What am I supposed to make of that?" asks Professor Rasmussen, flabbergasted, glancing at everyone in turn, but locking eyes with Jennifer, who sat very still, her face ashen.

"It is very strange," acknowledges Don Alvadoro sympathetically. "After saying this message to me the second time, this Jack Goodfellow turned and hobbled off into the darkness of the alley. I was only too glad to be rid of him, to be honest, but after closing the door I thought maybe I should come and get you, Señor, that it might be best for you to deal with this man in person given the strange circumstances. But when I opened the door, Jack Goodfellow was gone, gone in five seconds. I looked up and down the alley. I stepped outside and walked about for a bit, but there was no trace of him. It was like he had vanished into thin air."

For a minute, everyone at the table remains silent, thinking about what Don Alvadoro has just told them until Amber speaks up.

"Hey, Don Alvadoro," she says, somewhat hesitantly, "with all the strange stuff that's happening here tonight, it's like got me thinkin', you wouldn't know if by any chance the El Gitano is haunted, is it? Like with ghosts? I mean, it's an old building and all."

"Señorita," says Don Alvadoro, bowing courteously, "it's so interesting you ask that. From time to time, I hear people making similar comments. There are unusual happenings here at El Gitano, it seems. Why, it has even been said that I myself am a ghost," laughs Don Alvadoro. "Imagine such a thing, it all makes me wonder sometimes just what is going on."

Graciously taking his leave, Don Alvadoro now turns and walks back across the room, disappearing behind a door of heavy wood planks that closes quietly behind him. He has no sooner gone, however, when a vague up-swell of sound catches Jennifer's ear. So incipient and faint is this sound that she cannot decide if it comes from within the walls of the El Gitano or without. Akin to a low and constant drone at first, it begins to grow louder in pitch. What Jennifer hears, in fact, is the approaching din of a general ruckus, a hubbub of shouts and yells all breaking free in the street outside.

As she listens, Jennifer can see the expression on Glass-Eyed Johnny's face begin to change, for he too hears the commotion, while Professor Rasmusen gazes around the room to find some explanation for the noise. "What is that?" he asks.

"It's coming from outside," decides Amber, her ear catching the shrill whistle of a bottle rocket, its loud bang bringing on a rowdy chorus of cheers.

"It's happening," says Jennifer softly, a kind of frantic excitement in her eyes.

"It's the backlash," attests Professor Rasmussen, now staring intently at Jennifer.

"Yes," states Glass-Eyed Johnny, slamming down his beer glass on the table. "Got it!"

And with that, as if heeding some instinctual call, everyone leaps up. Professor Rasmussen pulls out his wallet and drops several bills on the table for the tab before following his companions as they rush into the next room, wriggling into their jackets, joined now by other patrons, all of them wending in and out among the tables, close on each other's heels as they file past the bar and toward the door, pushing their way outside into the unfolding fracas clogging the street.

Instantly caught up in a human lava flow, those who have left El Gitano find themselves dragged and jostled along, staggering and stumbling, then finding their footing, the crowd growing larger as the moon overhead shines down on a sea of people marching with fists in the air, a bottle rocket shooting high above them, its comet tail of sparks culminating in a bright explosion. Rapidly two more bottle rockets now race overhead, exploding, dropping a thin haze of smoke through which an upside down American flag can be seen waving on a pole, its bearer shouting: "Bring the bastard down!" This as the crowd seethes with fury, growing more and more irate as a chant breaks out: "Bring him down! Bring him down! Bring him down! Bring him down!" As the outrage of the people grows, voices peal out from every direction, the anger obvious, the disgust writ large on a small sign held by an old woman who wears a babushka and who lifts up her sign proudly for all to see—FASCIST PIG! People applaud and cheer this sign, helping the old woman to move along as she lurches forward awkwardly, her lips pulling back as she stammers, "Learn, pig! Learn from what is the sorrow and death of the old country!" The welter of the crowd continues to grow and the uproar is accompanied by a man rapidly beating a drum strapped around his shoulder, while the woman at his side beats time on her own drum, her long braids bounding, her eyes flashing. The drums pound with a cadence that seems to keep time with the resounding shouts that come from everywhere at once—"Bring him down! Bring him down! Bring him down! Bring him down!" And with that, as if to bring the Dictator down by proxy, a man leaps into the air and throws a fist into the face of the Dictator on a sign that reads LIAR! As the sign buckles, the nostrils of the Dictator spurt streams of blood, which a reporter, astonished at this phenomenon, begins to photograph, this as the crowd grows louder and louder, a growing hullabaloo that sparks a tinder of no return.

Meanwhile, rumbling down a side street to join the crowd comes a wagon in which a guillotine stands tall, its glinting blade hanging high between two wooden uprights, a word scrawled on the blade in red, congealing paint—*Liberté*! The men and women who accompany this guillotine wear clothes of solid black, some having donned black balaclavas that shroud all but their eyes, while others are notable for their tricorn hats, their faces masked by neckerchiefs tied behind their heads. The leader of this group, however, walks out in front of the wagon, a tall figure poised and erect, a man of somber dignity whose white hair flows back off his head in heavy locks that curl in sickle shapes behind his ears. His jet-black *justaucorp*, although frayed and scuffed at the elbows, is nonetheless impressive, even lustrous, and while this garment is too severe to suggest actual elegance, it complements his ebony walking stick, atop which sits a skull of solid gold. Proceeding with firm, measured steps, the man in the black *justaucorp* possesses a demeanor of complacent scorn. His eyes shift from side to side, his bearing formidable. With every step he takes, he hits his ebony walking stick against the ground, producing a resounding BOOM! It is not unlike that of a base drum, but made more splendid by the fact that its reverberations are felt in the flesh even more than they are heard.

Bit by bit, the wagon with the guillotine emerges from the side street, rolling slowly into the crowd, its appearance at once triggering a loud boisterous cheer as people leap about and give vent to wild hoots. On hearing this hullabaloo, a pack of dogs, seemingly conjured up from traces of mist, now rise from the bed of the wagon in which the guillotine stands, gazing about with fierce and searching eyes before leaping off into the night, their ribs protruding, their tongues lolling out. As the dogs disperse among the crowd, they let loose a howling harangue before heading toward a forming line of men in riot gear appearing in the distance. As if in reply to the howling dogs, a barrage of whistling bottle rockets shoots up overhead, scoring the night sky with spark-shedding trajectories. Seeing this, the people in the street shout all the louder, joining the howls all around them with savage urgency, one and all calling for the Dictator's head—BRING THAT BASTARD DOWN! LYING PIECE OF SHIT! TRAITOR! HAIL TO THE PUSSY GRABBER! SLIMY PISS-POT! CUT OUT HIS TONGUE! DUMB FUCK! STOP THIS HATE MONGER! ENTITLED ASSHOLE! OUT FOR HIMSELF! HE'D PIMP HIS OWN DAUGHTER! GREEDY SLIME BALL! SMASH HIM! HE'S A RACIST! DOESN'T KNOW HIS ASS FROM HIS ELBOW! PUT

HIS HEAD ON A PIKE! LYING CHEAT! HE'S SELLING OUT THE
NATION! COCKY KNOW-IT-ALL!   MR. SHIT FOR BRAINS! A
FASCIST! SHOVE HIS BALLS DOWN HIS THROAT! CONNIVING
MUCKWORM! IN BED WITH RUSSIA! HIGH TREASON! LINING HIS
POCKETS! THE DIPSHIT IN CHIEF! SNOOTY ARISTO! HE'S A
TURNCOAT! SCREWING US OVER! FULL OF SHIT! ENOUGH IS
ENOUGH! LET'S GO! LET'S MOVE! NO MORE OF THIS! LYING
THROUGH HIS TEETH! SON OF A BITCH! GET THE PITCHFORKS!
YA-HARR! CHEESY CREEP! KNOCK HIM INTO THE NEXT WORLD!
LET'S LOCK THE BASTARD UP! YEH! LOCK THE BASTARD UP! LOCK
THE BASTARD UP! LOCK THE BASTARD UP!

And as this chant continues . . .

BLOOD DIADEM

. . . the street swells with more and more people, sirens begin to wail with air-raid arias and the throng of angry marchers surges forward, heaving against the wall of polycarbonate riot shields that greets them up ahead, carried by yes-men goons sworn to do the Dictator's bidding, mindless drudges with arthropod antennae sprouting up from their helmets, twitching erratically, the arthropods outnumbered by the mob of people roiling toward them, a fierce, unruly menace, a multitude of faces over which a searchlight sweeps, revealing men and women lashing out, shouting, determined, caught up in the mayhem, the beam of the searchlight illuminating a teenager who hurls a chunk of cinder block through a plate glass window—while elsewhere another window smashes—and another—shards of glass cascading down and crunching underfoot as people run, dodge, rush about, all carried forward on the turbulent swell of what they are—the struggling, the exploited, the artistic, the ignored, the poor, the free-thinking, the broken, and the decent people who have had it up to here—all running hard against the goon-squad lackies at whom the Dictator angrily barks orders from a safe location in his plush abode, yelling at a television screen which he has stared at for hours, his little pig eyes glazed and wincing with contempt as he grabs a toy walkie-talkie given to him by General Au-Pair and into which he now bellows. His voice, however, is lost in a crackling storm of static, drowned out by the blaring of sirens, smothered in the uproar of revolt, whose loud and thundering dissonance reaches every corner of the night.

Sparking desperate calls of *Mayday! Mayday!*—the crowd in the street gives no ground and goes berserk, yelling, marching, lighting fires and throwing rocks and bottles that go flying through the air, only to be met by cannisters of teargas fired back in return, causing a mass of bodies to briefly recoil and then redirect its wrath in another direction, fists flying against the goons as the goons retaliate. A man holding a sign about global warming is body slammed to the ground, while another espousing freedom of religion is punched in the face. A woman who claims that her body is her own business gets grabbed in a chokehold and kneed in the kidneys, and yet the more the goons waylay the crowd the more riled the crowd becomes, exploding in a kaleidoscopic rumble of punches, pummels and vicious blows, the woman in the chokehold clawing the face of her attacker, her hair getting yanked as a man with an axe handle runs to her aid and clubs her attacker, the whole scene a jarring backdrop of fights and curses and wild rage, as squad cars try to corral the crowd and a man's jacket gets ripped from his back as he wriggles free from the goons, only to be tackled, skidding on the street and piled up on, clubbed and kicked until his blood runs through the nooks and crannies of the asphalt, pooling up in small red puddles.

Blazing at fever pitch, more and more people now rush out into the open and join the fray. Certain pockets of agitators have reached a critical mass, flipping over a car and torching another, while from a window several stories overhead an upside down American flag unfurls with the word SOLD emblazoned across it in black spray paint. The young couple holding this flag scream bloody murder, yelling at the top of their lungs to "Kick the Dictator's fucking ass! Give him hell! Show him who's boss!" While another man who leans out a different window cries: "He's a traitor! Traitor!" Flinging open yet another window, someone else shouts: "He's a shithead! Bring him down!" And soon more and more onlookers are hanging out their windows, cheering the tumult down in the street, exhorting the crowd to cut loose, to go wild, to take no more shit, to say fuck it all—creating an aerial cacophony in which voices boom and echo: "Hang the rich son of a bitch! Lambaste the dumb fuck! Box his ears! Fight on!" The hostility, indeed, is unrelenting, and not to be outdone are a half dozen people on a concrete balcony who now hold up a large depiction of the Dictator's face on which is written a single word in big block letters: ASSHOLE! And this is the word that the people on the balcony now begin to robustly chant, their voices bouncing off the buildings and resounding up and down the street: "ASS-HOLE! ASS-HOLE! ASS-HOLE! ASS-HOLE!"

Back on the ground below, meanwhile, the conflict grows more brutal and bloody. At one particular locus of action, a jumble of people struggles to break through a stubborn line of goons, but the Dictator's henchmen dig in their heels and push back, producing a clash of brawling bodies, a tooth-and-nail gridlock, a nasty bout of fisticuffs in which Jennifer Golembeski loses her balance and stumbles, just as the powerful swing of a nightstick cuts through the air and grazes her forehead, blood suddenly streaming down her face as her flesh splits open and she topples backward seeing stars. Although her feet have gone out from under her, Jennifer nonetheless looks straight up into the face of her assailant, only to find, however, that the face of the man fades in and out, blurred by the blood flowing into her eyes perhaps—or perhaps because the blow to her head has made her mind play tricks on her. Whatever the reason, the face that hovers over her distorts and rearranges, suddenly filling out with the exact features of the Dictator, a sneering, pig-eyed mug at which Jennifer has just enough time to spit before another resistance fighter trips and falls on top of her, knocking the wind out of her as she blinks away the rivulets of blood running into her eyes.

As the pandemonium continues, the paramedics on the scene don't know which way to turn. A fragment of crowd at this point has broken off and run down a side street while a phalanx of helmeted goons gives chase—only to find themselves ambushed by a roving band of gypsy punks lobbing Molotov cocktails directly at them, the punks having as backup a contingent of computer geeks who pop out from the shadows firing effective and powerful slingshots. Arrests are made fast and furious and the paddy wagons on the scene sag under the weight of handcuffed radicals and roughed up freedom fighters. As the ever-wailing sirens blare, the crowd grows more hepped up than ever, shouting and yelling to rally and revolt, while those resisting arrest are joined by still more people who jump the goons from behind in a rough-and-tumble riot of kicks and punches and billy clubs and cries, a contagion of rage boiling over, stoked by the Dictator and the scions of maggots who abide by The Man—while the people, poor chumps, get backed into a corner, grumbling, waiting, itching to make contact with that last final straw that will pull out all the stops on the *vox humana* from hell.

SHOCK TREATMENT

*T*he Dictator, while on his way to the Golden Putter Gold Club for a round of golf, spoke with Chanticleer Gazette reporter Wayne Radcliffe, who was accompanied by his recording assistant Jimmy Dalton. The interview, granted to The Chanticleer Gazette by way of a personal request, was conducted in a private conference room at the Balmy Breakers Hotel, West Palm Beach, Fla. What follows is a verbatim transcript of that conversation as recorded by The Chanticleer Gazette. No editing for either content or clarity was undertaken.

CHANTICLEER GAZETTE: Good afternoon, Your Excellency, thank you for taking time out from your busy executive golf schedule to speak with us today.

DICTATOR: Yeah, we fixed that, see, I'm here. I figured it. I could have been out on the green right now, riding in my golf cart, my 656th game of the year, but nobody knew that. You were over there in that, what, that whole deal. Now you're here. They could've gotten us, the Mexicans, but they didn't do it. They weren't paying. Nobody knew they weren't paying. I knew it, though. I said it. I said we'll make them pay because it turns out we'd just rolled out a list, like what Thomas Jefferson did, lists. He liked to get things done. Great American. Like me. He had lists to get things done. I predicted it. The concept is right. I thought of that, you know.

CHANTICLEER GAZETTE: Yes, well, we're delighted to have this opportunity to talk to you, Your Excellency, and I'd like to begin with the social unrest that's breaking out around the nation. The opposition to your regime seems to be growing. Protests are turning violent and rioting is breaking out in several cities. What is your assessment concerning the agitated state of the nation right now?

DICTATOR: Look, it's incredible. It's fantastic. We're making so much money. Maybe they can't help themselves, but I went to college. I know things. The leaks, too, I'm going to know that, who's wiretapping me, but maybe they can't help themselves. We're great again. Look how good it's been. The people go crazy over me because it's a lot of information that I predicted, mostly after the committee. General Au Pair was there. He saw it on the front page. He read it. I didn't read it. I'm busy, you know, in meetings, lots of paperwork. But what I'm talking about is my instinct. We're great again, all of America, it's like what the president of France said, but he really didn't say it. I said he said it, but not really, but he winked at me, which is more than saying it, yeah, if you understand these things. So it's going to be interesting because he knows I won. The pictures, the crowds, you remember, and it so happens that smart people understand me, but that wasn't in the newspaper. They couldn't be bothered, they made it all about the leaks. But I wasn't referring to Felix the Cat. I never mentioned Felix the Cat. I didn't say that, so why do people feel I have to apologize? Wait, wait though, over the next coming period of time, you'll see, I happen to know how life works. Tens of thousands of people, they cheer for me, they line up, cheering. I saw a man at a rally—and this is the truth—he was cheering so hard for me his teeth fell out. In Harrisburg, Pennsylvania, it was. Good people out there. And that's the greatness of how it is when things get proven so much that nobody knows it better than anybody else. That's why we're going to have a big military parade. We're going to do that. Big! Tanks! Soldiers marching! Fighter jets flying overhead! Maybe dropping some napalm jelly. It's not so bad, napalm jelly, I know more than anyone about napalm jelly, you can get a few burns, everybody knows that, but it's the greatness what matters. We're great again.

CHANTICLEER GAZETTE: Felix the Cat?

DICTATOR: Well remember it's the real story because that's where the whole—the number one horrible thing was showing I know what I'm talking about, like with Brussels, like Sweden, but Felix the Cat, it's been good, we talk about classified information, that's his job. So why are people so upset? Felix the Cat, if you want to know the truth, he really knows more than General Au Pair, and I like General Au Pair, he's a great guy. Great guy. I have to admit he plays with himself too much, but look what he did with Benghazi. Was it Benghazi? They dropped that headline, I never saw it, and people say it was more than that, so I'm forming a committee on it. Me and Felix the Cat, we'll study the matter. It's a serious problem, serious. But I don't like the leaks, it's bad, what you go to prison for if you release stuff like that. Or take the NATO costs, all that money these countries owe us. I said it, I was right, and Felix the Cat didn't deny it, that's what we get paid for, our intelligence, spying. The whole country believes me because they know I inherited a mess, all that stuff with the—the statistics of the mess, I mean we have opioids, and whatever happened to that Pakistani guy? I mean, I need to be treated fairly because of the purposes of my particular justice, everybody knows.

CHANTICLEER GAZETTE: I see, thank you for those insights, Your Excellency. I'd like to move on now to your former Minister of Foreign Relations, Tillerman Tyro. As you know, before he was fired, he had visited the fledgling democracy of Fredonia, where he pledged his support for the new era of self-governance that had been established there. The Fredonian president, however, had some stark words for Minister Tyro, stating that the policies which you yourself have enacted here at home have made a mockery of our Constitutional rights and destroyed our credibility as democratic paragon, making us, and I quote, "a total joke in the eyes of the world." How do you respond to these assertions, Your Excellency?

DICTATOR: Look, since then I don't know where he's gone with it, but Tyro was at the meetings. He knows. All that expertise he's got, it's really something, and there's no picture of him with Lee Harvey Oswald. None. Think about that. No Oswald. Not like that wetback down there in Texas with those skank daughters of his that I wouldn't even touch with *your* dick. Nothing like my daughter, Daughter Ditzy Doll Eyes. She's a prize and you know it. You've seen her. A prize! Did you get a load of her ass? It's like I told that shock jock, if she weren't my daughter I'd be humping her all day long. Hot stuff, you want it, there she is, and that shock jock knows it, for whatever he's worth, the sleazebag. He sees a lot of hot ass. He knows that daughter of mine stacks up. Good bloodline. That's what it is, and so where does some greasy little nacho chip get off trying to play in the big leagues—with thoroughbreds like me? Me! It's a disgrace. He couldn't see I was right. But I'm right over and over. Look at Kentucky. Kentucky proved I was right. I was there two weeks ago in a massive basketball arena. It was packed. Thousands of people. They're cheering me because they believe in me, highly respected people who have to go to the back of the line because they don't know anything other than—no, I'm not blaming, but the mess, the jobs, trade, the Middle East. They saw the picture of Oswald, and so we have an understanding. They know what he's up to, but I put that wetback in his place. Now he bends over backwards to kiss my ass. Why? Because I put him in his place. You see, that's leadership. That's why he gave that news conference on the surveillance. A lot of information. The scope of it, people plotting against me. It's the Dark State. Everybody, even, who, yeah, my Nazi friends, they knew about it, but that other dick, Prince Penis, he's bringing down the whole party, him and others. So that's why we have Tillerman Tyro, wonderful man, I'm just saying.

CHANTICLEER GAZETTE: But you yourself fired Minister Tyro, Your Excellency, I'm sure you recall.

DICTATOR: Yes, he's fired! He got off message. He talked up the Chinese like they were normal human beings and then went and said that Vladimir Puttenesca was a rat-faced thug, that Russia was the world's greatest kleptocracy and we were going down the same road. That was bad. Bad. I know Vladimir Puttenesca. He said nice things about me, I believe him, and what he is is a saint, a saintly man, wears a crucifix. What does that tell you? He's good. Not bad. Good. Wonderful man. He'll hang the Muslims upside down from the trees and let the wolves tear them apart. The gays too! You've seen his muscles. A truly great man. Great. Fantastic. Like the pope maybe, that's the kind of greatness going on. So we can't have Tillerman Tyro saying I want to create gulags out in Kansas and that I'm ready to bump off anybody I don't like, like that whore bitch porn star with pictures of my dick that's nobody's business. I should have liquidated her long ago, but I didn't, you see? I'm not the—it's what you have to do, you have to get in people's faces, slap them around, and so if somebody disappears it's that you don't miss the people who disappear because they're not there, right? Political opponents, liberals, if they disappear, so what? I don't make them disappear, and who's to say they're dead anyway? Nobody misses that kind of riffraff anyway, it's better for the country, and when I'm made dictator for life like President Gee Whizz out there in China—over there, you know, with his chopsticks and that wall, wow! What a wall! Look at their wall! So big, a big, beautiful wall! That's how it is. President Gee Whizz even has ivory chopsticks from the tusks of elephants that my own kids shot dead. Shot them in the head with big guns. Very big guns. They blast the elephants dead. Tough, my kids, they're tough like me, and the ivory, that's free trade! I bet you didn't know that. I know more about free trade than anyone. So when I'm dictator for life there won't be any need for gulags or even health insurance, it's going to be so great, so much money, and Vladimir Puttenesca, he knows this, I called and congratulated him, I let him know what a good job he's doing, look, look at the pretty eggs, the ballerinas, that's Russia, and that's why he clamps down on Pussy Riot. I can't blame him. Rioting pussies—bad, bad. He's afraid of them. I'd be afraid of them, too. Rioting pussies, it's worse than Mexicans and blacks and California all put together! Which is communist, by the way, California. Bet you didn't know that. I know more about communism than anybody. So I fired Tillerman Tyro, yeah, it was tough. But then again, he might have known Oswald. Who's to say he didn't know Oswald? I might have read it. Then you have real trouble.

CHANTICLEER GAZETTE: But getting back to the president of Fredonia. He made a damning statement about our nation and your regime. What do you—

DICTATOR: Name what's wrong! It's the fake news and people, all the people, they agree with the sources that admit the country isn't buying it. I have great instinct. I found out that things aren't incidental in China and the wall, their wall, you see, you can't blame them. But our wall will be greater. Bigger! Look, their wall you can see from the moon, that's nice, but our wall you'll be able to see from Mars. Mars! We're going to Mars. Did I tell you that? We got the rockets and there's people working on that, and the evangelicals, they're praying for it, actually praying to go to Mars. Jesus might be on Mars. They say he's everywhere. So if we need a delegation up there, they're going up there, to Mars. They can handle it, but there might be statues of the Beach Boys up there already, I read that, and I know more about the Beach Boys than anybody, but that president of Fredonia is a disgusting pipsqueak from a little piece of shit country. Garbage. That's what it is. He can only wish that he was going to Mars. But I'll show him who's boss, I'll set him straight. That's what I do. I'm from the old school, we beat the crap out of people. Good people. Hard working people. We don't care. I've ripped off so many people I could care less.

CHANTICLEER GAZETTE: But with all due respect, Your Excellency, when Tillerman Tyro was confronted by the president of Fredonia, he not only agreed with the Fredonian leader, but went so far as to call you a fucking moron, saying, and I quote, that your "head was so far up your ass it would take a 20-ton knuckle boom to pull it out." Might this have had something to do with his being fired?

DICTATOR: Fired! He's fired! If you look at what's going on, my base is stronger than ever. Unbelievable! It's been proven because I campaign better, it's like golf, and who knows this better than anybody? Felix the Cat. Because there is no collusion, and so I actually think that it's turning out—that it's going to—because there are no real Russians. The stories you guys wrote, then dropped, was that you? It's bad for the country, so the sooner it's worked out, all the stuff that happened with these indicted people, I don't even go that far. It's been proven! It would have been a whole different— it's different, like stroke play. If you're going to a golf tournament, you have to play, and the only thing I can tell you is that you go places and the whole thing is a witch hunt. It's like my, my, where did that guy go? That communications guy—it's all about how they came after him. He did the fandango! That's what he did, he had no choice.

CHANTICLEER GAZETTE: Your Excellency, are you feeling okay? Should we take a break and resume later?

DICTATOR: Feel great! Everybody knows how I came out and said it. The rocket man should have been done for, wasted, including all that stuff and whatever happened when you look at the things I did. I saved coal! It's everywhere. That's because of my genes. People will tell you the biggest problem is the made-up Russians, but not in West Virginia. They're rolling in money, so much money. But I'm the one! Their GDP, their average—so fantastic—I think there's a lot of talk of doing fantastic. But it didn't work for the purposes of hopefully thinking what I've done on this particular matter, which is no collusion. There was no collusion. No collusion at all. So they were coming after me, undercutting my cheeseburgers, so I can tell you this because the story is—when you look at guns or the—it's . . . I believe it! Thanks to my genes! So I said to them, "Good, let's go." I created the jobs.

CHANTICLEER GAZETTE: I see, yes, that's certainly interesting, but since you—

DICTATOR: Of course it's interesting, it's got to be interesting, the way of how it gets done. You take a beauty pageant, all that ass, all those chimichangas bouncing around. It's interesting, it's more than interesting, just so you understand, but it's business and I'm a businessman, I'm Mr. Business, and my lawyer signed off on it. There's lots of businesses I run, let me tell you, all over the world, and I talked to all these people, millions of people, such good people, and its going to be very popular to have all this money, so much money, you see, they got it in West Virginia now, the money. Thanks to me. So what I'm saying is they need beauty pageants down there to make it interesting, beauty pageants and coal. Then you'll get the bipartisanship.

CHANTICLEER GAZETTE: Ah, yes, if you say so, Your Excellency, but another point I wanted to address, since you brought it up, does concern the matter of collusion.

DICTATOR: Hmmm.

CHANTICLEER GAZETTE: As you know, many people charge that you have colluded with hostile nations in order to enrich your own personal fortune and in the process have jeopardized our national security and undermined the nation's credibility and moral authority. Some people have even made the case that you're guilty of high treason. How do you respond, Your Excellency?

DICTATOR: Wait! Wait! Beyond the testimony people have the privilege of saying we ended up with a gag order. When you can do something, buy something, it's not about—I got a mandate! Bigger than anyone knows, can even calculate, and the indictments, the plea bargains, it's a lot of different things, trying to stab me in the back, that's what they're doing, because they lost. Losers! There were no Russians coming back into the country. You can do a lot of different things. How could I even talk to them? But I know more about the issues than anybody else. I know the details, I do. Taxes—I know the numbers! Better than a CPA. I'm rich. But they wanted me to answer for that. These are sick people, so now we have the—you watch, it's a witch hunt, and people have no idea how—look, we need the wall! You saw this, the set up, and the Russian whores, they don't launder money, so it could be half the people who are going to these whores. So I'm moving in both directions to get rid of the chain lightning, because I don't want kids to get shot in school. I just want more guns, lots of guns, guns make you tough. But if the Russians say nice things about me, it wasn't my deal. I was a great student, that's how I did it. I'm a natural genius. Ask Vulpine News, they'll tell you. So the money will be flowing in, more money than people can count. So what's currency manipulation? What's money laundering? What's kicking people out of fixed income apartments? It's business. I'm treated unfairly, dishonestly, by the news media. They're ripping off this country, but China, too, and with Broadcom they steal my tanks! But we're doing the parade. It's going to be big! Big parade! Huge! That's why there's no collusion, because the Japs will go drop a bowling ball on the Puerto Ricans and whose cars are they going to buy then? Not our cars. We can't sell them any cars. No electricity in Puerto Rico. Too bad. No electric cars. Too bad. But those jabbering spics, look, I gave them paper towels and that's more than they deserve.

CHANTICLEER GAZETTE: I see, yes. You mentioned China, and recently you had tough words for both China and North Korea, yet in spite of our trade deficit with China they remain a stabilizing force in the region, particularly when it comes to North Korea's nuclear ambitions. How do you reconcile your tough words with continuing to maintain our diplomatic leverage in the region?

DICTATOR: They're shithole countries! Stinking shithole countries like Africa. But I like the Chinese, the man there, their leader, President Gee Whizz, you see, there's good chemistry between us, but it all should have been handled 30 years ago before that pudgy chink got whatever hands he's got on those nuclear weapons, and so when the oil is going in and with the chow mein commodities I say I do what I've always wanted to do, which is, you know, it's a nuclear menace, including Instagram, so I look at the whole trade thing differently than many people, that oil, that $350 billion deficit, it's ripping us off more than any Shylock in the history of the world or even the sweatshops where the little peons make my daughter's straight jackets. Great product, by the way. Excellent product. If someone loses his marbles, goes nuts, you can get him into one of these straight jackets in less than a minute, that's why they're called Minuteman Straight Jackets. It's a brand name, it's patriotic, a sign of greatness. Thanks to my daughter, Daughter Ditzy Doll Eyes. I'm a brand name, too, a better brand name, thanks to me. Best brand in the world, but the press doesn't report on that, it's the liberal media, controlled by hippies. They're in the Dark State, you know, like Darth Vader, they never went away. Only Vulpine News tells the truth because people have no idea of the unbelievably great job I'm doing. Health care! Taxes! But you guys lie about it. Fake news! But I'm doing the deals on the great capabilities and essentially something so terrific that they didn't show up. It was too great for them, the Saudis, the French, everybody. Where were they? What happened to that Pakistani guy? Nobody can tell me that. I would've sent him Air Ribs. Then what would he do? He'd get the message, like China, like North Korea. I got tough with how they never thought I'd be able to get payoffs to a porn star over the line because that's the tremendous scandal of the mess I was left with, by which I mean phony Russia for the purposes of who was pissing on my head! Who does that? Where are the Russian whores? It's locker room vigilantes! It's those hitmen at the FBI! It's that attorney general dipshit who's got only one ball and yet he goes and throws his weight around recusing himself like he's hot shit to save his own ass. He's the lowest of the low! No loyalty! No loyalty!

CHANTICLEER GAZETTE: Your Excellency, you don't appear well, you're trembling. Perhaps that's enough for today.

DICTATOR: I know what's going on, it's the Dark State. It's real, the people, even high school students are in on it. They're marching out, playing hooky! What's up? Why? Because a few of them get shot to death? Their parents are raising idiots! They could have tackled the gunman—it would have been fifty to one, a hundred to one! I would have charged right in at the gunman—gun or no gun. Charged right in! Because people know I'm fearless—that's why they wouldn't let me fight in Vietnam! Did you know that? I was too fearless, the morale would've suffered, and all these other soldiers— they were clowns, peace freaks, working class losers who didn't have two nickels to buy their way out of those body bags. They'd go to pieces if they saw how fearless I was. So the Army didn't want me. They gave me a deferment. But I was ready for the rice paddies, for the guns, but they had to keep up morale so I couldn't go. I was dying to go! Instead I had to hang around New York fucking a lot of babes, trying not to get venereal disease. Talk about scary. That's living on the edge, risky—more risky than Vietnam! But still I got to serve my country—look how I'm serving it! But Vietnam was a waste anyway because even as it was happening the Russians were sneaking into the country. I tried to warn the generals. Nobody could see it, but the country, it—look, there were little naked trolls with pink hair and Rat Finks, that's right, that was the conspiracy, the beginning of the brainwashing, and by who—the Russians! I hounded them down! On submarines they were, and driving Jaguars. Nobody listened and it was plain as day despite the sugarcane, they wanted it. The Bay of Pigs! And we did nothing about the Russians, they were right under our noses! Just waltzing into the country. Very bad. Bad. They say collusion with Russia, it's crazy. Lies! And all the while I was roping them in, tying up so many Russians—by the score! I can't remember how many. I was doing the spy stuff. They wanted to give me a medal, but I shouldn't be talking about that, it's classified stuff, but that's how I got debriefed on the plutonium, and it was smuggled by plumbers on whose yacht? You'll never guess! Aristotle Onasis! People don't know that. He's rich! Small world. But I knew it all, all that and more—all the Russians, I knew them, and Kuryakin, yeah, he was good, he switched over to our side. Hardly anyone knows that, but I knew, I knew, and the people in Iowa knew because they know better out there, because even a blind person can legally carry a gun in Iowa, it's true, they're ahead of the curve! Is that so difficult? We're great again!

CHANTICLEER GAZETTE: I see, well, I'm sure I've already taken up too much of your time, Your Excellency, it would be an honor to continue this at a later date—

DICTATOR: You didn't ask me about ISIS! I know more about ISIS than anyone! It's one of the threats I told everyone about now that they know I'm right when I say it. My instinct, and so you got Sharia law at Disneyworld, and that mouse—is he a rat? Do we know that? I know more about rodents than anyone. They're wiretapping me when busloads, whole busloads of square dancers got shipped out to

Vermont to vote illegally. So you can see what's going on? They're bringing down the country.

CHANTICLEER GAZETTE: Square dancers?

DICTATOR: No, you fucking dipshit! I can't tell you, but there are so many elements in that dossier and some people didn't say a word. Everybody laughed, even though there's going to be a war, did I mention that? Sure as shit! Big war! Big! Hell and fury—and then you'll see who cares about collusion! So do you know what I do at breakfast? I wrap up the Koran in a big piece of bacon and light it on fire. Then I eat it! I eat it with an Egg McMuffin! That's what I do! So how's that for being tough? Tell me! So there's going to be a war. You've got to show people what's going to happen to them because if you don't they dance in the streets otherwise. I saw them on TV, the Muslims, in Amish country, dancing in the streets and raping Amish girls, that's what they do. That's why Pennsylvania needs to vote for me or the whole deal with the Middle East, the 7 trillion, it'll default to Russia on account of the cheese. They're making all this cheese, making it in Russia now, but its intellectual property. The House Intelligence Chairman knows that. It's no secret. There was no collusion. Never any collusion. No collusion and no money laundering, no money laundering to speak of—no money laundering! No collusion! No hush money either! I didn't even eat the Russian cheese. I like American cheese.

CHANTICLEER GAZETTE: Well, on that note, Your Excellency, it was a pleasure to speak with you, and I'd like to thank you for devoting some of your valuable time to this interview.

DICTATOR: Yeah, it's good. Everything's good. Of course it's good, because I'm the Dictator and you're just worthless garbage, garbage from the fake news, I know that, you know that, and I know more about Mars than NASA.

CHANTICLEER GAZETTE: Thank you again, Your Excellency.

DICTATOR [continuing to talk as he rises from his chair and leaves the room, accompanied by a large contingent of body guards]: You'd better thank me, jerk, because the only reason you're here is because of me, so good riddance, dumbbell, and don't forget I know they're watching and anything I predicted other than that is exactly where it goes despite the Hatch Act and the emoluments and even when Germany was over here with that runt Brunhilde woman. So what if she speaks Russian and has a PhD in quantum chemistry—I'm rich! Rich! That's what I am! And it's the greatness of what's going to happen when the hicks and the KKK all drive across the state lines and then they'll buy the Russian cheese and the steel, and we'll send that rocket man south of the border and make the Playboy bunnies pay for it and then—then wait! You'll see! There won't be a seat left in the house and Schwarzenegger will be fired! Fired! Out on his Austrian ass! Not even an American! Fired! Like Tillerman Tyro! Like Michael Skinflint! Like Fandango! Who didn't last three days, the mangey wop! Couldn't even *do* the fandango! All of them ganging up on me! A plot! Conspiracy! Even that she-devil porn star! She put voodoo beans up my ass and then put my dentures in a glass full of piss! Nasty! Nasty woman! So many nasty women! Those rioting pussies! So many you can't even grab them all! Nasty! Nasty like that pantsuit princess chuckling away up there in Chappaqua as she watches me do all the work! That's what she did! Rigged the election so I got caught holding the bag! Me! Left with a mess! Incredible mess! That's how they did it! Just look at it all! Unbelievable mess! All the mess left by that half-breed jungle bunny who wasn't even born in this country and—and—and look! I'm telling you, I did the—there were the documents! Studio 54! Area 51! There's the evidence! He wasn't even born in this country! He wasn't even from this planet! The Air Force knew it! The generals knew it! But I had to call them out on it! Make them admit he was from that—that galaxy! Maybe Mars! Did I tell you we're going to

Mars? Another place! That's where! Out of the solar system! It's far away! How do you think he did it! No one else would do it but me! From a UFO! I'm not afraid of UFOs! I'd run right in! I'd do it! But I'd make sure they had Pizza Hut! That's how you deal with space creatures! You can't just—

[Door slams.]

CHANTICLEER GAZETTE: Whew, my God . . . Did you record all of that for posterity, Jimmy?

JIMMY: Sure did. In fact, the mic's still on.

CHANTICLEER GAZETTE: There it is for the record, Jimmy. That man is a blithering idiot, the mother of all assholes, no wonder the nation's going belly up.

JIMMY: I'm with you on that, bro. What do you say we get some lunch? I think it's time for a beer.

CHANTICLEER GAZETTE: More like a boilermaker for me. Getting stuck listening to that jerk is hell on Earth, it's like being in a madhouse.

JIMMY: Ha! I'm with you in Rockland, my man.

RHONDA REDWING AND THE WHIRLWIND MAN

Returning from a late-night walk along the banks of a woodland stream, Rhonda Redwing gazed up thoughtfully into the stars. This moment of contemplation was especially important to Rhonda Redwing, for to linger amid the shadowy stillness of the trees and hear the stream ripple faintly in the background helped to calm the foreboding that nettled her heart, the sobering apprehension that always occurred when the Whirlwind Man was about to pay a visit. Anticipating his arrival, Rhonda Redwing now picked up her pace, walking steadily through the woods, climbing up a rocky bluff and then nimbly working her way down the other side.

Knowing that the Whirlwind Man preferred to be in darkness, Rhonda Redwing entered the small gray house where she lived and did not turn on any lights, but instead made her way through the house carefully to the kitchen cupboard. Opening it and reaching inside, she felt about until detecting a hurricane lamp, which she removed and placed on a bare trestle table. Next, fumbling about in a drawer, she popped the cap off a metal cylinder and withdrew a wooden matchstick, striking it on her belt buckle, filling the room with a hissing glow.

After removing the glass globe from the hurricane lamp, Rhonda Redwing turned up the wick and touched the match to it, watching the flame take hold and sprout upward, the room around her dimly revealing itself. After replacing the globe on the lamp, she then glanced at a clock on the kitchen counter and went to the sink and washed her hands before opening a jar of walnuts, popping a few into her mouth. Chewing slowly, she stared at the flame of the hurricane lamp and considered how the Whirlwind Man would never mention a specific hour at which to meet her, but always put his arrival in terms of how many hours after dark the encounter would occur— two hours after dark, or three hours after dark, or however long. In addition to this, she puzzled over how the Whirlwind Man even managed to be at her house at all, for he always showed up on foot, which sparked the suspicion that he had ditched his car somewhere and made his way to her by walking roundabout through the woods. She also had the sense that he almost always arrived early and that he would linger about outside, remaining under the cover of darkness, waiting, biding his time, keeping himself from view until it suited him to walk up to the door and knock.

Knowing neither from where the Whirlwind Man came nor what he wanted, Rhonda Redwing realized that had he been anyone else she would have been on her guard and rebuffed the man, telling him to go away. But from the first night he had shown up at her door, she saw that this was a man trembling with fear, his sunken cheeks taut, his blue-green eyes pleading. She was too surprised to speak to the man and could only stare as he mumbled a few words and then walked away. But as she watched his tall figure drift off into the shadows, she was given pause and could not dismiss him. The urgent look in his eyes and his high-strung state of mind had provoked in her a feeling of kinship she could not explain, convincing her that in the end he would be back again to see her.

After this first encounter with the Whirlwind Man, she awaited his return for many days. She recalled that his fine blond hair was so thin it seemed to cling to his head by a kind of static electricity, and she thought about the soft but earnest reach of his voice, which struck her as soulful and sincere. What did he want with her? What did he want to talk about? Such questions ought to have been foremost in her mind, but overriding them was the simple anticipation of his return. This alone seemed to matter, and so when once again, a couple weeks later, a knock sounded at her door very late, she was not surprised, but looked up from her cross-stitching and listened, permitting herself a brief moment to do nothing before rising from her chair.

When she opened the door, the Whirlwind Man offered no greeting but stood nonplused and abject, as if he had been imperiously summoned. Only when the silence grew awkward did he speak, declaring openly that he was scared, his mouth twitching while his eyes blinked with embarrassment. His voice, however, was firm, and Rhonda Redwing—without hesitation—asked him what he was afraid of. Her question came instantly and naturally, as if their conversation had been ongoing and established, which caused the Whirlwind Man to look into her eyes, his expression changing, revealing the dark torments holding him at bay, his features marred as if by pain. As he struggled to answer, his chest began to swell, aching with something hidden and pent up.

Stepping aside, Rhonda Redwing invited him to enter, then walked into the kitchen to boil water for tea, the Whirlwind Man following, taking a seat at the trestle table as she put the kettle on the stove. The tea she had prepared was her grandfather's recipe for berry-mint tea, and once it had steeped for several minutes she offered the Whirlwind Man a hot mug of it. As he brought the mug slowly to his lips, she could see how the aroma seemed to put him at ease, his eyes closing as he inhaled it, at last taking a sip.

So began Rhonda Redwing's encounters with the Whirlwind Man, encounters that occurred only at night with the house in darkness. At first, very little of what the man said seemed to be of any account to her, partly because at first he said very little. But as the weeks went by the jigsaw of his words began to piece together in the manner of a portent, so that in the end it was not simply she who was serving to calm his riled state, but he who had emboldened her, who had brought her to the brink of a vital moment linked to something inherent in his words, so that she was caught unaware and had to confront it. And yet, she hesitated, finding herself at a juncture whose options were to either spare herself the obvious crisis of this man and tell him there was no further point in continuing their meetings—or adopt him as a man of paleface war paint, a man who claimed to hear the siren song of fossils and to breathe the wind-borne cry of bears, a man who with his eyes welling uttered that the polliwogs in the swamps had melted away, that the dreams of salamanders had turned to ash, and that the puniest comeuppance in the world had hitched itself to a bolt of lightning, igniting the blood of everybody with a fiery iridescence. Over and over, as the weeks went by, she had heard the wild declarations of the Whirlwind Man and watched as he hung his head and took it in his hands, saying mournfully, "We're all on the reservation now." Ultimately, she could not turn this man away, and so once again, tonight, she waited for him beside the glow of the hurricane lamp.

When the Whirlwind Man at last appeared, he was breathing hard, his eyes frantic and beseeching. As he paced about the room, he became so jittery he could hardly steady his hands to unzip his jacket, and although he was eager to speak, his words were stymied, a dizzy spell of despair closing in on him. So apparent was his distress that Rhonda Redwing went to him and took his hand, leading him to a sofa where she urged him to lie down.

"You are taking sides with yourself," she cautioned him.

"And you are Rhonda Redwing," he replied, his voice cracking. "You are a Mohawk, but what am I? What am I?"

"Tonight, you are someone to protect my dreams," she said.

The Whirlwind Man closed his eyes and spoke with them closed. "There are shadows entrenching in me, such terrible things," he said.

"Where do they come from?"

"Everywhere at once, like heat lightning, no one place, but . . ."

"But?"

"The finishing touch, there's always a lightning rod," replied the Whirlwind Man.

"You cannot help yourself," reassured Rhonda Redwing, "that's just how it is. Submit to yourself."

"I'm afraid. I've been afraid for weeks, for months."

"I will try to help you," offered Rhonda Redwing. "Tonight, listen, you will hang from that large maple outside the door. I'll tie you up to a huge branch there and you will hang there all night so that your feet cannot touch the ground, so that you are lifted off this world."

"What will happen to me?" the man asked, his eyes wide and rapt.

"You will confront a storm, I think. It will be harsh and brutal. But you know this, I think. Haven't you already found yourself losing your balance, almost falling down?"

"I saw a pressure-cooking high rise with larvae squirming out the windows," blurted out the Whirlwind Man. "It was a cold, white citadel, one of hundreds standing one behind the other . . . a necropolis, a graveyard of bleached concrete."

"Shhh . . . I will prepare you, I will help," said Rhonda Redwing. "Stick out your tongue."

The Whirlwind Man looked at her, unsure, then obeyed. Taking his tongue between her fingers, Rhonda Redwing gave it a firm tug, saying, "There, now I have removed your tongue, say nothing else, just keep quiet."

After telling him this, Rhonda Redwing went into the basement and returned with two earthenware jars stopped by wide corks. Each was a preparation she had mixed together only a couple days before. Kneeling down beside the Whirlwind Man, she placed the jars on the floor and opened one of them. The dark material inside was a black paste that smelled of bear grease and charcoal, and into this she dipped her fingers, after which she began to carefully paint the left side of the Whirlwind Man's face, starting at his hairline and filling in his brow, but stopping dead center in his forehead, creating a bisecting line. Carefully, she then moved lower and smeared the bridge of his nose, progressing down over his one nostril before fanning out the black paste under his eye and up over his temple, after which she darkened the whole of his cheek, his jaw, his chin, while delicately tracing the line of his lips halfway across to the midpoint, dipping her fingers into the jar again and again as she needed to.

After wiping her fingers with an old dishcloth, she now removed the cork from the second jar. The paste inside was a rich, red color, a cool mixture of clay, beet juice and berries, which she now scooped out on her fingers and dabbed on the Whirlwind Man's forehead again, this time on his right side, again beginning by spreading the color along his hairline and working her way down from there, covering every aspect of his face just as she had done on the opposite side, making sure the red color met with the black in the center of his face, continuing all the way down to his chin. When she had finished applying the contents of the second jar, the man's face stood out completely red on one side while the other remained solid black.

Pausing a moment, Rhonda Redwing now took a few seconds to consider the appearance of this man. Apparently satisfied, she then, without warning, yanked the man's shirt out of his pants, causing him to recoil, his eyes growing wide when he saw she held a gleaming hunting knife directly over him. Stabbing the knife through a portion of his shirt, she tore and ripped at the material, cutting away at it until a jagged piece was removed. This piece she carefully wrapped in a leaf of tobacco, saying, "I will put this under my pillow tonight."

The Whirlwind Man did not respond, and Rhonda Redwing took his hand and brought him to his feet, telling him she would now prepare him for the tree. After fetching a long length of rope along with a few faded bath towels, she and the Whirlwind Man went outside, where she began wrapping the Whirlwind Man's shoulders and armpits with the towels, tying them together in snug–fitting rings. This was a measure that would provide padding against the rope, which she now looped around his body in the manner of a harness, creating a double crisscross that she cinched tight and knotted between his shoulder blades. Confident that the Whirlwind Man would not dislodge from this harness, she then walked to a toolshed and dragged out an old wooden stepladder which she opened and placed under the thick limb of a large maple.

The Whirlwind Man waited until she now told him to climb to the top of the ladder, to the highest step, which he did, balancing there tentatively as the Mohawk woman below took the end of the rope that was trailing behind him and tossed it over the limb overhead, catching the end of it as it fell and pulling it to take up the slack between the limb and the man. Then she tossed the end of the rope over the limb again, and pulled, repeating the process yet once more and pulling so that the rope coiled firmly around the limb. Next, she took the end of the rope and drew it up tight, tying it around a smaller tree a few feet away, securing it with her own version of a timber hitch knot. After doing this, she went and shoved the ladder out from under the Whirlwind Man's feet, watching him drop down and then get jerked upward at the shoulders, the rope catching him at the armpits, his body swinging to and fro. Gazing up at the Whirlwind Man, she saw the half-black, half-red face she had created, the man staring down at her, hanging there helplessly. With his body still swinging to and fro, she quietly turned and walked back into the house. There she undressed and got ready for bed, taking the tobacco leaf in which a piece of the man's shirt had been wrapped and placing it under her pillow. After crawling beneath the covers, she then took a deep breath and, stretching out as she did so, quickly fell asleep.

The Whirlwind Man, meanwhile, hung suspended in the darkness, dangling from the tree outside. With his tall frame looming in the shadows and his red and black face stark and unsettling, he looked every bit like a displaced scarecrow that had been picked up by a strong wind and hurled through the air before landing in the branches of the tree. Frozen and phlegmatic, the man's features showed no sign of life, having taken on the rigidity of a mask, although his eyes, despite being downcast, were bright and staring at the ground. As a breeze picked up, the ground beneath him began to shift about, moving this way and that as the Whirlwind Man twisted one way, then another, caught in the ebb and flow of the wind, everything around him beginning to veer off its axis so that he had to struggle to keep up with it, and couldn't, his eyes shifting about as he completely lost his bearings.

Soon the Whirlwind Man heard the teeming roar of a cataract grow louder and louder while the green-gold streak of a firefly flew straight at him, so bright as to be blinding, a prelude to bearing witness, for the Whirlwind Man's eyes now caught sight of a glittering marquis hung out to dry with the pulpy face of a demagogue grimacing with fury and hate, but lavished on by the patsies and pushovers who feed off the cud of tweets where talk is cheap and for whom the bright and crooked billboards of America splinter and slither down into the scalding loam that is the advent of Aka Manah, transistors sparking an overload of blazing copper filaments that weave a wavelength of lies reeking with the offal of an end-game primate gutted on the altar of his own stupidity—the Dictator.

With eyes growing wide, the Whirlwind Man hears the harsh friction of insects fiddling to the tune of Nero's encore, a farrago of scratchy strains that echoes over the bottomed out hulls of ships run aground on misty shoals awash with orange rinds and swizzle sticks and plastic jugs and bones, while a lowly foghorn blows, sounding the depths of dying men forgotten on rusted gurneys crowding green-tiled corridors or stuck in the solder of melted circuitry or left to rot hanging on factory joysticks, their fingers twitching to ovations of canned laughter, the brain-dead cocoon of the American dream, the habitat of human flyspecks hatching the hot air and show-biz bluster of a crass and ignorant blowhard—the Dictator.

Aghast and staring, the Whirlwind Man confronts a maze of open ditches and gaping metal pipes flaming with a toxic chrism that ordains the bloody contents of a gigantic wave going rogue in a turbid roar across the tops of shopping malls and stadiums, its towering fathoms curving upward and crashing down, an oily smear of brute force crushing the glassy-eyed electron that sees in every direction the flotsam of a stillborn limbo in which a lost and fearful nation becomes a clinging vine entwining itself around the haywire helix of an autocratic idiot who gobbles up fried chicken while his well-heeled connections wink and nod at the inside joke of patriotic flag wavers bought off for chump change at the hands of wily profiteers who with the slick stroke of a pen unleash the soundbites of Hydra-headed piranhas gnashing away at the last gasp of freedom writhing under a rigged gavel slamming down with the unbearable weight of distortion and lies and double speak and all the sickening in-your-face bullshit that is the power of propaganda and the slave trade of brainwashing—the Dictator.

With sweat trickling down his brow, the Whirlwind Man at long last cannot escape a young woman's dark eyebrow rising in a moonlit clearing as the far away harangue of a tyrant turns into a herky-jerky sideshow of unseemly fits and starts, a rambling screed gone off the rails with a bad case of the blind staggers, the man's cloddish feet reeling about as his nose rips with snorts and he pulls a face of such ill and vile ugliness that America's children cringe and freedom fighters spit in disgust and self-respecting women stick their fingers down their throats as if to puke because the sonic boom of revolution is underway and despite whatever's happening here you do know what it is by the telltale shots of firing squads and petrified lockdowns and the trashing of Lady Liberty drawn and quartered across a land wallowing so deeply in robot religion and dead-end suffocation that Golgotha itself shrugs it off as hopeless because already emerging out of the billowing smoke and flame walks a toothless hag in a tattered shawl joined by the shadow of a large black dog where there is no dog, arbiters from the underworld who make their rounds among smoldering ruins and crumbling abutments, the blood-drenched streets glistening as they twist along through the ongoing uprising that is still on the march and crushing all those pretty boys of wealth and condescension whose Father of Lies goes lumbering away with his little pig eyes pricked open by fear, a troubling chill cutting through his guts, the evil eye at hand or all of whatever that brings to the fore a deadweight pratfall and the final crash of a man crumpling to the floor, the kerplunk and splat of a shitting invalid—the Dictator.

As the night wore on, the Whirlwind Man felt himself draining away until at last the night began to gray with the first signs of dawn and the forest came alive with the uplifting sound of birds. Up early and stepping out of her house, Rhonda Redwing had slept well and deeply, and now eagerly approached the Whirlwind Man, who still hung suspended from the tree where she had tied him, his body barely moving in the still air, his eyes closed. As she approached him, Rhonda Redwing considered his haggard face and stubbled chin, and quickly dragged her stepladder up beside him, drawing a knife and cutting him free, bearing his weight as best she could as she helped to ease him down the ladder to the ground, where he collapsed on his back and stared at the sky, which was now taking on a faint touch of blue.

"Am I alive?" he asked, his voice raspy.

"You are alive."

"I saw horrible things," said the Whirlwind Man, swallowing. "I don't remember all of them."

"Here," said Rhonda Redwing, unwrapping the piece of the man's shirt from the tobacco leaf which she had placed beneath her pillow the night before. "Take this," she said, pressing the piece of shirt into his hand, "it will keep you safe now."

"Horrible things are happening . . ."

"You must rest now," she advised, stroking the man's forehead with the backs of her fingers, noticing how tightly he was clutching the piece of shirt she had given him.

"What is going on, Rhonda Redwing?"

"You have gone to the vision world, it was calling you, I heard it."

"This will end badly," declared the Whirlwind Man. "I know it—*here*," he emphasized, thumping his heart.

"Of course," she agreed, her face calm and solemn.

"I don't understand," said the Whirlwind Man, shifting about uneasily. "I don't understand what's happening."

"Shh, it is like you said," confirmed Rhonda Redwing, her gaze directed momentarily at the woods beyond. "It is just like you said," she repeated, her face a combination of sadness and indignance, "we're all on the reservation now."

TICK ... TICK ... TICK ...

E ven though the Dictator can be found milling about the Excellency Suite, the room is deep in darkness, a murky overlay of shadow which at points is impenetrable. The Dictator has refused to turn on any lights, which is curious, for as a rule he always has a craving to be in the spotlight, to be illuminated and on display, for he is a kind of weapons-grade class clown who, when it comes to demanding attention, really has no peer. Thus, it is noteworthy that he has now retreated into the shelter of a dark corner. Hidden from view, he pokes about in little ways and wanders aimlessly, clearly furtive, but overtly copping a bold and stubborn attitude as well, a fugitive in denial, one might say, but more to the point—an imbecile at loose ends who cannot figure out exactly whose bluff he should call.

Perhaps the Dictator's diminished presence of mind stems from the fact that the resistance and all its underground offshoots have rattled him beyond repair. Perhaps he is feeling a tad too much heat. Perhaps he is more frustrated and on the ropes than usual because the coalescing hatred of this tyrant is sparking flashpoints that are ever more brazen and disruptive, an opposition force that is growing right under the Dictator's nose, a rebellion which to the Dictator's mind equates to political and personal effrontery so extreme it constitutes a kind of political manslaughter and sacrilege all rolled into one. To squash and defeat the unpatriotic vermin who dare to march under the banner of "the people," the Dictator resorts to his usual default setting—a maniacal ego firing on all cylinders, a double-down attack mode whereby he applauds in stupendous fashion every command his pea brain has given, however idiotic or self-destructive, his thoughts now rolling through his skull with wild abandon, thoughts all a-tumble in a sludge fest of mental disarray as the Dictator reflects proudly on one of his more heinous accomplishments—the zero-tolerance immigration policy which he has mandated with great manliness throughout the land.

Indeed, impressed by the brutality of this policy, the Dictator gloats with grim pleasure over the strongarm tactics used to rip families apart and yank children wailing and screaming from the arms of their mothers as soon as they set foot in the Land of the Free, children who exist as mere fodder for the Dictator's human trafficking schemes, a solution that, if not final, will at least stem the rising tide of that inferior gene pool bubbling up from Mexico and Central America and anywhere else south of the Rio Grande. An infestation, that's what it is to the Dictator's mind, parasites crossing the border in droves, all of them crashing the wonderful party of American greatness, bandidos that John Wayne himself would have shot dead on the spot with his lever-action Winchester. And who, after all, could be more American than John Wayne? Or so the Dictator's reasoning goes, for he is determined to stop this infestation in its tracks, and if innocent children happen to mysteriously vanish at the hands of government goombahs, well, "What of it!" croaks the Dictator. The cries of frantic children and parents are actually music to his ears. The little buggers should be gone without a trace, he concludes. It's nobody's business but his what happens to them, his and his alone as the supreme and incontestable ruler. And yet there are those elusive and insidious leaks, as always, the inside tips and hearsay that have revealed the abducted children are being detained and processed in high-security internment camps, domestic black sites, remote and foreboding places with signs that read: OFF LIMITS! NO TRESPASSING! ENTER AT YOUR OWN RISK! Indeed, those gallant reporters and cameramen who attempt to shed light on where the abducted children have gone and expose the cruel conditions imposed on them have found their cameras smashed along with their noses. Nevertheless, the dogged persistence of the press has revealed that certain children have been tagged as potential rapists and drug dealers and that these unfortunate lads (and lasses) have been put on buses with blacked out windows and then fast-tracked to Arizona, where Loco Joe, yes, good ol' Loco Joe, stands by the gate of his concentration camp, rhythmically slapping a billy club into the palm of his hand as he readies himself for his new arrivals, ready to tan the hides of the little tykes because regardless of what a zero-tolerance immigration policy might mean to other people, for Loco Joe it means all out sadism, which is all well and good as far as the Dictator is concerned.

Images of human anguish caused by the zero-tolerance immigration policy now dance merrily in the Dictator's head, just like sugarplums, a testimony to the obvious truth that he is strong, that he is tough, because don't forget, for the Dictator it is all about showing people what he's made of. So how dare these weak and namby-pamby bleeding hearts get in his face about human rights and the well being of children? The thought of such opposition, this resistance, as people call it, makes him bristle, for those who refute and condemn his immigration policy are actually chipping away at the man's mental bulwark, the very underpinnings that enable him to rule by divine intuition and self-serving decree—a scenario so intolerable in any other capacity but the presidency that it would have gotten the asshole thrown out on his ear.

But as for those snivelling do-gooders who recoil at seeing children abused and traumatized, the Dictator denounces them as not knowing shit about children. Aren't they getting a wonderful eyeful of his own kids? Didn't they see what a great parent he is? His daughter is, without question, an undeniable goddess, a tempting morsel whose hot ass the Dictator would regularly boast about, while as for his sons, Tweedledee and Tweedledummer, they are the epitome of perfection, titans of . . . of . . . yes, well, of perfection! For they are the greatest and most gifted fellows! The best in everything! The very best! So where do people get off raking him over the coals? He knows all about the rearing of children. He has what it takes to raise kids. The proof is in the pudding. And lest anyone forget it, his third son is but a child himself, yes, a child. So how can anyone levy charges of callousness and cruelty upon him when it comes to the needs of children? Can't they see what a fine role model he is for what's his name? That third son of his? Only a child, but . . . Suddenly an avalanche of doubt comes crashing down on the Dictator. He can't be sure if he actually *does* have a young child, come to think of it. And does he have another daughter? Somewhere? By yet another marriage? He cannot quite recall that either. But this young son of his—is he real? The Dictator can not verily recall, for his cognitive flywheel has just popped free and is sailing away all on its own, leaving the man mumbling to himself that surely he must have a third son, and yet he is in a funk over what the boy's name might be. The dictator racks his brains to dredge up this name. It is a name, he believes, that suggests wealth and prestige, a name that has something to do with royalty maybe, a name that is suitably grandiose and pompous. Is it Viscount? Is it Duke? Can it possibly be Chevalier? Hmm. It is with stark befuddlement that, try as he might, the Dictator cannot say for sure if he actually has a young child and what that boy's name might be. He suspects he does have a young son, but strictly speaking it is hard to recall any meaningful or specific interaction with this fellow. He seems to merely flit by the corner of the Dictator's eye at times, an etiolated pixie who is gone before the Dictator can squarely get a bead on the chap. All of this is strange, to be sure, and the Dictator begins to brood, not only going over it all in his mind, but going so far as to wonder whether the boy in question is actually some sort of hobgoblin haunting him. Growing more and more rattled by these thoughts, the Dictator shudders as if somebody somewhere has walked across his grave—or had spat on it.

To clear his head, the Dictator begins to think about cheeseburgers, but even cheeseburgers, despite being sufficiently stacked with salty pickles and dripping hot grease, do not stave off the insults and recriminations with which his lips are quivering, for as the Dictator lumbers through the shadows of the Excellency Suite he grows more and more angry, more petulant and cantankerous, and it is all on account of those political gadflies who dare to obstruct his rule, who expose the racist venom behind his immigration blockades and who even have the foul audacity to criticize him in public, exposing the brilliance of his initiatives as really nothing more than garbage. But not only does the Dictator resent such people for what they have said, he also flies off the handle because they are peons, middle-class peons, even low-class peons, peons who don't have anywhere near the money that he has, and yet there they are, throwing their democratic principles and fancy book learning full in his face, railing about all that bogus malarkey called separation of powers. Damn elitists, that's what they are! Losers! Don't they see that real Americans don't want powers separated? Real Americans want big, strong power. Real Americans, like the rodeo clown picking his nose out in Casper, Wyoming, or those wondrous money-minded stockjobbers selling worthless securities on Wall Street, *those* Americans want power that was like missiles! Powerful! To blow things to pieces! There are things that should be blown to pieces, the Dictator reminds himself, growing exasperated, trembling, spitting nickels as he grits his teeth at a cavalcade of enemies lying in wait in every corner, no-good shitheads who make no bones about calling him out as a liar and a fraud who is driving the nation down a wretched abyss.

But he'll show them, the Dictator stubbornly resolves, for he hits on the idea of proclaiming himself Dictator for Life, of having himself coronated as a supreme ruler who until his dying day will be nothing short of a king! And what could be better than that? That will be his ticket to not only absolute power, he reasons, but to unconditional respect and adulation. No one will dare harass him and give him grief if he's a king. They'll know enough to genuflect and bow down, like in the movies! And since a king can hold the fate of someone's life in his hands, anyone who opposes him will and must fall in line, they'll think twice about challenging his rule. He'll put people to death! He'll be just like that commie leader Gee Whizz over in China, who granted himself a lifelong tenure of power with a snap of his fingers! Power! Big, beautiful power! Power for his whole life! And to think Gee Whizz did it without giving two shits whether 1.3 billion Chinese liked it or not. So there! Well-well, the Dictator considers with shifty-eyed satisfaction, so what's to stop him from doing the same thing? He'll get Vulpine News to start promoting the idea. He'll get the machinations of tyranny to play fully into his hands so he can woo over those vulnerable saps who attend his rallies. The chumps at his rallies will gladly buy into a lifelong dictatorship. It'll make them feel important. They already let the rich freeload on their backs year after year as it is, so it only makes sense to keep a good thing going, the Dictator reasons, to strike while the iron is hot, to establish a dictatorship for life and see that it is fully sanctioned and upheld. What better way to do even less work than he does right now? He won't have to answer to anybody. He can watch television, eat junk food and go golfing to his heart's content, though he will, of course, still be out to make obscene amounts of money. He'll have all the time in the world to expand his cat's cradle of deals and transactions, a global shell game that has landed mountains of laundered cash square in his lap.

Of course, speaking of all this laundered money, the Dictator knows full well that no one is supposed to know about it, that no one is supposed to know about all the back alley deals and corrupt finagling, and yet, unbeknownst to the Dictator, there are several people who *do* know, such as a jewel thief moonlighting as a cabbie in London, a reclusive writer with a broken arm in Pennsylvania, and a recently defected Russian double agent whose code name is Kolossus. These and other people hold pieces in the puzzle of the Dictator's criminal activity, and while each piece in and of itself is limited in what it might reveal, these pieces are starting to fetch fat little pouches of money as investigators bid on them. Starting to suspect that people are being bought off and that he is being double crossed, the Dictator is greatly troubled. He detests and loathes anyone who would even *consider* selling him out. Such people are rats, including those Russian whores who pissed on his head all night in a Moscow hotel room while he begged them to wiggle a silicone bougie up his ass. Such people are sneaky, even whores, even though he paid them. All such people are dangerous and unpredictable, all of them having sufficient dirt on the Dictator to make his life miserable, to compromise his power and to clobber him with a legal and public relations nightmare. Such people, the Dictator grumbles, are better off out of the picture, non-existent, liquidated—with no one the wiser.

Shifting his feet and tilting his outstretched arms like a toppling windmill, the Dictator now looks hard into the shadows with his little pig eyes, the darkness seeming to have a cavernous quality that extends well beyond the walls around him. Although he will not admit it, the Dictator finds this darkness disturbing. Were he to stray into it, he fears he would get lost and not be able to find his way back. It makes him uneasy, this darkness, its depth and gravity seemingly capable of exuding at any moment the dank and wormy air of a charnel house.

Stiffening brusquely, the Dictator shudders, but still refuses to turn on the lights, for he prefers to stew unseen, in the shadows. It is one of those rare moments when the Dictator does not want to be the center of attention. He does not want, if truth be told, to give himself away, for the Dictator's fears and frustrations are mounting, fueling his desperation to a red-alert level. He needs someone who can reign in the willy-nilly matters in his head and elsewhere and oversimplify them. If this can be done, he might feel capable of conquering his bugbears with just a few bold and bellicose tweets. To aid his cause, he first thinks of calling General Au Pair, but General Au Pair will merely do magic tricks or perform a little hat dance or punch himself in the head as he attempts to endear himself, which is, of course, very much to the Dictator's liking, but the general doesn't count for much in the way of reassurance. For that, for big, strong reassurance, the Dictator needs his political oracle, a man renowned for his piercing analytical mind, his flashy diamond rings and his Durga-armed grasp of all things under the sun— political, economical, legal, scatalogical, etc.

The man the Dictator wants is Bugeye Upchuck, and to summon this latest entry into the revolving door of sycophants stepping up to kiss his ass, the Dictator walks over to a filing cabinet and takes out a shallow bowl of dull brass. This he puts on his desk, setting it down near the wall of Lego blocks that represents the wall he keeps promising to build along the border with Mexico. Next, he opens a drawer in his desk and takes out two Ziploc plastic bags, one containing dried skunk cabbage and the other pulverized rat droppings. Taking a healthy pinch from each of these bags and placing it in the brass bowl, he stirs the contents with his finger. Then, with a long-stemmed butane lighter, he produces a flame, touching it to the mixture in the bowl, watching as a red glow appears and trails of stinky smoke begin to rise.

His preparation completed, the Dictator now gets down to the business of calling forth what he believes is one of the most profound minds on the planet, an intellectual giant who sets the heads of talk show hosts spinning with his proclamations and opinions, and who without fail can manage to credibly and decisively advise the Dictator simply by telling him what he wants to hear. Now that the burnt offerings of skunk cabbage and pulverized rat shit are smoldering away, the Dictator throws up his arms and cries out, uttering a command he knows by heart:

Oh, Great Counsel,
From New York to Waikiki,
Bestow your pearls of wisdom on me
And I will favor thee!

So cavernous is the darkness around the Dictator that when he is done speaking he half expects his words to echo, but hears nothing, and waits, and as he waits he grows impatient, the silence testing his ears until he imagines he hears the sound of someone drawing near, someone discreetly approaching, although Bugeye Upchuck has yet to appear. So eager is the Dictator to commence this meeting that he feels physically bruised by each second ticking by, waiting, waiting, fuming at the thought that someone other than himself might be monopolizing Bugeye Upchuck's time, while never considering that it is the middle of the night and that the man is likely asleep.

In due time, however, the Dictator hears what might be a faint rustling, a papier-mache bat wing, the muffled lisp of old parchment or even the crinkle of dried flowers. Glancing toward the door, the Dictator thinks he detects movement and begins walking in that direction, treading as lightly as a sluggardly clod can tread. On reaching the door to the Excellency Suite, he sees that it is ever so slightly ajar, revealing a faint vertical line of light from the hallway beyond. The Dictator, certain that Bugeye Upchuck is on the other side of that door, holds completely still, barely breathing, on tenterhooks as he awaits the slow and meticulous arrival of his confidant.

That confidant, without so much as touching the door or its adjacent jamb, now begins to squeeze himself through the narrow opening that exists, for he is able to fold up his whole body like a piece of shabby origami, bending it in on itself and flattening it out, his arms and legs collapsing, steamrolled into an absolutely even plane, a kind of cubist abstract thinner than a pizza. The man's head, which resembles a skinless wiener, but is soft and pliable like a water balloon, also oozes through the crack in the door, a flabby discus that hangs there for a moment before filling out again, growing into a round orb. Hollowed into this orb are two strange, protruding eyes, and below the eyes there is a pinpoint dot where the mouth would be, a tiny speck from which fleshy little lines fan out, leaving no doubt that this puckered aperture is an anus. Moving nearer to this anus, the Dictator gawks at it while giving it a sniff.

Perverted renifleur that he is, the Dictator, his nose twitching, inhales the stench of this asshole as if it were ambrosia, detecting a rank septic smell that is very familiar to him. The smell is that of an obfuscating miasma spreading across the land, one which has attracted large numbers of dung beetles that feed off the shit it promises. Like the dung beetles, the Dictator also is enamored of this stench, relishing it no less than the zesty pungency of piss from Russian whores as it streams down his head. For now, however, it is the odor there in front of him that captivates the man, the odor of stale shit smutch, the essence of the miasma perpetuated by the Dictator and his cohorts, including Bugeye Upchuck, who time and time again has put his shoulder to the wheel for the Dictator. Thus, the Dictator's reverence for the anal asterisk before him is very high indeed.

"Good to see you, Bugeye Upchuck!" hails the Dictator.

The aperture in Bugeye Upchuck's face squirms about as if touched by a live electrical wire, its circular membrane contracting and expanding as it emits a little symphony of farts.

"I can't understand you, Bugeye Upchuck!" says the Dictator.

To which the aperture, try as it might, can produce nothing but gaseous sputters.

"Let me lubricate you!" suggests the Dictator.

Rummaging about in his desk, the Dictator at last lays his hands on a bottle of Slick Sensorium sexual lubricant, an item he likes to keep handy, and which happens to be the exact lubricant used by Russian whores to facilitate the insertion of a bougie up his ass. As he proceeds to draw a bead of clear, glistening fluid along the length of his middle finger, the Dictator feels confident that this will loosen up Bugeye's tongue. Like a deviant Jack Horner, the Dictator now takes his finger and plunges it into the awaiting asshole before him, thrusting the finger in and out with the same crude disregard with which he will grab a woman's pussy.

"Take that! Take that, baby! I'm giving it to you, huh? Huh? Huh? See!"

Bugeye Upchuck, meanwhile, is sucking on this thrusting finger with a notable look of bliss on his face, for this is no mere dietary indiscretion—not at all—but rather a necessary sustenance common among certain slime balls who are never their own men, but who must feed off each other for their own advantage. Thus, it is no surprise that when the Dictator pulls his finger out of this asshole and finds it encircled by a soggy onion ring he immediately gobbles it down.

"Yum! Yum! It is so good to see you, Bugeye Upchuck!" exclaims the Dictator, smacking his lips. "You must help me!"

"Mein Fuhrer, I can talk!" replies the buggered Bugeye with great relief.

"Yes, yes," acknowledges the Dictator. "I'm a miracle worker, I work miracles with everything. But I need you to help me."

Bugeye Upchuck remains silent and the Dictator looks the man up and down, noticing the jaundiced yolks of his eyeballs daubed in the center by a bit of blue, as well as the anal aperture, which is now well lubricated and begins to widen, making way for two front teeth that drop into view like a portcullis. Then Bugeye speaks: "Before we begin, Your Excellency, I do have a gift for you."

"A gift!" says the Dictator, looking pleased.

"Yes, Your Excellency, it's a book," says Bugeye Upchuck as he removes a black leather-bound volume from inside his suitcoat.

Book! thinks the Dictator with disdain, for he lacks the intellectual chops to read through a single paragraph much less a whole book. "I don't like books," says the Dictator caustically.

"But Your Excellency," replies Bugeye Upchuck, softly petting the book as if it were a pelt of luxurious sable, "it's not just any book, no, not at all, but a deluxe graphic-novel version of *Mein Kampf*. Lots of pictures, not so many words, just the way you like it. You have a soulmate in this book, Your Excellency, trust me. Read it, take heart in it, and take action!"

"Hmm, I'm a very busy man, the busiest man in the world, but I'll try to make time for it," says the Dictator, taking the book in his hands.

"Thank you, Your Excellency, thank you, you won't regret it. Now what is on your mind, Your Excellency? The hour is very late."

"What do you say about all the hateful people out there?" begins the Dictator. "They threaten our national security. They're nasty, hateful people. Bad. Hateful. Bad, especially the women. This nonsense about equality and respect. They make a big deal about it because I grab their pussies, but do they grab my crotch? No! That's because they don't really want equality. They're too weak, too pathetic to grab my crotch. So I do them a favor, the biggest favor of all for these women, women who won't grab my pecker. I host beauty pageants for them! Big, wonderful beauty pageants, big cities where everybody sees them—millionaires, publicity agents, members of the Golden Putter Golf Club. Thanks to me they get to show off their booty on stage because I love women, I respect them, but now they're ganging up on me, hustling the vote with all kinds of women—black women, Hispanic women, even ugly women. I've seen them on TV. Fatty Arbuckles. It's disgusting. They have no shame, and now they're recruiting girls, 16 years old, 17 years old, twat that's still in high school, going after them, turning them against me, turning them into firebrands. It's like burning the American flag, that's what it is, a threat to national security. But they won't grab a guy's pecker. They're weak! Weak!"

"They don't grab your pecker, but they've got you by the balls— Yuk! Yuk! Yuk!"

"Is that a joke?"

"Your Excellency, forgive me," says Bugeye Upchuck, "but all these lawsuits, so many women, they're coming out of the woodwork—models, TV contestants, hotel maids, and even a porn star who says you were shagging her. A porn star, Your Excellency! What must Primo Bimbo think? *Does* Primo Bimbo think? And what of that little boy of yours, what does he think? This is not exactly the behavior we seek in role models for our children, but then again, perhaps children are better kept in cages like we do along the border! Yuk! Yuk! Yuk!"

"I'm talking about the women," says the Dictator, scowling, "the women rising up against me, it's un-American, and every woman against me is turning three more women against me."

"It's a problem," agrees Bugeye, "and the lawsuits don't help, so many women accusing you, such vicious litigation, but we'll discredit them all, we'll attack them on the issue of character, one by one, break them down. As a former prosecutor, that's what I know how to do. We have to be tough, hard, mean. That's what women understand, take it from me. I'm a good holy Catholic, so it was hard to cheat on my wife, but I did it. I did it because I'm tough, tough on crime and tough on women. I've got toughness on my side. You've got toughness on your side. We're tough. That's how we have to be. Look at former Senator Grinchgin. Senator Grinchgin had his wife served divorce papers while she was lying in the hospital dying of cancer. Now that's toughness for you. That's how you treat women, show them who's boss, right to the end. So there's nothing to worry about. We're tough."

"So we stick it to the women and we win the lawsuits, is that what you're saying?"

"We win the lawsuits," reassures Bugeye Upchuck, "and once we do that you will have again endeared yourself to millions of women by being tough, very tough, though there is another matter."

"What other matter?"

"There is, Your Excellency, the matter of Kolossus."

"Who the fuck is that?"

"Don't you know? There's a buzz going around about somebody named Kolossus. This is very high-level information, very privy, I thought you would have been apprised."

"It's up for discussion."

"I trust," queries Bugeye Upchuck, "that you do pay attention during your daily intelligence briefings."

"You'll know soon."

"Your briefings have been dumbed down into little tiny bullet points, Your Excellency. Was there no bullet point about Kolossus lately?"

"Stay tuned!"

"Your Excellency, this is serious, have you really not been informed about Kolossus?"

"Yes, Kolossus, big discussion about him, sure, big."

"Good," says Bugeye Upchuck, "then you know Kolossus is dangerous, dangerous to you."

"How? Why?"

"Speculation is rising that Kolossus has been paid off by the Dark State. He's a recent Russian defector, Your Excellency. I'm given to understand he had been working as a double agent for many years and has now come over to our side completely. He has burned his bridges with Russia for good and has dropped off the intelligence grid completely."

"So what's that got to do with me?"

"Your Excellency," sighs Bugeye Upchuck, "Kolossus might have what the Dark State wants. It's thought that Kolossus possesses a certain raunchy videotape in which Russian whores are urinating on the head of an eminent American, the most well-known of all Americans. If the reports are true and should this tape come to light, Your Excellency, the collective stomach of the nation might turn in a big way. Even the legions of walking dead staggering blindly behind you might waver in their loyalty. Trust me, no one wants to see their revered leader exposed as a perverted clown, a degenerate jackass. The videotape would prove catastrophic. The Paris Hilton sex tape would be a day at Bible school compared to this lollapalooza. It would erode general support and wreak national havoc. Think of the distraction. It would devastate our momentum going forward. Such a video would be a gift of red meat for the resistance. Already everywhere you look there's a new provocateur cropping up. There's something in the air, Your Excellency, which just might be revolution. But as for Kolossus, if he has this videotape, it also begs the question of what other incriminating information he may possess, what other evidence against you he may be willing to turn over."

"We need to stop Kolossus, can we get him?"

"If there's nothing to fear," suggests Bugeye sagely, "then we need not fear Kolossus."

"Where the hell is this Kolossus? He can't just come waltzing into this great land like some border rat from these shithole countries. It's illegal! Zero tolerance! Where is this lowdown sneak, Kolossus? He's a threat to national security, a terrorist! How do we take him out? Where is he? Send in a drone!"

"Your Excellency," begins Bugeye Upchuck with notable measure, "Kolossus has been an expert intelligence operative for a long, long time. You don't just go out and find Kolossus. He's probably got five different passports and is nationalized in five different nations. A man like this is a global shape-shifter, a polyglot, a man with multiple identities, backgrounds, talents. He could be a surveyor in Romania, a cost accountant in Spain, an inventory clerk in Toronto. My point is you could be looking at Kolossus square in the face and not know it. He's that kind of guy, well connected in the most discreet and influential ways. He's come up through the ranks of Russian intelligence. He apparently has the supreme knowhow of an exemplary double agent, knowing the Russian game like the back of his hand while having integrated with the very best spies in the United States. The man is one to be reckoned with. You can't just go drop a bomb on him."

The jowly slabs of the Dictator's cheeks begin to redden. His countenance is stern and grim, producing a pout of disgust. "Then what about that chink! Can we bomb *him*?" the Dictator yells, virtually exploding.

"What chink?"

"That Pillsbury Doughboy mop-top chink running North Korea, can we bomb *him*?"

"Your Excellency, you can't just—"

"Don't tell me what I can't do!" roars the Dictator. "I'm the supreme, indisputable leader! The chink shafted me! He reneged. I gave him show time, free publicity, and a giftbag. It was a nice giftbag! A red velvet giftbag tied with a satin ribbon. Primo Bimbo tied the ribbon. She can tie great ribbons, you know, the most big, beautiful ribbons. So I filled the giftbag with Gummie Bears and Hershey's Kisses, a Bruce Lee action figure, even an Elton John CD, and then the pudgy little jerk goes and reneges on the whole deal. He won't dismantle a single nuke! Won't verify anything! He won't even meet with my people! Won't return our dead bodies—and he keeps building nukes! He treated us bad! Bad! But he took the giftbag. He's probably eating the Gummie Bears right now and listening to Elton John. So why shouldn't I bomb the shit out of him? He screwed me out of a Nobel Peace Prize. I could have gotten it! For the nukes! We could have had peace! Now he says he won't dismantle any nukes. I called him, I did, I called him to settle things. I said about the nukes, the nukes, dismantle the nukes. And he said no way. No! That's what he said. So it's his fault. He told me to take the nukes and blow them out my ass! He called me a one-wheeled rickshaw! He called me a midget rooster! He called me a deep-fried disco ball! So it's time to blast him off the planet! Bomb him! Waste the two-faced nutjob!"

"So many enemies," acknowledges Bugeye Upchuck, nodding in agreement, "so many people who want to put you out of commission, but starting a war with a nuclear power can have serious ramifications."

"Then I'll start a war somewhere else!" barks the Dictator.

"Ah, Your Excellency," commends Bugeye Upchuck, the jaundiced yolks of his eyeballs bulging bigger than before, "you truly *are* a genius."

"Of course I am! What's the point of a big military parade—missiles, tanks, M-16s? What's the point of all those Airborne Rangers if you don't use them? It's like spending a lot of money on one of those big, beautiful steaks from the Golden Putter Golf Club and then not eating it, just staring at it. Stupid! We got the bombs, we got the bombs! Boom! Boom! We use them!"

"I take it then," surmises Bugeye Upchuck with a sly wheedle in his voice, "that your sentence is for open war."

"War! Tough, strong open war!"

"Nothing works better, Your Excellency, to rally the people," agrees Bugeye Upchuck as his tongue—or perhaps a small turd— briefly protrudes from the anal starburst centered above the knob of his chin. "No one will dare defy you in the face of war. War is the foremost refugee of patriotism, and it's so easy to start a war. People will gladly accept colorful lies about going to war rather than scrutinize facts and analyze them. Package the war in patriotism and people will lap it up like strawberries and whipped cream. In America, there really *is* a sucker born every minute. The Gulf of Tonkin resolution enabled the nation to charge full tilt into Vietnam—based on torpedo attacks that may never have really happened! Yuk! Yuk! Yuk! The invasion of Iraq was perpetuated by a propaganda campaign worthy of Herr Goebbels. Instead of opening their eyes and looking at the facts, Americans pulled the sheets over their heads and cowered in fear over weapons of mass destruction. Yuk! Yuk! Yuk! Of course there were no weapons of mass destruction. So we must contrive a colorful, jingoistic lie, Your Excellency, it's always more desirable than the plain truth, and people love your lies, they can't do without them, and you, of course, are the best liar around, Mein Fuhr—I mean, Your Excellency. So concoct the right lie and you can start your war tomorrow. Americans will fall all over themselves to embrace a show of force. It's been proven! Give them a green light to be gung-ho and they'll be gung-ho. Then all your other problems will fade away."

"They ought to be gung-ho! And war," ponders the Dictator, "you're right, war will get all these nasty, hateful people off my back. I'll go to war and if they're still against me it will be treason, high treason! Then we can hang them, right? Or strangle them with piano wire, can we strangle them with piano wire? Or we'll just hang them from light posts, including that son of a bitch Kolossus!"

"It's all for you to decide, Your Excellency. Your word is final and absolute. You are the Dictator," says Bugeye Upchuck, closing his eyes and nodding with saintly deference. "War is a win-win situation for you. You get to strut around blustering as a tough, happy warrior and yet have no actual skin in the game. None at all. Let other people get their arms and legs blown off, for war is not the ken of we the privileged."

"So right you are, Bugeye, so right, because war is my prerogative, war is mine to make!"

"As is your destiny."

Destiny.

Now this is a word that slowly sinks into the wormy cheese of the Dictator's brain. It evokes great pageantry, a Technicolor sea of cheering people who are beside themselves with adoring zeal as they heap cheers and tears of joy upon a man who is both their savior and world conqueror—the Dictator. With the blubber of his lower lip unfurling, the Dictator's jaw drops down until his mouth hangs open and he stares deep into the darkness of the Excellency Suite, the faraway look in his eyes growing more and more distant until it becomes removed from anything connected to reality, for the Dictator has now, as they say, zoned out. He is, in fact, consumed by an image of himself wearing a toga of purple silk and a laurel wreath that crowns his head as he happily gathers wool on a high mountaintop, the firmament above him bright with colors of violet and gold, the clouds breaking apart to bestow upon him shafts of radiant sunshine, while off in the distance the gray puffs of little mushroom clouds arise. Proudly and indolently, the Dictator strolls along gentle paths strewn with flowers cast at his feet by shapely swimsuit contestants who smile endearingly at the man, their teeth preternaturally white while their pussies are up for grabs. Yes, it is good to be the Dictator, and as this idiot sinks deeper and deeper into the grandeur of his own delusions Bugeye Upchuck decides to depart.

Walking over to the door, he stops and carefully sidles up to it. Crimping himself tightly with a shrug, he retracts his head between his shoulders and then begins to shorten all four limbs. His arms and legs, like pliable sticks of licorice, crease and flatten down in a series of accordion pleats, while his torso deflates and collapses, a precursor to the changes soon underway in the skinless wiener of his head, for the man's noggin is also compressing, dwindling down into a thin, rubbery pancake. Once he has reduced himself to a one-dimensional cutout, Bugeye Upchuck aligns himself with the crack in the door through which he entered earlier, squeezing himself through it and slithering away.

MEETING THE HIGH PRIESTESS

E ver since having agreed to meet with the high priestess of the Covenant of the Golden Moon, Jennifer Golembeski felt slightly on edge. The high priestess was someone she had known only briefly and so it seemed odd that she should suddenly call her and ask to meet somewhere they could talk privately. They had had only casual interactions in the past and, at a loss to explain her motives, Jennifer was waiting eagerly when the high priestess knocked on her door.

Seeing the high priestess standing there immediately put Jennifer at ease. Although the woman's bearing was erect and even prim, she moved with a relaxed air. She seemed comfortable in her own skin, having nothing in her manner that was off-putting or pushy, which Jennifer found reassuring. The woman's eyes were a soft, inviting blue, while her hair, brown and naturally wavy, fell to her shoulders in a simple and becoming way. Her demeanor was composed and engaging, her features pleasant, though they changed to a look of concern when she saw a raw gash running dead center across Jennifer's forehead. Given pause, the high priestess now stepped forward, raising her hand and gently brushing back Jennifer's hair, exposing a coarse band of scabbing marked here and there by small seepages of blood. In places the wound was sprouting black filaments of suture, while all around its edge there appeared a reddish-pink tinge.

"My God, what happened to you?" asked the high priestess, wincing at Jennifer's injury.

"It's nothing, it was the riot," Jennifer explained. "Everybody was in on it."

"Are you okay?"

"Just sore."

"It's so regrettable that this happened," commiserated the high priestess. "I fear you'll have a scar."

"It's no big deal."

"I hope you didn't suffer anything more than this," inquired the high priestess, with some apprehension.

"They roughed me up in jail for a couple days, but they had to let me go. I can't afford a smart phone or the Internet or anything, so they couldn't nail me on anything, there was no record of anything. They didn't know anything about me, so they couldn't drum up any charges. They were pissed."

"So you just happened to be out there that night, out in the street?"

"It's a long story, but I was out there."

"Had I known of your injury," said the high priestess, looking kindly at Jennifer, "I would have brought some healing herbs for a poultice, something to revitalize the flesh, an emollient I concoct, it's very soothing."

"It seems to be healing," replied Jennifer, adding, "slowly but surely."

"Had you remained in the coven, you would have learned about many of our treatments for wounds and ailments. We place a lot of emphasis on natural remedies, and on healing the spirit as well," noted the high priestess, eyeing Jennifer closely.

"The meetings were interesting," commented Jennifer, at a loss for words. "But I've had a lot going on, so I kind of stopped going."

"That's understandable, but I missed you all the same."

"But we're both here now," said Jennifer, her voice perking up as an invitation to talk.

"Yes, and I'm glad for it. I appreciate that you agreed to meet me and hear me out."

"Do you want to sit down," asked Jennifer, "in the kitchen? There's really no where else to sit."

Walking into Jennifer's kitchen, the high priestess noticed a clean, spare room with a bunch of ripe bananas on the counter. To one side of the kitchen sink stood a bottle of Dawn dish detergent, while on the other sat a dish rack with a pink sponge lying inside it. In the corner of the room was a square wooden table with two simple chairs that had been painted green long ago. After sitting down, the high priestess for the first time noticed a scratch-off lottery ticket stuck to the refrigerator door by a pentacle magnet. Wondering as to why someone would buy the ticket and not scratch it off, she looked at Jennifer and as their eyes met she detected the same freewheeling passion in her gaze that was there at the covenant meetings, the same windswept look of someone who could not settle down.

After Jennifer took a seat across from her, the high priestess began by asking a question: "Do you know when I realized I was a witch?"

"I couldn't begin to say."

"It started when I was a young girl," began the high priestess. "In my early years, I grew up in Amsterdam, on the outskirts of the city. I speak Dutch, though I don't have any occasion to these days. Anyway, off in downtown Amsterdam there's an old church, the Zuiderkerk. I never went to church, my parents were very laid back and saw no point to it, but I loved it when the bells of the Zuiderkerk would ring. They would carry across the city, their sound inviting and lulling. I didn't think about them consciously, they were there more in the background of my mind, part and parcel of the moment, though they made a claim on my awareness to some degree, whether I was riding my bicycle or playing with friends, often they were there, ringing away. I couldn't even say at what specific hour they rang or if they rang randomly. I was growing up with them, you see, they were part of me, so much so that one night as I slept I dreamed I was hearing the bells. I recognized them immediately, a comforting, ethereal sound, the bells of the Zuiderkerk off in the distance. Except something wasn't quite right. Although there was no mistaking them, I detected something different in the bells, something offkey, and I realized they were out of sequence, that they were ringing backwards, as if some confused bell ringer were pulling all the wrong ropes. It's hard to explain. I had a strange and disconcerting feeling, and the dream in a way lingered through to morning when I awoke. A little later that morning, I learned that my grandmother had died.

"At the time, I was too young to grasp any connection between those backward ringing bells and the death of my grandmother, but in some abstract way I sensed the two things were connected. This was the beginning of many instances in which the bells of the Zuiderkerk would go tolling backward in my dreams, becoming portents of something about to happen. I heard them ringing the night before the space shuttle Challenger exploded and before the 1989 earthquake in San Francisco, and before the attacks on the World Trade Center. I never knew what the bells were foreshadowing exactly, but I was always on my guard. The bells were never wrong. Yet they weren't always dire, mind you, I heard them the night before I met my future husband—rather than love at first sight it was more a revelation at first sight.

"As these bells continued throughout my life, I tried to understand this experience. I wasn't having a premonition exactly, I'm not psychic, but after much thinking about it I concluded there was something magical happening, that out in the world there was some magical force that was real and alive, and it could not be dismissed just because I didn't understand it or was not fully aware of it. I greatly respect the hard facts of science, I do so wholeheartedly, but I became convinced that there is much more to all the things we think we understand. Even in something like photosynthesis, no matter how well we explain it, I detect an element of magic in the process that we perhaps do not fully grasp. So I began to take a skeptical view of life, becoming more attuned to the mystery around me, so that the more I considered my place in the world, the more I was awakened to natural and ineffable connections, until it just so happened that my unrealized identity was leading me toward Wicca. I learned that I was more humbly fundamental than I had thought and that my wisest ancestors were not those heavy-handed people making pronouncements about God during Biblical times, but rather those hardscrabble people who were painting on the walls of caves by torchlight long, long ago, people who embraced the mystery of themselves and the world around them."

Listening closely, Jennifer presumed that the high priestess's words were meant to pertain to her some way, that there was some message being spelled out for her. She struggled to add up all the things that had been said, but couldn't find the sum. Looking beseechingly at the high priestess, her only response was to say that her own reasons for thinking about joining the coven were maybe to put herself to good use.

"And was that the only reason?" asked the high priestess kindly, patiently, as if she had all the time in the world.

The woman's inquiry was so perfectly mannered and her eyes such a soothing blue that Jennifer couldn't resist staring at her, fearing that if she gave a less than adequate answer she would prove disappointing. Tongue-tied, she admitted that she might have had another reason but couldn't quite recall.

"I suspect so, too," said the high priestess with satisfaction, leaning forward as she continued. "In fact, I more than suspect it, I know there was some other reason, and it's because the night before I met you the bells of the Zuiderkerk once again went ringing backwards through my dreams, and it was you they were foretelling."

"It *was*?"

"On meeting you, I knew it without a doubt."

Never taking her eyes off the high priestess, Jennifer spoke as if in a trance. "And was I a good foreboding or a bad?"

"You're genuine."

"What do you mean?"

"Your purpose is intact, that's why I heard the bells, that's why you sought out the coven."

"I read about the coven in a newspaper that somebody had put out with their recyclables, and there were girls in high school too who were into Wicca and stuff. I learned a little about it. One of them gave me a CD by a group called Inkubus Sukkubus, it was witch and pagan music. But," said Jennifer, hesitant and uncertain, "I don't really know anything about a purpose."

"But I do."

In wonderment, Jennifer stared at high priestess.

"Sometimes," the high priestess continued, "the hardest thing to see is ourselves. People get full of distractions. Plus you're young and coming to terms with the world, which kicks up a lot of dust. From where I'm sitting, what I see is a person with something inside that wants to flex its wings, but if you're not sure what that something is then it may be difficult to liberate it."

"But you know what it is?" said Jennifer, only half asking.

"You yourself know, if you'll be honest with yourself."

"But I am," said Jennifer defensively.

"I have no doubt you'll be honest if you're called upon to do so, so let me call upon you now. Tell me, did you enjoy the coven meetings you attended? Be honest."

"They were okay."

"Just okay?"

"Like interesting, so-so. Everyone was smarter than me."

"What were you hoping for? What did you want from these meetings?"

"I'm . . . not sure."

"What scene did you envision that would have been better than so-so, that would have turned the meetings into something you would have really liked?"

Raising an eyebrow, Jennifer smiled playfully, but said nothing.

"Tell me," coaxed the high priestess. "What are you thinking? Be honest."

"I wanted to dance naked out in the moonlight off in the woods."

"Go on, please, explain it more."

"It's me and all the other witches and we're dancing naked in a circle, and there's a crackling fire at the center. On my head, I have a ring of flowers braided together like what hippies used to wear, and as we dance around in a circle there's a drum beating, or at least I hear a drum, and I feel good because I'm exposed to the sparks of the fire and the leaves on the trees and the moonlight that's touching my whole body everywhere so that it's like washing me clean. I realize I can let loose and that there's nothing to be ashamed of because all around me it's happening with all the other witches, and so I feel at home, like I belong. Then we all join hands in a circle around the fire and it's like we create a magnet that attracts the power of the moon and the fire and it's good, it can help me. I'd like to think it can help me."

"Help you in what way?" asked the high priestess.

"I'm not sure," admitted Jennifer.

"All women want to be empowered," said the high priestess, "but what you're partial to, I believe, is energy. There are currents of energy running all around this planet, raw and primal energy, fickle at times, but very strong. I suspect you're attuned to these currents because of forces within yourself, because you have the ability to insinuate yourself into the greater energy around us and to connect with it, and if you can connect with it you can direct it to its full effect. It's a sign of the highest magical power to do this, only a rare and gifted witch is blessed this way."

With a kind of giddy confusion playing out in her features, Jennifer looked around the room and then back to the high priestess. "Are you . . . what you're saying, are you saying that I'm a witch?"

"You are, and I think you recognize something inside yourself that speaks to this fact."

"But, wait . . ." said Jennifer, her voice faltering as she tried to come to terms with something that seemed to be shifting under her feet, "I never went through the initiations."

"It doesn't matter in your case."

"Is this why you wanted to see me, to tell me I'm a witch?"

"Not exactly," explained the high priestess, "I'm here on behalf of a friend of mine. He has a great knowledge of witchcraft, this friend. He has read books and books on it, and studied ancient texts and manuscripts. Throughout his life he has gotten to know all sorts of practitioners. He has been conducting research for years, a very learned man, and while not a witch or practitioner himself he's often instrumental in bringing about the casting of spells and curses. It's a very serious business, one that I don't particularly agree with. You know the Wiccan Rede, 'An ye harm none, do as ye will. And ever mind the Rule of Three: What ye send out, comes back to thee. Follow this with mind and heart, and merry ye meet, and merry ye part.' It is what I abide by, though when it comes to curses I acknowledge there are different views on the matter. More to the point, however, is that my friend wants to enlist your services."

"My services?" blurted out Jennifer. "What kind of services?"

"I understand your surprise," said the high priestess with a note of sympathy. "I'm dropping everything on you at once, I know, but my friend, he's a colleague of sorts, he's making this out to be an urgent matter. I've been dealing with Norman long enough to know that if he's pressing me on something it's with good reason."

"That's his name, Norman?"

"Norman Modrak."

"And so this guy wants me to do what for him?"

"To put a curse on someone," answered the high priestess, her words uttered with such forthright calm that Jennifer did not react at first.

"But this guy doesn't even know me," said Jennifer with a tad of pique, "and I don't know nothing about curses."

"I told him about you," admitted the high priestess. "I told him right after I first met you. He knows that I dreamed about the bells ringing backwards before our first meeting, and I told him I detected something very special in you, an uncanny potential. He wanted to meet you. He takes such matters very seriously. But you stopped showing up at the meetings and it never came to pass. If I were a Bible thumper, I would have tracked you down and hounded you to come back to the coven, but we're not like that in Wicca. In the end, I was quite surprised when Norman called me recently and asked about you, asking about that girl, that girl, he said, the one the bells foretold. He was very worked up, which is unusual for him. He all but begged me to see if I could track you down. I got the feeling something big was in the works, and so here I am."

"Well I'll be dipped in shit," said Jennifer softly.

"It can't be all that bad," laughed the high priestess, and as she brushed back her wavy brown hair and crossed her legs Jennifer found comfort in her look of intimacy, realizing that outside of Amber Lamphere this was the only person who had ever really cared to know one meaningful thing about her.

"But still, I don't know how to do a curse," stated Jennifer, "and anyway, who's this curse on? What's it all about?"

"Both of these points are key," responded the high priestess, looking serious now. "For one, this is not something you need to commit to here and now. You're under no obligation to agree to do this. I have no idea of what this curse is or the person it involves. My not knowing is by choice. The particular details will be a matter between you and Norman Modrak. He'll tell what you need to know, and if you're willing to go forward the matter will be in your hands. If not, simply decline the offer. You'll want to consider all the implications of this closely, and that's partly why I'm here, to fill you in, to prepare you so that you have some idea of what to expect. But Norman Modrak isn't in the picture yet, he'll come later. So are we square on things so far?"

"I think so," said Jennifer, eager to hear more.

"The second matter is the curse itself," the high priestess informed her. "Although I don't know the exact nature of what Norman Modrak wants you to do, I have a hunch it's something formidable, something that could be taxing in terms of both your physical and mental stamina. This is not the province of the average person, what you're thinking of doing. This is going to the extreme, attempting to to see just how much energy you can conduct, and then to see if you can control it, to direct it to your purpose. Imagine if you were a surfer on one of those big 70-foot waves in Hawaii. Just to stay on it, riding it, might be scary, especially if you've never done it before. Now think about trying to control that wave, that energy, to control its direction. It's impossible, you say, but that's your task, the impossible, except there's one variable, one thing going for you that the surfer doesn't have—she's in the physical world, but you'll be on a metaphysical plane. Yes, you will be connected to the physical world, but not completely beholden to it because you'll be a conduit for the energy you'll be tapping into, energy that goes above and through our world, and if you pull it off, you'll be able to influence reality as we know it, your curse will take effect."

"But—"

"But how do you do it?" said the high priestess, anticipating Jennifer's question. "That's the critical question, and one for which I don't have a definite answer. A curse such as this, the kind I think Norman Modrak is proposing, requires that you come to terms with the world's energy in your own way. There is no cryptic manual somewhere to tell you what to do, no arcane or hidden advice. You have to discover it within the process you embark on. You have to open yourself up to all the forces of nature while keeping in mind one specific task, your curse, what you want to happen. If you get overwhelmed, you'll drown in the process, you'll be good for nothing. You must be extremely flexible, it's a very delicate dance, you must know when to lead and when to follow the energy you submit to. You must also believe fervently in what you're doing, the curse must be an ardent commitment. Anybody can follow directions, but not everyone can find their own way. These are two different things that require two different kinds of people. It's not a matter of being smart, Jennifer, but of being aware, hyper-aware, so that you know just what's what and what you need to do."

"I'm not sure I understand."

"Going forward with this isn't easy. You'll learn by the process itself, you'll be learning on the spot. I can provide preparation and suggestions if you want to attempt this, but I can't do much more."

"I think I want to do it," stated Jennifer, growing more open to the idea.

"You won't know for sure about that until you hear the specific request. But understand," stressed the high priestess, "if you take this on, it all begins with your mind. You need to open it very wide. Shake up the tumblers of your brain, break down the conditioning and indoctrination of your whole life, the littlest things even. Open up to other influences and channels of change even if you don't know what they are. Submit to the energy around you and grow comfortable with it. Let it pass through you and awaken you. Then let it sweep you up, however disconcerting this may be, however uneasy it makes you. You must ride that wave of energy. You must blot out everything and let yourself go. This will be intense, it will take a toll on you, and then comes the hard part. You must impose your vision, the curse you want to happen. A fusion between all this energy and your own will needs to happen. At that point you're on your own."

"So I just try to do it, is that how it works?" questioned Jennifer.

"If you're wholly attuned to everything that has been happening, if it has all been going the right way to the utmost, then it's possible the next step forward will suggest itself. I wish I could be more definite about it, but none of this is cut and dried. If you want to proceed, you'll find out from Norman Modrak whom you're putting the curse on and what it is exactly. He's not a malicious person, Norman, so I feel confident in saying that whatever he wants you to do likely has some principle or justification behind it, but you must wholly agree yourself to be successful, you can't agree simply on his behalf."

"So do we set up a meeting?"

"That would be the next step."

"And the bells in your dream, it's all like you told me? You think I can really do this?"

"I think you have unusual potential."

"Okay then, I'll meet with him, but I have a job, you know, so we need to have the meeting when I'm not working."

"I'll contact Norman and make the arrangements. I know he'll be glad to meet you. But there's one other thing you need to know that can help with this. When you execute this curse, you'll need to go to a designated spot to do it. By that I mean the right location, one that offers the best chance of success. A curse should be performed outdoors and at night. Do it when the moon is full. The spot you'll be going to is very natural and isolated, an out of the way and rugged place where the land is giving off vibes, where the energy is concentrated. There are such places, you see. Native Americans are very much in tune with this kind of thing. In fact, to help find the best spot I contacted a friend of mine. Her name is Rhonda Redwing. She's a kind of medicine woman. Actually," said the high priestess, pausing to scrutinize Jennifer from a slightly different angle, "you resemble her somewhat. But my point is that Rhonda Redwing recognizes the deep vibes that exist in the Earth itself, in the rocks, the canyons, the trees, the streams, the lakes, the life force itself, if you will. I shared with her my objective, meaning *your* objective, and asked her if she knew of a place where the energy was particularly apparent, where it might best serve the enacting of a curse. She thought of several places, but there was one in particular that she believed offered an ideal combination of male and female energy coming together, a place of both rock and water, a place with a large vista that would provide a clear view of the moon. It has no specific context in Haudenosaunee culture, it's not a sacred spot, per se. Rhonda Redwing discovered it while hiking a few years ago, searching for bearberry shrubs and other medical plants. She was hoping to find a slippery elm tree, but never did. Nevertheless, she found a place where the land is imbued with power, the collective power of time immemorial. That's what you want."

"Rhonda Redwing," pondered Jennifer, saying the name aloud. "Is she on the rez? Onondaga? Akwesasne?"

"No, she lives off of the reservation, but it's curious you bring it up. As I was speaking to her, she seemed in a somber mood. At one point she happened to say that we were now all on the reservation. I'm not sure what prompted it, perhaps the current political strife, perhaps the ecological collapse that's looming nearer. She said that when the trees start dying from the tops on down the end of life as we know it on this planet is at hand. In any case, I think I know what she means, sadly, about all of us being on the rez."

After reflecting for a moment, Jennifer posed another question. "And where is this place then, where I do the curse?"

"She gave me a map," answered the high priestess, and reaching into a canvas pocketbook embroidered with bright geometric designs she withdrew a piece of paper which she unfolded and handed to Jennifer.

"The map looks clear enough," said Jennifer, examining it, "but I don't know where any of this is, where the starting point is."

"I'll give you directions to the starting point, it's fairly straightforward, but the hike will be demanding, you'll need to allow yourself enough time."

"Maybe I'll check it out beforehand, I mean, if I decide to go through with this."

"A very good idea," commended the high priestess, "especially as you'll be making this journey at night. In fact, it will be rather late at night because when you're putting a curse on someone it's best that the person be in a deep sleep. When people are asleep, it's most likely their psychic guard will be down, that's when they'll be most vulnerable to a curse. So it's best to aim for the wee hours. It's another point to keep in mind, something to give you an edge."

Nodding that she understood, Jennifer bit her lower lip for a moment as she mulled the matter over. "It all sounds good," she said at last. "I'll at least meet with Norman Modrak and see what he has to say. I can't promise anything, but I guess it's something to consider."

With a look of deep appreciation, the high priestess got to her feet and thanked Jennifer for her cooperation, promising she would contact Norman Modrak that evening to make the arrangements, adding, "It may take him a few days before he can get up this way, but I'll keep you informed."

"We can meet at El Gitano Bar and Grill," suggested Jennifer. "There's a backroom there that's very private."

"I'm sure that will do."

"Don Alvadoro runs the place, he keeps everything under his hat."

The high priestess said nothing, though her eyebrows went up with an approving look. Then, after putting the strap of her pocketbook over her shoulder, she stood there, seemingly so straight and formal that Jennifer half expected her to bow, but instead she held out her hand and firmly took Jennifer's, holding it as she expressed her great pleasure at having been able to meet again. Surprised and flattered, Jennifer made a barely audible reply.

The high priestess once again noticed the scratch-off lottery ticket stuck to the refrigerator and the pentacle magnet holding it there. Not revealing any reaction to it, however, she walked to Jennifer's door and said goodbye, parting in one of those civil but slightly awkward moments when there really is nothing left to say. Then, descending the common stairwell that went down from Jennifer's apartment she listened to the dim echo of her footsteps until she reached the bottom landing, at which point she heard a voice above her and looked up to see Jennifer standing there, leaning out over the top railing.

"By the way," Jennifer called out, "if you get a chance, tell Rhonda Redwing I said thank you for the map."

MAKING A PACT AT EL GITANO

Four days later, Norman Modrak walked into the backroom at El Gitano Bar and Grill and found Jennifer waiting. He was surprised, however, to find her in the company of another young woman, Amber Lamphere. Jennifer, on assuming that the man walking toward her was Modrak, showed equal surprise at finding another man tagging along. It was an unexpected situation that made for strained introductions and greater reserve on everyone's part, a situation that was hardly helped when McPherson, the man in tow with Norman Modrak, noticed the wound running across Jennifer's forehead and, as if unable to contain himself, uttered, "Whoa, you really *did* pick up every stitch."

Offended and surprised, Jennifer was at a loss for words until angrily retorting, "And what is that to fucking you?"

Witnessing this exchange, Norman Modrak stared at McPherson in astonishment and wondered what had come over the man. Recognizing the need for damage control, he told Jennifer in his most mollifying tone that he was sorry to see she had been injured and hoped she was recovering. McPherson likewise was about to express his concern by way of an apology when Amber suddenly spoke.

"It was the goons of the Dictator, that's what did it to her," she blurted out, her indignance obvious. "They whacked her with a billy club, they could've killed her. It was during the riot."

"Indeed!" responded Modrak with great empathy, shooting a brief but telling glance at McPherson before again engaging Jennifer. "I hope you're not in pain. The abuse suffered by ordinary citizens under the Dictator's regime is an absolute outrage."

"I'll say," chimed in Amber again, but Jennifer said nothing and the silence at the table became a brief impasse until McPherson offered to buy everyone a round of drinks. Accepting the offer, Jennifer and Amber ordered gin and tonics while Modrak selected a glass of La Maldita Garnacha from the wine list. McPherson opted for a Scotch on the rocks.

As they waited for the drinks to arrive, small talk passed back and forth with Modrak asking how the food was at El Gitano. Amber raved about the seafood burrito while McPherson, who had been perusing the menu, noted that any place serving tripe and beef hoof soup sounded like authentic Mexican, to which Amber replied that a lot of the recipes at El Gitano where very old and that Don Alvadoro, who ran the place, could tell you what kitchens they came from hundreds of years ago.

"That could be why some people think Don Alvadoro is a ghost, because there's ghosts in this place," boasted Amber, "we even saw one the last time we were here."

"A ghost?" exclaimed Norman Modrak, watching Amber smile somewhat coyly as Jennifer kicked her under the table. "How interesting."

Not saying a word, Jennifer looked closely at Modrak and then at McPherson. Modrak, dressed all in faded black, looked like a destitute lounge lizard, but to be fair, with his graying hair and considerate behavior he had something avuncular about him. Almost overly polite at times, he might have come across as fawning were it not for something inscrutable about him, this coupled with a mother lode of self-assurance that gave the man a certain clout. McPherson, on the other hand, would have been easy to label as a stodgy tight-ass, his Oxford shirt and tacky wingtips being pretty much dead giveaways, but then again, he was a man who in his own way seemed almost too unassuming. Jennifer sensed there was more to the man than met the eye, and although she had a liking for Norman Modrak she knew instinctively that McPherson was the better man to be in league with. There was something definite and able about him, even though he rubbed her the wrong way.

When the drinks arrived, McPherson raised his glass to Jennifer and, attempting to smooth over his prior blunder, said, "Here's to getting well."

"Yes, to getting well," seconded Modrak as glasses went up all around, with Amber smacking her lips and saying, "That tastes good. For me and Jen, you know, gin's our only weakness—like Dr. Pretorius!" she added, looking pleased as Punch at having dropped this reference.

Giving a muted chuckle, Norman Modrak took a decisive breath and said, "Well, now that we're all together, I guess that brings us to the matter at hand, though I must admit, Jennifer, I thought we'd be meeting in private."

"Me too," replied Jennifer, shifting her eyes toward McPherson.

"Yes, I see your point, but the endeavor we're here to discuss has been instigated by my friend here, he's here because he has a stake in the matter, so he was eager to meet you."

"And I have a stake in Jennifer," put in Amber, "she's my friend."

"I appreciate that," said Norman Modrak, "but this is a sensitive matter, something that, when you get down to it, is a deeply private matter."

"We can keep a secret," pledged Jennifer.

"I don't deny it, but the matter of a curse requires the utmost discretion, the utmost confidentiality. It's always best that way."

"We don't have a problem with that," said Jennifer, digging in her heels.

"But I think my friend might find it problematical were the matter to go beyond us three," persisted Modrak. "As I said, he's the one behind this endeavor."

"In which case," interjected McPherson, sipping his Scotch before he continued, "I think maybe it's best to approach the issue in a different way."

With Modrak deferring, Jennifer narrowing her eyes, and Amber smiling, McPherson looked down at the table as if deliberating. "Just so I completely understand," he said, raising his eyes toward Jennifer, "I trust that when you got hit in the head you were out in the street protesting."

"We all got caught up in it," said Jennifer.

"But protesting against the Dictator is, I'm assuming, something you did very willfully."

"Let's just say I hate his guts," said Jennifer, her tone eerily solemn, "and now that my face is disfigured I hate his guts even more."

"That's right," butted in Amber, "we'd skin him alive if we could."

"Then we'd tie him to a whipping post," added Jennifer.

"Then we'd stick it on anthill squirming with thousands of fire ants," warned Amber.

With each of these statements Norman Modrak's eyes grew a little wider while McPherson concluded: "Then I think it's safe to say the Dictator is not one of your favorite people."

"He's a rat," declared Amber, "a lying, murdering rat. Go ahead, Jen, tell them what happened to Rosa."

"Who's Rosa?" asked Modrak.

"Rosa Cortinas," said Jennifer grimly. "She's dead."

"What happened?" inquired McPherson.

"She was from Mexico," explained Jennifer. "We worked together in the same factory. We were friends. But the Dictator's goons got on her trail and came after her. We had an escape plan in place. Everybody was there to help, but we lost her. Something went wrong. She never met up with us."

"We're part of Action Underground," clarified Amber, clearly proud of the fact.

"We wanted to help her," Jennifer went on. "We thought the plan was a good one. We rehearsed it and everything. But in the end the Dictator's creeps got her. They beat her up, they raped her and then they killed her. She was found hanging from a highway overpass with a noose of barbed wire around her neck."

"I'm very sorry to hear about your friend," stated McPherson soberly. "I'm glad you tried to help her. Sadly, this is how dictators operate. First they go after someone in a social gray zone, someone most likely not to be noticed or cared about, so having an anonymous immigrant disappear fits the bill. Under a dictatorship, society will be tested to see how much it will bear, how indifferent people will become to the fate of their fellow man, because if they turn a blind eye then it won't be long before people who are more in the mainstream start disappearing as well. They simply drop off the map, maybe somebody finds them dead in a ditch or never finds them. They constitute isolated cases at first, cases shrouded in contradiction and ambiguity, but sooner or later a dictator's full reach will hit home. Sooner or later it's somebody next door who disappears, your friend's husband, your neighbor's wife. They simply go to work one day and don't come back. Were they murdered? Tortured? Who knows? But what the Dictator knows is that the best way to cheapen life is to start going after people whose lives already appear cheapened. And so the first victims might be desperate refugees, their children getting ripped from their arms or conveniently dying in custody. It's intimidation, it's state-sponsored kidnapping. The kicker, however, is that it all gets predicated on some sick and twisted interpretation of the law. Of course, as Thomas Hardy wrote, 'There are many triumphs of justice that make a mockery of law.' So in a very real sense that's why we're here, to seek your help in seeing justice triumph, to hit the reset button, to move the nation back toward freedom and basic human rights, to get out from under the thumb of a fascist pig."

"Wait a minute, you guys," said Amber, her brow furrowed. "Wait a minute," she repeated, looking from McPherson to Modrak and back to McPherson, at whom she wagged a finger. "I'm thinkin' about something here. Are you who I think you are?"

"Who do you think I am?" asked McPherson, curious.

"What I'm thinkin' is that you're the Dark State, because all this what you're saying sounds like it could be the Dark State to me."

"I can see where it might look that way," agreed McPherson, given pause for a moment, "but we're not the Dark State, although it would be fair to admit we share a similar interest."

"Which is what interest?" prodded Jennifer, listening very closely.

"One might call it an interest in national security," McPherson replied almost offhandedly.

"But what do *you* call it?" Jennifer pressed.

"I call it defending the fundamental rights of a free society from a power-hungry tyrant who's determined to wreck and trash everything our nation stands for," declared McPherson, heating up somewhat.

"If you'll allow me," Norman Modrak now interrupted, "these points are well taken, very much so, but before we go any further it's important to understand that there can be no breach of trust here. It must be clear from here on in that we all keep this among ourselves, all *four* of us," he stressed, looking at McPherson for any sign of objection.

"I would agree," nodded McPherson.

"And you, Jennifer, you're on board so far?" inquired Modrak.

"That's what I'm here for, the high priestess made everything clear."

"Amber?" said Modrak with some reluctance. "I trust you can stay mum about this."

"Mum's my middle name, just ask Jen. When it comes to keeping secrets, we're the cat's nuts."

"Then let's get to the heart of the matter," said Modrak, "which is the curse, which is to be enacted on behalf of my friend here," he noted with a dodge of his head toward McPherson. "He came to me with a request and I offered to oblige. Fortunately, my contact with the high priestess has brought us all here this evening and has brought you, Jennifer, to the fore as a desirable enactor of this curse. The high priestess believes that you are particularly capable of living up to the task. It will not be an easy one. Nevertheless, the high priestess has put great store in your potential, and I hold her opinion in high esteem. This curse, mark my words, will be on a grand scale, but what I've heard here tonight, what has come to light regarding the personal dynamics involved here, gives me great reassurance that whatever powers of witchery you possess, Jennifer, they will measure up and they will very likely prove successful."

"And that task is . . . ?" questioned Jennifer.

"As the high priestess mentioned," reminded Modrak, "you are not committed to anything. Our proposal is for you to consider, and you can agree to it or not. If not, there are no hard feelings, we simply finish our drinks and go our separate ways. However, we will keep all of this strictly among ourselves if that's the case, as if this meeting never occurred."

"Agreed," said Jennifer.

With that, Norman Modrak gestured to McPherson, who now began to speak. "In the simplest of terms," McPherson explained, "there are forces of oppression eating away at the fabric of our democracy, destroying the bedrock on which our nation was founded, scrapping fundamental rights and freedoms. This totalitarian threat, whose clutches we are in right now, seeks to thwart the individual and smother free thinking in any way it can. By destroying our free press with a meatgrinder of lies and relentless propaganda, putting our journalists in cages and enlisting foreign autocrats to kill them, and by constricting our free will through intimidation and heinous violence, the goal is to create an alternate reality in which people not only submit to the prevailing authority, but even gladly begin to relish the process of submitting. It's all about the fiefdom of money and power controlling the serfs and vassals, doing it brazenly on the one hand and yet often so insidiously that the average serf doesn't even know he's being controlled. This threat is real and it's happening now. It's happening at the hands of a dictator whose insatiable hunger for absolute power allows for no restraint. In our media he must be omnipresent, but he craves omniscience as well by using technology and any means he can to know when there is even the slightest waver in absolute loyalty to his cause. Like Caligula, he sees himself not only as an infallible ruler, but as a god, and he enables this delusion through frightening machinations. He has employed surveillance networks utilizing the most menacing technology. Security grids are plotted with random checkpoints to nab people. Facial-recognition cameras and cell phone sniffers are strategically placed without our knowing it. Databases are built up with voice prints and secretly obtained DNA samples, and there are scans that can even identify the gait a person has as he walks along in a crowd. Such data are gathered subtly, usually without our knowing it. It's Big Brother on steroids. It's the Internet of things, which may sound like a clever idea, but does it mean that your car is subject to GPS vehicle tracking by someone, somewhere, while you're none the wiser? Someone who wants to know your every move? Dictators have always been dangerous people, but the danger in our nation right now is critical. The world-wide web is a reality, but when a malicious spider, in this case the Dictator, begins to weave and control the strands of that web, he will do so to devour anyone he doesn't like, in which case we're doomed as a free society. So when we see warning signs such as these, we don't take chances. We strike and strike hard. In this case, we're bypassing the conventional means by which to incapacitate someone and instead we're trying something new— witchcraft. A curse can't be scanned, it can't be traced, it can't be sampled. So if you want to avenge the death of Rosa Cortinas, and the deaths of many others, enacting this curse will enable you to do so."

"You mean . . ." began Jennifer, appearing flabbergasted, "you mean it's *him*, that's who I'm putting the curse on?"

"Hot diggity!" yelled Amber, quickly lowering her voice. "Jen, you've got to do it. This will be so cool. You've got to cast this curse! I know you got the stuff to pull it off. I feel it every time we get in bed together, I go weak in the knees. And you know what Lorenzo is always saying, that guy from the Himalayas with the crazy poncho, he says you got some real freaky mojo. He says it every time he's at Smitty's Tavern."

"Amber, please."

"What? I know what a zinger you are, and Lorenzo says that stuff about freaky mojo for a reason. When you told me you had the makings of a witch it all became clear to me. You do! I realized it— and you do, too, admit it. You got the power to make this work, and who better to curse the Dictator than you? You can cast some kind of curse that will maybe shrink his head down to the size of a golf ball!"

Clearing his throat, Norman Modrak now spoke up. "Let's not get overly ambitious," he cautioned, "curses have limitations like everything else."

"Better yet," continued Amber, "put a big ugly snout on his face to go along with his little pig eyes."

"Amber—" said Jennifer with startling firmness, "that's enough, please."

Retreating behind a complacent smile, Amber now looked fondly at her friend and said no more.

"Executing a curse is not a simple matter," Norman Modrak stated with some severity. "As I'm sure you gathered from talking with the high priestess, it can be tricky and demanding, with no guarantees. The object of the curse, as you now know, is the Dictator, while the objective itself, well, not to put too fine a point on it, is to kill him."

"That is the general outcome," interjected McPherson, "though the exact mechanism of death is totally at your discretion."

Looking sternly now at both Jennifer and Amber, Norman Modrak followed up by saying, "The choice of whether or not to proceed is completely yours. We'll respect it either way."

Speechless, Jennifer looked back and forth from Norman Modrak to McPherson and then considered Amber, saying softly, "Is this the thing we want, Amber?" But Amber simply closed her eyes and drew her finger across her lips as if sealing them shut, after which Jennifer looked up at the ceiling for a moment and recalled the spark that had mysteriously jumped out at her the last time she had been sitting there, right after the apparition had appeared. She then turned and looked at the jukebox, recalling the music that on that same night had come blasting through it all on its own. And she recalled as well the horrible murder of Rosa Cortinas and that strange message which Don Alvadoro had delivered to Professor Rasmsussen—*She's the girl.* Taking a slug of her gin and tonic, she now drew a deep breath and thumped her glass down hard on the table, saying with resolve, "Okay, I'm in. I'm going to launch that fucker to the moon."

Modrak, with something of a sigh of relief, raised his glass of La Maldita, but said nothing, while Amber, raising her gin and tonic, also said nothing, though McPherson, a bit late in following suit, raised his glass and said in an oddly warm and endearing tone, "Good luck."

"I believe you've been informed," said Modrak to Jennifer after they had all sipped their drinks, "of a particular spot where the curse is to be carried out."

"Yes, Rhonda Redwing drew a map for me."

"Ah, Rhonda Redwing, I've heard of her," acknowledged Modrak. "I hope to meet her one day."

"I guess I would too," said Jennifer.

"It would be nice if we could all meet again," mused McPherson, "but such a situation would be highly unlikely, so on that note I think it's best we part for good."

"Yes," agreed Modrak, taking a last opportunity to advise Jennifer on what was coming next. "At the next full moon we want this curse to get off the ground. You'll be feeling your way, coming completely out of yourself. Nothing will be predictable or certain. No matter how unsettling things get, bear with it, know that we're counting on you. I trust Amber will be there for support, but she can't intervene. She needs to go off on her own and leave it all to you. No matter how unpleasant she thinks things are becoming for you, she needs to let it play out. This will be grueling and it's probably not a bad idea to have her along with you. We will all hope for the best. The high priestess will contact you for some last-minute counseling, but you can't divulge any particulars to her."

Jennifer agreed and after they had all finished their drinks, and after a few lingering concerns were clarified and addressed, then the discussion at the table was marked by a more unified rapport.

Everything was settled and the plan set in motion, with Jennifer insisting there would be no backing out. The die, irreparably cast, was now tumbling toward the next full moon, and as Modrak and McPherson got up to leave they shook hands with their young confidants and walked out of El Gitano never to see them again, except when Amber stormed outside onto the sidewalk and yelled after them as they were walking away.

"Hey! You guys, if we pull this thing off do we get anything? I mean like money or somethin', a kind of reward? We'll be doing the whole world a favor, you know!"

RALLY HO!

Hurry! Hurry! Hurry!
Step right up!
Be first in line!

As the doors to the Ninth Circle Stadium are flung open, young and old alike jostle each other to rush inside, their eyes wide with anticipation, for all around there is a carnival of sights and sounds besieging them. Yes, it's rally time, folks, when those who are self-condemned by ignorance and delusion begin to swarm, the lowly and the lofty alike having come together in search of the Dictator, that demented Pied Piper who leads them on by tweeting his tunes of rage and arrogance, a man of reckless abandon who views everyone and everything with savage disgust, excepting, of course, his own imperial rule. As a long stream of his devotees scurries into the Ninth Circle Stadium, they gad about and don't know where to turn first, for all around them there is no shortage of distractions to indulge these mooncalves. There are booths in which guns with live ammo can be fired at pictures of political enemies and civil rights leaders, there are dartboards whose targets are racist caricatures of Jews and black people, and there are pyres upon which the effigies of liberal judges and advocates for socialized medicine are set ablaze. To go along with this fiery entertainment there is also the book-burning bonfire, where all sorts of subversive reading material goes up in flames, particularly books on evolution, global warming and fascism, not to mention such dreaded books as *The End of America*, *The Hand Maid's Tale*, and *1984*, whose pages one man tears out with his teeth and spits into the fire. Yes, delights and entertainments abound for these churls and nincompoops. Gazing up with child-like wonder, they are also treated to the sight of a man dangling from the top of a huge telescopic crane. From the ground up, this crane is festooned with colorful lights blinking on and off, and although the man dangling from this apparatus nearly blends in with the night sky, his blimpish form is nonetheless recognizable as that of radio blabbermouth Bum's Rush Limburger. Strapped into a heavy-duty harness typically used for livestock, Bum's Rush sways about at the end of a thick steel cable. With microphone in hand, this human ball of grease is conducting a live broadcast for station WASP, flooding the airways with pugnacious talk and all sorts of fightin' words, words that barge forcibly out his mouth, bringing with them a strong whiff of combustible swamp gas, a noxious vapor that has caused the man's body to bloat so severely that his skin is stretched tight like that on a fat Brägenwurst sausage. A windup chatterbox whose diarrhea of the mouth gushes forth in a bottomless loo of swirling nonsense, Bum's Rush Limburger blabs and blabs, bolstering his petty tirades and crackpot polemics with angry pomposity, a voice that simply must be heard because this guy, lest we forget, is *the man*. As a cheerleader for iron-fisted, autocratic rule, he has made the airways his soapbox, a venue where he can blab and blab and show his listeners that he is the orneriest demagogue this side of the Pecos, that he is the meanest, most wily endomorph south of the Montana picket wire, that he is the rootin-tootinest tough guy to ever pull a cap gun on a wooden Indian. Indeed! And yet the fact remains that Bum's Rush Limburger is really nothing more than a spouting spittoon of insipid drivel not heard since the heyday of Bedlam with all its wailing madmen.

Be that as it may, Bum's Rush Limburger keeps blabbing on and on, dishing out the pablum that keeps his bottom feeders happy— while remaining unaware that high above him a large flock of vultures has begun to gather. Just barely discernable to the naked eye, the vultures circle about, gliding on plumes of hot air that rise up from below. With their wings stretched wide, the birds float effortlessly in endless and easy loops. Endowed with limitless patience, they appear to be stealthy and quiet beings that seem to maintain a kind of radio silence, although their eyes are decidedly peeled, awaiting a rosy decapitation they seem to know is coming.

Birds of prey aside, however, back down on the ground the rally continues with a special appearance by that world-renowned female Frigidaire, Primo Bimbo. At this very moment, in fact, she can be found climbing to the top of a tall ladder, where she steps out onto a small platform. After blowing a kiss to the gawkers below, she readies herself for a high-wire act unlike any other. With silver pasties on her boobs, she wears a hot pink thong and has a faux donkey's tail pinned to her ass. Before her there stretches a beeline of tightrope wire under which there roils a large pit of muck and shit and fuming chemicals that burn the nasal membranes even from afar, a deathtrap that would test the mettle of the most seasoned circus pro. Nevertheless, Primo Bimbo knows that the show must go on, and to showcase America's downfall in all its sordid buffoonery she now jiggles her boobs so that the silver pasties on her nipples swish about. The crowd cheers. Then she makes a flamboyant gesture, flinging both arms upward, a gesture that seems to say: "Look at me!" The crowd cheers some more.

Next, with arms sticking out at her sides to maintain her balance, Primo Bimbo proceeds with the discipline of a finely tuned automaton, an apathetic sleepwalker who now places one foot in front of the other as she steps out onto the tightrope. Keeping her eyes straight ahead, she makes every footfall a measured act of precision. Never flinching, never hesitating, she displays no hint of concern. Her self-control is impressive, to be sure, for she is utterly committed to the daredevil antics at hand. Thus, it is surprising when Primo Bimbo's eyes, ever so briefly, stray downward, stealing a glance at the deadly brew beneath her. Despite this lapse in attention, however, Primo Bimbo never falters in her footwork, continuing to cross the tightrope with deliberate and artful aplomb.

Standing amid the cheering crowd, Senator Mitch McConman is relishing the chance to gawk at Primo Bimbo, suddenly finding himself in a fit of schoolboy lust. With his hands in his pockets, he can't resist toggling his dick back and forth in his pants, his eyes bulging even bigger than usual, his eyeglasses fogging up as he hopes against hope that in some dark corner of the Senate Chamber he can maybe, just maybe, get it on with Primo Bimbo. Indeed, with a goofy leer, Mitch McConman tells himself that if the Dictator can fuck porn stars on the one hand and then sign Bibles for tornado victims in Alabama on the other, well isn't it a case of anything goes? Isn't it perfectly within reason that Primo Bimbo might put on a cowboy hat and yell *Yahoo!* as she rides his dick reverse cowgirl? Because Mitch McConman, poor bloke, is desperate, so absolutely desperate to get that little something that he just can't get at home.

Yet although the sexual fantasies of this long-lusting hick are neither here nor there when you get down to it, what is worth noting is that Primo Bimbo's downward glance at the mire below her has activated this morass in unforeseen ways, the surface of this toxic cesspit now coming alive with flickering sheens of greenish yellow and fiery vermillion, while slippery creepers of liquified flesh wriggle their way across the gloppy fluid, branching out amid stiff currents that suddenly turn choppy, as if some ill wind were at large. Here and there, huge bubbles begin to drift up from the depths of this vile pit, resting briefly on the surface before they go floating off into the open air, people craning their necks to watch them as the bubbles gain in altitude, going up and up before bursting with a bright flash, releasing a blizzard of spores and microbes that are free at last to double down on the helix of extinction.

Not quite sure what to make of this display, the rally goers on the ground below scratch their heads, barely having time to ponder the matter before recoiling in shock as the skeleton of a huge prehistoric beast now rears itself up from the filthy ooze and fizzing scum before them, the creature's enormous boulder-like head swiveling about on a spine of giant vertebrae pocked and stippled by the ravages of time, its long jawbone studded with jagged teeth flashing their menace, their power, while within the eye sockets of the creature's skull the gawkers find themselves mirrored in a dark night that reveals just how puny they really are.

"Psst!" says Hank Bunghole, who stands among the gawkers, whispering to his buddy, Billy Duntzkapp. "Where's the Dictator, Billy? He needs to get a load of what's happening here, Primo Bimbo's trippin' up."

"I don't know, Hank, I haven't seen the Dictator nowhere, but I hear tell he'll be appearing on stage later on. But for now just look at that big, bodacious swamp creature comin' out of that dang-blasted pit!"

Indeed, the long-dormant abhorosaurus has now heaved itself into full view, an agile mass of interconnected bones arriving from a lost world, its anatomy perfected for sheer destruction, its mineralized claws flexing with spidery ease, sharp and steely and ready, while the powerful jaws cleave shut, then fly open—gaping wide as the head of the beast rises toward the little morsel tottering on the tightrope above it. Primo Bimbo, for her part, is scared shitless, her balancing act going to pieces as she quivers like jelly, flails her arms and then, after some herky-jerky movements, slips and tumbles headlong into the jaws of the abhorosaurus. As if sucked into a four-dimensional atom smasher, Primo Bimbo smears the air with a blur into nothingness and is gone, vanished, nevermore, her invisible *poof* now zinging around to all four points of the compass.

The crowd cheers hesitantly, wondering if this is all part of the show, observing what appears to be a subtle smirk in the jawline of the abhorosaurus, the creature now slowly turning its head, the empty eye sockets feasting on the crowd with a dark, intimidating stare. Growing uneasy, people quickly move on, many of them seeking solace farther along the way at what is sure to be a hit—the Superior White Man Exhibit.

Yesiree. How better for a man to determine his self-worth than by touting the color of his skin? Throughout Dixie and elsewhere, in fact, you will find no end of honky honchos still singing the praises of that antebellum conceit that God has clothed the white man in the epidermis of divine purity, that such bodies are the very color of angels' wings! Yet even among the idiots who believe this ridiculous crap, there is no question that for the purest and most inimitable whiteness no one can hold a candle to the star of the Superior White Man Exhibit—the one and only Senator Oily Graham Cracker, a man who stands out whiter than a ghost from the tunnels of Nordhausen, his tongue a white glowworm that hangs from milky plasticine lips. Hailing from the great Palmetto Bug State, Senator Cracker is a man who takes pride in his "Southern heritage," a man who will gladly uphold the legacy of walking on the heads of black people as he retrieves a cool mint julep or purchases a new hoop skirt for the lady of the manor. "A skirt that is," laughs Senator Cracker as he stands proudly atop a slave auction block, flamboyantly waving a bullwhip, "a skirt that *is*," he repeats with dogged emphasis, "bought and paid for by poor nigger suckers in chains!"

The crowd heartily applauds this brute ingenuity, pressing nearer to hear more.

"It was the best of both worlds, the Old South!" declares Senator Cracker with his honey-dipper tongue, a man so white that the whites of his eyes have totally eclipsed his irises, a man made even more ghoulish by the fungus gnats that clog his ears and which now begin to emit an eerie glow. "In the Old South we did God's bidding!" yells Senator Cracker. "Why we saved the black people from themselves by making sure they stayed pickin' cotton and didn't try no fool notions of going off and trying to make something of themselves. That's right, we saved them! Like any good Christian would! We kept them and all their pickaninny children slaves! Slaves like in the Bible! And we wouldn't tolerate no Spartacus! We would beat sense into them niggers like with this here bullwhip that I'm holding in my God-fearing hand. So it didn't get any better than the Old South! And that's how we all got to be on easy street and got ourselves to be friggin' rich without lifting a pinky! That's the glory of the white man for you, that's the glory of the days gone by!"

The crowd is starry-eyed, speechless, on the verge of weeping at such spirited oration, while Senator Cracker passionately wraps up: "And this here bullwhip, this here bullwhip you see in my hand," he states, beginning to choke up, "it's but a thing of the past now, a remnant from a golden bygone age, an age when Aunt Jemima was in the kitchen making me some grits and all was right with the world. But we can say goodbye to this here bullwhip now," blubbers Senator Cracker, tossing the bullwhip away with a wistful gaze. "But mind you, mind each and every one of you, let me say that getting rid of this whip don't mean shit in the end! Not shit!" the Senator shouts, his lips pulling back in a snarl. "It don't mean shit because the white man's on top and he's going to stay on top, whip or no whip. He's going to stay on top because we got lawyers and legislators who can forge manacles of fine print and doublespeak that are stronger than iron chains! And so let it be known to all you people here tonight that we're not just going to keep black people down in the shit, because—so help me God—we're going to create a lily-white caste system that's going to keep *everybody* down in the shit! Tons and tons of white people included! Because we've overcome our prejudices! We're inclusive now, got it? We're inclusive in despising everybody and keeping everybody in the shit! Anybody who don't have the money to buy their way into the club and don't get to sit with the *man*, well then they're in the shit! And so mark my words, this whole nation is going to become one big salt mine, one big sweat shop and plantation all rolled into one, one big company town with overseers at the top just like me! And that's how it should be, damn it, from sea to shining sea! Amen!"

The crowd breaks out with sustained cheering and loud vociferous hurrahs. Having been tossed the red meat of racism, these myrmidons of state control now want nothing more than to find a scapegoat for the raw fury welling up within them. Bursting at the seams with an urge to belittle, harass and attack someone, they search about desperately, hoping a journalist might be at hand, someone they can gang up on and viciously beat to a pulp, for these dolts and slackers do not want their lives enriched by thoughtful inquiry into sound and responsible government, just their base instincts aroused, and how better to do this than by attending one of the Dictator's pep rallies? One of his patriotic masquerades? Indeed, the show must go on! And after watching Senator Oily Graham Cracker take a final bow, the crowd eagerly slouches on to the next big, beautiful, wonderful event—an appearance by that judicial juggernaut of the beer kegs, Justice Pigskin Hangover!

Hurry! Hurry! Hurry!

Step right up!

Sis-boom-bah!

For out comes a man waltzing about in black judicial robes, twirling like a ballerina as he pops into the air, landing on a makeshift stage that consists of several oak planks laid across two large wooden sawbucks. Twirling about on tippy toes, this man in the judicial robes pouts and tap dances. He is a man of solemn and dewy-eyed piety, with a fool's gold crucifix about his neck that is simply dazzling and clearly there for all to see. And why not! What better way to show the populace that he embodies sanctimonious scruples sung by the angels on high, for this man just happens to be Judge Pigskin Hangover (the Right Honorable, of course), a man divine in both thought and deed, who attended a private Catholic prep school of the first order, a bargain at $60,000 a year when you consider all the virtuous character it buys. So what's not to like about this man? In one vetting process after another, he has stated that throughout his college years he was a veritable goody two shoes. He lifted weights, he played sports, he studied hard, he studied *very* hard. He went to bed at ten o'clock and always said his prayers after a glass of warm milk. He was a bookworm, pure and simple, although he does admit, in all honesty, honesty, mind you, that at times he did "sip some beer" and that, now that he thinks about it, as best he can recall, there were particular occasions when he did, in fact, guzzle "lots of beer." Proof that he laments this transgression is made clear by the anguished and aghast look on his face as he admits it. Clearly the beer he has consumed, be it "some" or "lots," has haunted and plagued Justice Hangover for many years. It has weighed on his conscience. It has left him trapped in the big-time guilt trip of his own dark and brooding confessional. And yet, when it comes to his vicious attempts to force himself on women and fuck them, Justice Hangover is in full denial mode. He refuses to come clean. "Rape? Not me!" Indeed, he cannot countenance such outrageous accusations. "This is a plot by the resistance!" he sputters with nasty, sneering belligerence, a spectacle quite at odds with the legal deportment one would normally expect of a hotshot justice. "It's a plot by the Dark State!" he rants. He tells everyone, in fact, with no skimping on bombast, that it is all a plot to ruin his life, that his accusers are all in on this plot, and he dismisses the sworn testimony of these accusers out of hand, for such people are mere ciphers who have no place in the ongoing matrix of the judge's path to onward and upward success. Sweep it all under the rug, that's the judge's opinion, his nostrils pinching tight and kindling with a fiery red flush of indignance, although this redness may result from booze. In any case, all we know is that no one should dare bad mouth a grand and golden boy like Justice Pigskin Hangover.

Alas, when all is considered, however, it is no surprise that Pigskin Hangover has his naysayers, millions of them, in fact, people who give no credence to the man's sterling reputation, who not only question his parsing of legal mumbo-jumbo, but also his moral probity, for they are convinced by credible reports that the man is a drunken lecher who has brutally attacked unsuspecting women, a wretch who has been known to flash his private parts in public, particularly at women from what might be called "working class" origins. And then there are the rumors of his participation in orchestrated gang rapes in which women were drugged without their knowledge and rendered unconscious, rumors that do not exactly do the justice any favors. Indeed, for all too many people, Justice Hangover is a lowdown and two-faced rat. Then again, there are his defenders as well, those who cry foul. "No-no!" they cry. "This is not so!" they cry. For they deem the allegations against the Honorable One to be false. They side firmly with the judge and tell everyone bluntly to take heed and consider the exemplary tutelage that Pigskin Hangover has received from his earliest days, tutelage at the hands of the renowned Father Fondle and Bishop Bugger, gems of the Catholic Church who raked in scads of money while teaching little Pigskin at a ritzy private school made to order for the lad, a 90-acre playground for rich boys replete with heated swimming pool, cappuccino bar, recording studio, on-call masseuse (named Candy), indoor running track, golf course and even velveteen toilet paper, all perfect for a twerp like Pigskin, who has always been enamored by his own exclusivity. And exclusivity is, indeed, the hallmark of those who faithfully reside in Pigskin's camp, as attested by a chorus of fellow frat boys that now cries out: "How else do we produce the best and brightest minds in America if not by over-indulging ourselves, if not by testing the limits of our own excess?" What food for thought, this question! But not to be outdone, the Maryland Chapter of the Me-First Order of Stodgy Old White Men also gives a cry: "How else do we save the nation from the evils of minorities, the pestilence of diversity and the threat of empowered women? It's shameful! Disgusting!" These and other knuckleheads who stand by Justice Hangover remain convinced of his infallibility. They point to his exemplary education and notable accomplishments, they rattle off a rollcall of people in high places who can sing the praises of Pigskin, and they do, of course, set store by that golden crucifix around his neck, a reminder that Pigskin has been groomed and nurtured by not just anybody, but by "Men of God," the Jesuits in this case, including the famous classical scholar Father Donald Debris, a divine fellow who, when he is not delightfully in his cups, can be found poaching pheasants at a nearby game preserve. All of this, of course, goes a long way toward reassuring the supporters of Pigskin that he is a living, breathing testimony to all that is upright and good in the world, a legal titan who by means of his impeccable character is a priceless gift to the nation. Why even his chaste and cherished virginity has been championed by the justice himself on national television, the man having lately appeared on Vulpine News, his little missus perched beside him as he touts his sexual abstinence by advocating a stainless steel cock cage available on Amazon. Well! If this isn't Pigskin all over! Deary me, there are no two ways about it, he's a man among men, this fellow, a man who now, still dancing about on the oak planks laid across the sawbucks, does several dainty pirouettes before kicking up his legs and swishing his judicial robes to and fro in the manner of a cancan, revealing that he's buck naked under his robes, his little dick a sixpenny damnation that bobs freely about.

How people cheer for Justice Hangover!

Meanwhile, the abhorosaurus has been making the rounds, its huge skeleton clattering along until it spies Bum's Rush Limburger dangling from the top of his telescopic crane. Intrigued by such easy pickings, the abhorosaurus moves closer to this low-hanging fruitcake, the dark void of the beast's eye sockets intensifying with apparent scrutiny. Then, rearing up on its hind legs, it slowly opens its jaws and by degrees sinks its teeth into the ballotable bag of bullshit that is Bum's Rush Limburger. All across America, those tuned into station WASP hear the man scream—and then hear the spurting sound of hot sizzling grease, for Bum's Rush has been fatally punctured, his body deflating until it goes limp, hanging sticky and shriveled from the teeth of the abhorosaurus, looking very much like a used condom.

The crowd does not cheer, but grows a tad restless, getting the feeling that perhaps larger forces are at work here, that things aren't quite as scripted as they ought to be. A great unease settles in, perhaps even a grain of panic. Seeking comfort in numbers to assuage their discomfiture, the crowd now converges en masse on the stadium's main stage, shouting and chanting, champing at the bit for the main event—they want the Dictator, they cry out for the Dictator, they yank at their hair and scream for the Dictator. And as the welter within the Ninth Circle Stadium grows, as the crowd gets riled up into a teeth-gnashing fit, a woman recognized by all now takes the stage, provoking a loud cheer.

The woman in question is none other than Prissy Miss Conjob, the Dictator's personal wet nurse and one of his most staunch defenders. With a face that's a deep freeze of glistening ice, she grits her teeth in a forced smile. Always ready to go on the attack, she is shrill and nasty, her mouth a snake pit of twisted lies and stupendous feats of deception, all of which are accompanied by exhalations of liquid nitrogen that chill the soul. For her service and dedication, she is greatly prized by the Dictator, who would very much like to grab her pussy, but refrains from doing so for fear of getting frostbite, for he has seen the footprints of hoarfrost that this woman leaves wherever she walks and has watched as she picks icy graupel from her nose, so that in the end the Dictator thinks it might be better not to push his luck with this Arctic hellcat. Thus, the Dictator has contented himself with Prissy Miss Conjob's fanatical loyalty, holding dear the lies and absurd conflations she spins on his behalf, while she in turn kisses his ass to no end, as any power-hungry grub will do. So who better to take the stage at this gala event and introduce the Dictator? Who better among all the luminaries in the Dictator's handpicked looney bin to address the crowd than she?

With her teeth grinding in the hollows of her head, Prissy Miss Conjob now speaks out: "Welcome, mindless herd! We've got a really big show for you tonight! A really big show! And you look like a great crowd! I know a great crowd when I see one and I know you're a great crowd because the Dictator has made America great again! And if America is great again then you're great too! See how easy it is to be great! We're just great! All of us!"

The crowd, convinced beyond the shadow of a doubt of its own greatness, cheers and hoots like there's no tomorrow.

"Thank you, mindless herd! You're bigger saps than I thought!" continues Prissy Miss Conjob. "Remember that to stay ill-informed and not think critically is always the best way to lap up whatever bullshit the Dictator chooses to dish out! And we do love his bullshit, don't we? Because who needs to face hard facts when we can sink back into a lot of cozy lies? It's easy! It's just a matter of pretending that someday a little bit of that luxury which your billionaire Dictator surrounds himself with is going to rub off on poor slobs like you!"

The crowd, worked up into a hornets' nest of irrepressible excitement, breaks out in tumultuous applause.

"That's the spirt, mindless herd!" exhorts Prissy Miss Conjob. "With a champion like the Dictator leading you around by the nose you can rest assured that you're on the way to greater and greater greatness! Take my word for it, there's no need to actually look into the matter! There's no need to substantiate facts or weigh pros and cons! No need for reading and research and all that stuff! That stuff is for sissies! All you need do is simply swallow whatever line of shit the Dictator gives you! Swallow it hook, line and sinker, and you'll see how good it starts to feel once it's nestled down in your tummy! Because when you've got the greatest man in the world telling you what to do and what to say and what to think, it's your patriotic duty to be a pushover! And so without further ado, I give you the man himself, the man who has remade America in his own deranged and rotten image, the greatest of the great, the Dictator!"

The crowd, torqued up beyond belief, delivers an electrifying roar of approval that verges on mass hysteria as some people hyperventilate and piss their pants while others claw their faces in a violent act of self-flagellation, deeming themselves unworthy to behold the Dictator and to even breathe the same air he breathes.

At this point, an enormous movie screen that provides the backdrop to the stage on which Prissy Miss Conjob stands, now flashes like a stun grenade. Following this attention getter, an ornate collage of patriotic imagery unfolds and segues, backed up by a full orchestra as a CGI bald eagle now soars into view, gliding over the image of a slowly undulating American flag. Fading in and out of this scene are wholesome and tough-looking men (white men), whose garb suggests that they are true salt-of-the-earth types, welders and miners and stockyard workers from rural America, though they are really models from the Doo-Whop Modeling Agency in Newport Beach, California. In turn, interspersed with these images of tough-looking men, there are, of course, women (white women), whose expressions of sober grit and determination coupled with their very good looks and trim figures add spice to this visual tableau. Yet as it happens, these women are actually recruits from the Balls of Bliss Escort Service, a high-end call-girl operation where Primo Bimbo—back in those days no one will talk about—was a loyal and very busy employee, one who performed her duties well.

Erupting into shrieks and cheers and madhouse caterwauling, the audience watching this shit on the screen eats it up. To be sure, there are no party poopers here. Here in the Ninth Circle Stadium stupidity festers and reigns supreme, the excitement building as the sound of beating drums can now be heard, growing louder and louder as men in costumes resembling disheveled birds come stomping out onto the stage. Each of these men is thoroughly garbed in feathery leggings and downy doublets, the arms of each man constituting fully fledged wings, the feathers of which are bloodied and in places scorched black. As these avians flap their wings and twirl themselves around, the audience can see that the men wear elongated beaks similar to those of medieval plague doctors, their eyes circled by black greasepaint. As a background to this scene, the beat of drums continues, broken now and then by an occasional shriek. Indeed, there is a kind of growing suspense as these birdmen now draw in their wings and in unison begin to hop about in a clockwise circle, a circle that grows tighter and tighter with each revolution until there is no room left for them to turn. In the end, the audience is left to watch a huge feathery mass, one that is consolidated so tightly that the men within it can only jiggle to and fro. Nevertheless, there is a coiled-up power in this movement akin to the rocking of a regulator atop a pressure cooker, which adds to the anticipation that something, for sure, is going to happen.

As the beat of drums hammers on, the birdmen all at once let loose a gruff yell and jump back as they do so, creating an opening at their center in which the Dictator appears in a flashing puff of red smoke. Looking more embittered and glum than usual, looking, in fact, like an ogre who has just sat on one of his balls, the Dictator glances fiercely about, his little pig eyes fixed and beady, his nose open for combat. Flapping their wings, the birdmen who surround the Dictator now back off, allowing the Dictator to walk forward, which he does with a lumbering strut, nose in the air, chin jutting out, his haughty demeanor that of a man who will be catered to before all else, a man who commands all the subservience money can buy. In short, what the audience sees in the Ninth Circle Stadium is none other than the Dictator they have come to know and adore, that they rally around, a real grotty creep on whom all eyes are fixed, the rally goers wondering what he will do next.

With his face beet red and his piss-colored hair tousled and flipped in unruly ruffles, the Dictator struts about. He glares with his little pig eyes and begins by hurling insults right and left, vilifying his opponents and browbeating anyone smarter than he is. As usual, he is on the attack with a seething belligerence that he perceives as manly, lashing out at everyone and everything. With a sneer of the utmost hostility, he denigrates the women who have been scarred and traumatized by sexual predators, declaring them enemies of all the healthy and upright men in America, before going on to openly stoke the neo-Nazi fires of violence and mob rule as he lays claim to his own exceptional bloodline, touting his superior breed as one that the nation must emulate by ridding itself of the inferior genotypes flooding across the nation's southern border. Yes, the Dictator is on a roll, gleefully making faces as he now trashes the free press and then attacks in blistering fashion the growing list of turncoats who have at long last found enough courage in their hearts to declare the Dictator hopelessly inept and insane.

"Now that's a real president for you!" someone cries.

"That's a strong, tough president!" cries somebody else.

As a rolling wave of applause fills the Ninth Circle Stadium, people leap to their feet in a standing ovation, clapping wildly, watching as the Dictator gazes down at them, his frown squeezing his little pig eyes into smaller and smaller dots, turning them into little pips while his lips are thrust forward so far they get sucked up into his nose.

Next the Dictator begins to bellow loudly that he has racked up more accomplishments than any other leader in the land, that he has done more to make America great again than the last twenty presidents combined. He, in fact, rudely mocks his predecessors while holding himself up as the exalted peak of perfection, pointing a stern finger at his audience as he scolds them, telling them they have never had it so good. Never! And he tells them that things are going to get even better—incredibly better! Astoundingly better! It's a done deal, he says. The finishing touches are all in place! He's got his people working on it—all the best people! Strong, beautiful people! People who deliver! Because nobody has ever seen greatness like the kind of greatness that he, the Dictator, can produce, the man carrying on and on, an unabashed liar and bullshitter. But this is no impediment for the suckers in the Ninth Circle Stadium, who "Ooh" and "Ahh" as they listen, watching as the Dictator strolls candidly about, a man who needs no convincing that he is superior to all other men, a man cocky enough to believe he can always outdo himself, and to prove it he declares that he will now bite the head off a live chicken.

The people, ecstatic on hearing this news, cheer wildly and are still cheering as a musclebound man bulging with veiny biceps and well-oiled pecs walks onto the stage, his taut powerful quads quivering. Although he wears a black leather Speedo that just barely covers his crotch, he is no less notable for the black executioner's hood that covers his head, punctuated by two eyeholes from which his eyes look out. Clearly, this is a man with a daunting and formidable presence, a veritable giant, yet this bad-to-the-bone tough guy is partly overshadowed by the chicken that he holds before him, especially given that the chicken's head has been fitted through a hole in a tiny poncho of green and yellow stripes. Held tight in the grip of this man, the chicken can do nothing but turn its head about, its eyes frantic and confused.

Stepping up to the Dictator, the man in the hood extends his arms, holding forth the unfortunate fowl, while strains of a dated rendition of "Cielito Lindo" rise up. When the lyrics to this song kick in, sung in melodious Spanish that no one understands, boos and vicious catcalls ring out in the Ninth Circle Stadium. Nodding and simpering, the Dictator could have predicted this reaction and is unduly pleased by it, for it plays right into his hands, the mob before him working itself up into a hateful harangue. Then, in a snooty rail of disgust, the Dictator bellows: "This chicken is Mexicans!"

The crowd's fury can barely be contained.

"This chicken is Guatemalans!" the Dictator blares, eagerly awaiting the peals of outrage he knows are coming. "This chicken is the Costa Ricans! And Hondurans! And the goddamn Puerto Ricans who can't help themselves in the face of a little rain and wind! This chicken is the whole battering ram of subhuman shitheads, drug dealers and murderers that's laying siege to our borders!"

Hearing this, the audience erupts in bloodthirsty fury.

"And so what are we going to do about it?" asks the Dictator. 'I'll tell you what we're going to do. We're going to shoot to kill! Kill them! Kill them! Lethal force! That's what they've got coming to them! And our troops! Our great, beautiful troops, God bless them! I know they're ready to do the job! Ready to gun those suckers down like Rambo! That's how it goes! And if people thought seeing women and children put in cages was a tough break, wait until they see them tossed into coffins! Then nobody will have to worry about them and where they are. So we shoot to kill, that's right! We kill them! You know how it works, like with resistance fighters and protesters at my rallies—we beat the shit out of them! And if you want to tackle some fake news reporter and strangle him to death, go ahead! I'll pay your legal bills! And I'll pardon you if you kill him!"

Knowing that he must drag himself ever lower in the gutter to keep the base and brainless rabble before him happy, the Dictator now plays a game of one-upmanship with himself the likes of which no one has ever seen.

"Look at this chicken here!" commands the Dictator. "This chicken is all the shithole countries that threaten our God-fearing American way of life. This chicken is Mexico! It's El Salvador! It's France! It's even Canada! Yes, it's Canada, too! Because you can't trust them up there! It's your closest neighbors that stab you in the back because they know you don't expect it! So if we put a little parka on this chicken, it's Canada! We can make the chicken France too! And Great Britain, those whiners! Not to mention China! Year of the rat—every year! They're all rats over there in China! All of them! Shithole countries! But they're all chicken if you stand up to them the way I do! They know I mean business! They know the United States won't be pushed around anymore by sneaky pipsqueak countries picking our pockets! These countries will get in line and play fair or else! And if they don't, if they come across our borders, we kill them! And if that weasely president of France upstages me again, maybe we'll kill somebody over there in France to send him a message! Just the way the Saudis do it! I said I can shoot someone on Fifth Avenue in broad daylight and get away with it and that's just what the Saudi Arabians did! They took a page right out of my own playbook! They killed the fake news! Then walked away scot-free! But when it comes to Mexico and all those shithole countries south of the Rio Grande, I'm going to kill this chicken! Right now!"

Spurred on into a frenzy of nationalist pride and sheer lunacy, those in the Ninth Circle Stadium boil over with blinding rage, their malevolence breaking out into all manner of shouts, threats and vulgarities until bit by bit a chant catches on—"KILL THE CHICKEN! KILL THE CHICKEN! KILL THE CHICKEN! KILL THE CHICKEN!"

The man in the black executioner's hood, keeping a rock solid grip on the chicken throughout, can now feel its heart flutter, the eyes of the bird darting about, the feet of the bird scratching at the air from beneath the little poncho it wears as the Dictator opens his mouth wide and with the roar of the crowd ringing in his ears now thinks of himself as a gladiator in the Colosseum, his mouth encircling the chicken's head as he moves in for the kill. In one angry bite, his teeth crush the bird's windpipe, the death throes of its body held fast by the man in the hood as the Dictator shakes his head to and fro, his teeth tearing through the feathers, skin and tendons, a spray of blood hitting him in the face, prompting him to yank back and rip the chicken's head free from its body, which is now spurting blood and shaking uncontrollably in the powerful hands that hold it. Although the crowd is now cheering ecstatically, the Dictator is in a quandary. He cannot quite decide whether to spit the chicken's head out or simply swallow it. Feeling it squirm and twitch against his cheeks is distinctly unpleasant and he knows he needs to think fast. Spitting out the head would, of course, be a very dramatic act of disgust, one that certainly would be justified and approved. But then again, swallowing the chicken's head would be more manly, a gruesome and disgusting act that would make it clear that the Dictator is really and truly a tough and macho guy.

In the end, after working up a big gob of saliva and after some intense efforts on the part of his Adam's apple, the Dictator does, indeed, swallow the chicken's head, feeling it ultimately slither down his throat and into his big, fat gut. Watching all this, the crowd, in an uproar of dizzy and fanatical adulation, goes bonkers, cheering, clapping, whistling, convinced finally and fully that the second coming of America's greatness is at hand, for the Dictator is a man who has virtually self-beatified himself before their eyes, a man victorious and splattered with blood who, like the very best carnival geek, can grab and hold the attention of even the biggest numbskull.

"That's how we do it!" insists the Dictator loudly as the man in the black executioner's hood drops the chicken's body to the ground. "That's how we deal with shithole countries like Mexico, Guatemala and anybody else that gets in our way!" promises the Dictator. "That's how it's going to be! Wait and see! Yes! Wait and see! We got ways to deal with the mercenary cutthroats out to ruin our nation! But I can't tip my hand! I'm not stupid! I can't tell you what they are, but we got ways! Oh, yeh! You just keep watching! Kill them! That's what it comes down to! At home and abroad, we kill them! You'll see what I mean! At the next rally! You'll see! It might be in two days, this rally—maybe three! I can't say for sure, but it'll be whenever I have to take my next shit! That's right! Because I'm going to shit myself right on stage! It doesn't matter! Everybody already knows what my dick looks like thanks to that mean, nasty porn star I was fucking who went and tattled on me! So it doesn't matter! So at the next rally, you'll see! You will! I'm going to shit out a chicken skull into a chamber pot of solid gold! And so whoever did that before? Whoever did? Nobody! Ever! Only me! That's right, your favorite dictator--me! Me! That's what I said! Only I can do that! And guess who's going to be there? Go ahead, guess! Guess! You got three guesses! The ghost of Elvis! That's who's going to be there! We booked him! We did! It wasn't easy, but we got him! There are so many good and beautiful people that want to help me out! But the ghost of Elvis! That's not just anybody! You can't get any more American than Elvis! Elvis likes me! And he's going to wash off that chicken skull with Coca-Cola because everybody likes Coca-Cola, right? He's going to wash that chicken skull off and then I'm going to wear it around my neck like a war trophy—except it's better! Because I didn't have to go to war! I didn't have to go to Vietnam! Like the way I don't have to pay taxes either! Because it's great to be born rich! And that chicken skull, it's going to be tied around my neck with the braided hair of a half-breed killed and scalped along the Mexican border by—guess who! Loco Joe! Loco Joe himself! That's right! Loco Joe! You don't mess with Loco Joe! He's one of the best neo-Nazis we got! He might be there at the next rally too! We'll see! We'll see! You have to show up to find out! That and more! You never know! You have to be there! Stay tuned! And God bless America!"

Amid cheers and hoots and cries of outright worship, the crowd is now falling all over itself with joyous devotion. People reach out to the Dictator simply to bring their mortal flesh a few inches nearer to this paragon of leadership and wisdom. For others, their eyes nearly roll out of their heads they are so overcome by this Messiah of the Money who has deigned to grace their paltry lives. Betty Fizzlewit of Pockmark, Texas, is crying so hard her mascara runs in lurid streaks down her face, while Luke Beauvine of Sulphur Pit, Louisiana, unworthy sinner that he is, crosses himself feverishly forward and backward. The crowd, indeed, is overwrought and beside itself with glee and excitement, wriggling like a nest of silverfish. They just can't help themselves. But after things finally settle down and people are making their way out of the stadium, Billy Duntzkapp, a loud and fervent fan of the Dictator, finds himself "chawing" on something the Dictator has said, something that tests the credulity of even Billy Duntzkapp. Leaning over to his companion, Hank Bunghole, who is out of breath from cheering, Billy now states: "You know, Hank, I was thinkin'. Nothin' against the Dictator and all, but ain't it going to be a little tough to get the ghost of Elvis to appear? I mean, it sounds to me like a little bit of a stretcher, like the Dictator is pullin' our leg, for sure."

"I understand what you're sayin'," replies Hank Bunghole, "but I'm not ruling anything out, not with so much craziness going on these days.   Things just keep gettin' weirder and weirder, you know?"

THE WITCH GOES HUNTING

Very late into the night, Jennifer Golembeski and Amber Lamphere were climbing down a dry gully bed. Above them a full moon illuminated every stone and crevice they encountered. In a small gunnysack slung over Amber's shoulder, a flashlight was packed away, but with the moon a cornucopia of bright rays bathing everything in sight the flashlight was unnecessary. Everything was fully visible to the two young women, their passage marked by exceptional clarity. As the gully they were following now grew overly rugged, they decided to scramble up and out of it, proceeding along a tall line of trees bordering a meadow. After marching single file for a mile or more, they then made a silent detour down an old logging trail. Here the illumination of the moon enabled them to see distinctly briar patches that tugged at their jeans as they continued on. Now and then fallen trees, moldering and moss laden, blocked their way and they had to high step over them. At times the rough terrain and unruly thickets made for slow going, but before long Jennifer pushed her way through a cluster of Juneberry trees and into a clearing, a high plateau where the ground sloped downward and where a rocky escarpment jutted out from the hillside behind them. Off in the distance, the fiord-like tail of a lake could be seen, its leaden glimmer captivating like a jewel.

Having previously scouted out this spot, Jennifer could understand why Rhonda Redwing had chosen it, she could acknowledge its elemental combination of earth and sky, rock and water, all of which affected her deeply. It was a spot where the land did indeed give off vibes, she realized, and now, with the moonlight streaming down, she was eager to embrace the primal backdrop around her, whose indomitable presence now seemed to captivate her with its unspoken authority. To achieve this end, she recalled the advice of the high priestess and took it to heart. She began to open herself up completely, utterly, as if she were a conduit for the force of eons manifested around her.

Taking out a plastic bottle of springwater from her gunnysack, Amber offered it to Jennifer, who took a swallow and handed it back. Without a word, they both considered the vista before them and the plenitude of stars above. For Jennifer it was time to clear her head, to breathe in the existence of everything in sight, to submit to the undertaking at hand and flesh it out. Already she was trying to ease out of the moment, to depart from the here and now and move into that special realm where her viability would be compounded and set free. She told herself she needed to do this at all costs and she prepared by closing her eyes and jangling her arms until they hung limp. Warmly gripping Jennifer's arm, Amber now gave her friend an earnest look of encouragement before walking off with her gunnysack, disappearing into the night, while Jennifer again closed her eyes.

After letting her body go limp, Jennifer stood there for several moments, her head sagging to one side while her breathing slowed and evened out. With her eyes remaining closed, she began to suspect that she was losing her sense of direction, that there were suddenly no landmarks anywhere with which to get her bearings—

even if she had opened her eyes. She thought first that the late hour and a touch of fatigue were to blame for this feeling, but she gradually recognized that her equilibrium was altering along lines not so easily explained. Her body, ever so subtly, had begun to sway to and fro as if prompted by a pendulum swinging within her. Something in her told her she must synchronize with this movement, though in doing so she often found herself stumbling and losing her balance, but by the same turn gained a new and impending momentum, one that integrated with her movements slowly at first, but became irresistible.

Eagerly, Jennifer now gave herself over to what was happening, her mind drifting, her feet beginning to shift about until she began to stagger and wobble. To Amber, who watched from the shadows, her friend appeared as a kind of disjointed puppet who flouted the norms of standing upright, for given how Jennifer lurched and stumbled she ought to have fallen down many times over, yet avoided doing so as if by some highly dexterous ability. Although she felt more and more out of control, Jennifer could tell that her body was tapping a newfound source of power. She believed tremendous springs were coiling beneath her. She had the sensation of being sandwiched tightly between the earth and sky and found her state of mind so unsettling that she was tempted to open her eyes, but instead collapsed gently to the ground.

After briefly tossing and turning, Jennifer stretched herself out, her arms and legs extended and twitching until at last she grew still, becalmed for the moment and at peace, until she experienced a strong boost, a leveraging upward that caused a surge of butterflies to heave in her stomach. So definite was the grip in which she was caught that the ground seemed to dissolve beneath her and she found herself buoyed by a wonderful and frightening suspension. Although she succumbed to this strange power, she also found herself struggling to uphold her purpose, realizing that at any moment she might be whisked away along some wholly unrecognizable course. Thus, as if trying to discern an object through a swirling fog, she attempted to crystalize a specific vision. Determined to bring this vision to life, she at first found her efforts sketchy and haphazard, but in time they yielded the clarity she desired. Excited by her progress and becoming more confident, Jennifer now began to relinquish every aspect of her identity—what she was and who she was—understanding in a flash that it would not suffice to simply impose a curse upon the Dictator, but that in all ways she needed to become the curse itself, cancelling herself out in order to achieve what was to be not only a transformation, but a permeation as well, the two entities going hand in hand in a Mephisto waltz that was spinning her to the furthest limit.

Yes, she told herself, you can do this, go for his brain!

What began for Jennifer as an act of will power now materialized into a steady vibrant stream, a force whose direct emanation sprouted from her entire being. Staying true to her intention while simultaneously remaining abreast of the physical world, Jennifer's field of energy continued to expand until she began closing in on what she wanted. Shuddering with intense conviction, Jennifer could sense the diffusion of her whole existence, which was now reduced to phantom nerve endings that were surreptitiously teasing out the borderland of one man's mortality, intermingling specifically with a domain of flesh and blood, probing the channels between life and death. In the thrall of this endeavor, Jennifer shook repeatedly as if with a chill. Spasms racked her body from head to toe, and yet her throat filled with robust and gleeful noises, like those of an excited animal. She was on her game. She was going full steam ahead, while Amber, who sat in the shadows a distance away, watched her friend with deep concern, holding back the urge to take her in her arms. Little by little, however, Jennifer's body grew still again until at last she simply lay there in the dead calm of the moonlight.

By a delicate incursion, Jennifer was now encroaching directly on the Dictator's brain, swiftly making a run down the central sulcus before wriggling through various tissues and curious little byways. Then, through a rapid weaving of icy and invisible threads, she acted as a stitch in time, darting in and out of the entire cerebral cortex, doing so over and again until she left in her aftermath a spun-glass web that knocked the Dictator's delta waves off kilter and undermined his frontal lobe. Amid the fizzling squib of his neurons, she continued to reconnoiter, spiraling through ventricles and taking to task a host of blood vessels coerced into swelling and contracting through a rhythmic counter play until they were all but dancing to Jennifer's tune. The Dictator's brain, now primed by Jennifer's singular influence, suddenly lay fully exposed and vulnerable, a target for an even greater power, a lethal dynamism that quickly took over and would in time see things to their end.

On reaching this juncture, Jennifer suddenly suffered an impact so hard hitting it was akin to an explosive blast. She felt as if slammed down a bottomless pit, as if she were tumbling over herself in a sprawling freefall that left her breathless. Disoriented and with her strength draining away, her struggle for self-control went nowhere. She began to panic and wondered if she was dying. She wondered if she had gone too far in executing her curse, if she had set too much in motion, for now that the deed was done she found herself an expendable outcast, the victim of a ruthless chain reaction whose bounds she had perhaps overstepped. Jennifer's fear that she had taken things too far, however, really had no basis, for the repercussions she was experiencing constituted nothing more than the price one paid for a black magic alibi.

Amber, meanwhile, who the whole time had been sitting with her back against a large maple, now watched as Jennifer began to writhe about, a victim of keen and jarring forces, her arms flailing desperately and her feet shuffling. Yet despite the rigorous ordeal

Jennifer was undergoing, her voice carried clearly through the darkness, hushed but resolute, as she said: "Gotcha . . . I gotcha, you dumbass pig . . . It's curtains . . ."

Hearing this, Amber knew at last that the sojourn of the spell was over, and so she sprang to her feet and ran to comfort the bedraggled body that lay before her. Drenched in sweat and sullied from the damp ground, Jennifer rolled from side to side, her eyelids fluttering as she struggled to make contact with the world again. The touch of Amber's hand reassured her and she now opened her eyes, swallowing hard before saying in a halting voice, "So glad you're here . . . best of friends."

"It's okay, Jen. Take a deep breath. You pulled through. You did it."

"Yes, I did it," agreed Jennifer weakly, "I know I did."

Aching and tired, Jennifer attempted to lean up on her elbow while Amber squatted down, hugging her friend from behind and supporting her as she struggled to her feet. Although a bit unsure of herself at first, Jennifer, after standing for a moment, once again felt in control and capable. Her first few steps were awkward, but with each step her footing became more firm and she soon improved in both her mood and demeanor, so that by the time they had started back down the logging trail toward home they were sharing casual observations and making small talk, albeit in lowered and reverent tones, for their intimacy was now underscored by a sense of relief, the relief that arises when a person has had a close call and those things worth cherishing have their importance renewed. Such was the case tonight, for Jennifer's experience was just as much Amber's, each of them guided by a deep concern befitting "best of friends," friends who now paused briefly to rest in an open glade, sharing a drink of water from Amber's bottle and giving a last admiring look at the moon before moving on.

SAL RONGO SPEAKS AGAIN

Freddy's Bar, Brooklyn, NY

Jesus, Willie, how about setting me up with a beer, I'm a bundle of nerves, just walked here at breakneck speed, you see. I'm all worked up, I'm telling you. I was just sitting at home watching TV and I swear if you had turned it on you would have flipped your lid. It was like I saw the whole life of the nation go flashing before my eyes. It was all this crazy shit on the news like you wouldn't believe, these crazy ass reports that you couldn't make up even if you were on drugs—how for one the Dictator started off the day by harping all about voter fraud again, going on a tweet storm in which he claims that out in Iowa there were 40,000 scarecrows who voted illegally in the last election! I shit you not, Willie! It's there in black and white, an authenticated tweet which the Dictator didn't even delete. You heard me right—40,000 scarecrows! They crawled down off their posts and committed voter fraud! With the Dictator going on to say that nobody knows about this but him, him and Congressman Steve King-Kong of Iowa, who's another real fucking piece of work. King-Kong, you see, goes ape shit every time he sees a Jew or a black guy or a Latino. He's a wingding, Willie. Somebody wrote a tell-all expose on him and found out he does a stand-up comedy routine in blackface that he takes on the road all over Iowa to churches and tent revival meetings. He's a big hit! And this is the racist fruitcake that the Dictator claims knows all about the 40,000 scarecrows, a guy who don't know shit, a guy who's got his lug nuts loose upstairs and who actually took the Dictator's tweet to heart because he knows it'll win him favor when it comes to getting perks and pork and kickbacks under the table. He even ratcheted up the whole thing by saying that the 40,000 scarecrows in question are radicalized liberals who walked out of the cornfields knowing full well that the crows would swoop in and ruin the harvest, that this was yet another example of the mean and hateful actions by the left wing in this country to hurt farmers and starve Americans—and he says this out there in Iowa with the cameras rolling and with a straight fucking face, no less! So you tell me, Willie, just what kind of political skid row is this nation on here?

To me it's like the mental derangement of the Dictator has gone contagious, it's like some bizarre science fiction movie where one guy goes nuts and then anybody who gets too near to him also starts to go nuts, like just by being around the guy. It's like everyone's mental immune system got compromised and they don't have their resistance built up to fight it off, and so they're like falling prey to the rantings of a lunatic. One look at the Dictator and you can see he's nuts, and everybody's losing their marbles right along with him. Look at Bugeye Upchuck, for example. The guy was always a slippery little worm, but nobody ever would have said he had a screw loose. But now every time he opens his mouth it's like he's auditioning for a padded cell, chattering away with such ridiculous palaver that people just back off and try to get away from the guy, just like you would with any madman. We've reached a point where people have given up trying to reason with Bugeye Upchuck or anybody else in this merry-go-round of morons that makes up the Dictator's world, and it's a merry-go-round that's spinning faster and faster and more out of control, the case in point, Willie, being that by noontime the Dictator had released a statement that he's calling a national emergency, saying that there's a secret cult of Guatemalans who abide by the Mayan calendar and that they've got cocoons of extraterrestrial creatures that were left on the planet thousands of years ago by space travelers, and what the Guatemalans are doing is smuggling these cocoons across the Mexican border on account of it's their plan to get them all across by a certain day on that Mayan calendar, because that's the day these terrible monsters fight their way out of the cocoons and then start destroying the whole United States of America, after which the Guatemalans take over! That's the official statement, Willie! Official! It's got the Dictator's royal seal on it and everything, and he even signed it with his usual chicken scratch, but the press thought it was a practical joke, that some wiseacre was goofing on them. They really couldn't believe this shit and so they like had to vet the story ten times over before releasing it to the public. Meanwhile the Dictator won't walk back not one word of it, but is actually hyping up the whole thing as some kind of alien Trojan horse from another galaxy, saying that what the Guatemalans are doing with the cocoons is to take us all by surprise, which of course gives him yet another reason to start shooting off his mouth about building that stupid fucking border wall that nobody wants and which he can't keep his trap shut about not for five minutes, saying now the wall is needed to keep out the alien cocoons!

The nation is up shit's creek without a paddle, Willie, that's what it's boiling down to, and just when you think things couldn't possibly get any more fucked up they do! The Dictator's own people can't control him. The guy's a mental case. He needs to be hogtied and institutionalized, that's what I say. He's out of his gourd, off his rocker, a nut job who's wrecking the nation on all fronts with so much shit flying through the air it's like projectile vomiting coming down at you through a wind tunnel, hitting you full in the face! Everything and anything, Willie, a green light for polluters, a nuclear arms race with Russia, trade wars everywhere you turn, and global warming being relegated to an urban legend, plus all the endless propaganda and state-sponsored fascism, you name it, the guy's all but doing mouth to mouth on dead Ku Klux Klan members and setting the stage for a whole new era of Jim Crow, not to mention how he's buddy-buddy with any Jew baiter he can find, even has a reincarnated kapo serving as a senior policy advisor, while the Dictator's *foreign* policy is a gift, an absolute gift to our enemies, because the Dictator has left the nation's jugular exposed to anybody who wants to take a bite, the least of which is Russia, with Vladimir Puttanesca watching from afar and licking his chops, because the Dictator is doing more serious harm to this country than all the terrorist organizations combined could ever do in fifty years, and if anyone is pulling his strings it's Vladimir Puttanesca, the whole point of which was reinforced today with another breaking news story about some Russkie turncoat spy guy who's gone and flipped over to *our* side, but it's sketchy and hard to follow, but the story's seems to have some legs and people are starting to pin down the facts about it one by one. All these gumshoes from the press are looking into it and the picture they're painting is that some kind of big master spy pulled a major switcheroo and bailed out on Russia. People who got their finger on the pulse of these things say that there's lots of agitation in the Kremlin right now. Not happy campers, if you follow me. But the speculation here is that if this defector is as high up as people seem to think he is it's likely that he's absconded with a whole treasure trove of classified information and that one of the jewels in this treasure trove is bound to be a certain sex tape. Yes sir, Willie, the mother of *all* sex tapes, the one where the Dictator is flopping around buck naked in a Moscow hotel room while Russian whores take turns pissing on him. Now it might seem unlikely that a bombshell such as that would actually come to light, excepting for the fact that the people on TV reported there's this deeply embedded correspondent over there in Russia who was savvy enough to intercept a communique that spoke directly to the fact of the matter—that the sex tape was among the compromised secrets and was now fair game! That it's out of the country and potentially headed for the public domain! Now the guy, or woman maybe, who intercepted this communique has remained anonymous for fear of getting nabbed and packed off to Siberia, but the kicker is that what this anonymous person actually revealed about the communique is that it was intercepted from the Kremlin itself, meaning it didn't come from any old Russian on the street where you might be hearing the vodka talking, but somebody high up, and the experts reviewing the matter said it all has a ring of truth to it, a high degree of credibility, and there's even whispers from Russian insiders that Vladimir Puttanesca really has his knickers twisted about getting snookered by some Benedict Arnold who goes ripping off that sex tape right out from under his nose, that and all this other top-secret information that's been pilfered. But if you think Puttanesca was fit to be tied over it, that's because I haven't told you how the Dictator reacted. As soon as he heard about the defection and the fact that this sex tape featuring yours truly was out of Russia and likely making its way through different channels, as soon as the possibility got through his thick skull that this sex tape might go to the highest bidder or be up for grabs to premiere in the public sector, well the Dictator was knocked for a loop, utterly stunned and reeling, I saw it right there on TV, talk about a blockhead. I never saw his little pig eyes look so beady and frantic. The guy was in a dither big time, all because of this Russian defector.

Apparently the Dictator suddenly needed to somehow neutralize the whole Russian defector story, which really got under his skin, no question, really rattled him, and which when you think about it is total bullshit, highly suspect, because show me one single American who's going to be rattled if an enemy spy decides to come over to *our* side, honestly! For any upstanding American, this would be a *good* thing, but as anybody with two cents' worth of brains in his head can see, the Dictator is a shifty-eyed scoundrel, a rich fat cat who's been going behind the nation's back to sell us out at every chance he gets, all so he can get his grubby little mitts in the till. But this Russian defector story tells me things are catching up with him, that something's in the works, that this spy flipping thing might bring the whole dictatorship crashing down, because it was obvious the Dictator was in a tizzy over it and had to get ahead of the whole thing, try to give himself cover for whatever was going to start raining down on his head. So no sooner does the story about the Russian defector break than the Dictator wants to make an impromptu statement to the news. He wants all the networks gathered together right there and then.

But it's a big deal to pull something like this off, getting all the networks together, you can't just snap your fingers and have everybody hop to, I mean with it being so off the cuff and on the spot, you see, because all the Dictator's aides have to be informed, the Secret Service has to be briefed and ready to protect his ass, and all of it is made more harum-scarum because nobody knows what the hell is going on. The Dictator wants to make a statement to the press, that's about the size of it, and so a whole big conference room gets set up real quick with microphones and chairs and the right backdrop with the American flag and all the usual window dressing. Pretty soon, people from the news outlets start showing up until they're flooding into the place, wondering what's up, wondering what's so damn important. Are we declaring war? Did some important honcho die? Is there a national emergency—meaning other than the cocoons from outer space? Everybody's anxious to know, Willie, but I've got to tell you that when the Dictator walked out there on live TV and started jabbering away nobody had the slightest clue as to what the fuck he was talking about.

First of all, he comes hobbling out like he's being frog marched barefoot across red-hot coals. He's like twitching and jerking himself around with these weird little movements, and that sour puss of his is twitching too and grimacing, so that I'm wondering what's going on with this idiot. Does he have a bad tic of some kind? Does he got the shakes from a bowel obstruction? To see him was the most bizarre thing, Willie, it was actually scary, and I'm thinking who in God's name let this clown go on public display looking like this? Even when he gets up to the microphone he just stands there and his whole body starts contorting itself just like how he does it on his own when he's making fun of people who are physically handicapped, except this is worse and it's no act. The guy's one shoulder was jutting high up toward his head and his arms were all bent in odd ways like some broken stick figure. His fingers too were curled up and like frozen into claws that looked like they were trying to grab something. This was freaky shit, Willie, something was majorly wrong with the dude, and it was like he wasn't even really aware of what was happening, just squinting with his little pig eyes and doing his own little St. Vitus dance, while the camera goes panning around the whole room so you can see all the people sitting there dumbfounded, their mouths hanging open—like mine was! I was watching a guy who right before my eyes was giving new meaning to the word moron, and this was before he even started talking.

But when he does start talking hold on to your hats, that's all I can say, because he's bouncing all around like a pinball, he's all over the map, Willie, chewing the fat something fierce about producing American steel and how we need to start making steel toothpicks and soda straws and toilet seats, making them all out of American steel, and that he's got a fan club in India of a billion members who support this idea and they support it because they're in awe of the size of his hands, which he then lifts up for everybody to see and tells everybody to look at what big, beautiful hands he's got and that a team of doctors, the very best, most fabulous doctors, used his DNA to trace his hands back to Bigfoot, and then he says he knows more about Bigfoot than anybody, before he starts talking about his fan club in India again, saying that half the people in the fan club are belly dancers but he doesn't call them Pocahontas because you've got to see the beautiful asses on these women and they're not really Indian Indians anyway, so they won't scalp you like Pocahontas—and it just keeps going on and on, all this cockamamie horseshit coming out of the guy's mouth about how he has cut a deal with Harley-Davidson to make golf carts and all this other outrageous shit, and all the while people are noticing there's spittle dangling off his lip, and the only breather he ever takes is to now and then stop to pick his nose, I'm telling you, right there on TV! It was all so over the top, Willie, that if you like beamed this knucklehead off to the Whitney Museum as some kind of bullshit performance art all the uptown art snobs would be jumping for joy, because you never saw anything like it, the guy was losing it, standing up there teetering, looking like one of those inflatable bop bags that look like Bozo the Clown that little kids used to knock around, while the Dictator's face—holy shit, it was so twisted and distorted it could've been in a funhouse mirror, with this crooked smirk that was stretching halfway around the guy's head like some weird kind of fault line about to open up.

Believe me, Willie, there was some wild stuff going on here, something beyond the pale even for the Dictator, I mean the guy was in a bad way and it was freakin' me out, it was freakin' everybody out, you could see it on TV. Everybody supposed the Dictator was going to deliver some kind of reaction to the news about the Russian defector and that notorious sex tape that was on everybody's minds, but instead the guy goes off the deep end, with the closest he got to his sexual peccadillos being to give everybody a stammering lecture about having sex with a porn star! He got real pompous and arrogant and with his usual idiotic bluster he started saying how if you cheat on your wife with a porn star it's not really cheating because it's a business enterprise on account of it's the porn business. So it's like inspecting a casino you want to buy, though you may not actually buy it, he says, or like looking over a suite of offices where you want to set up operations. That's the logic of the guy, Willie, totally fucked up, which had me wondering if Primo Bimbo had these same opinions when she found out her hubby was dipping his wick into a triple-X starlet.

But as far as the Dictator's royal family goes, who the hell cares anyway, right? It would be best for the nation as a whole if the rest of these lowlife assholes dropped off the face of the planet just like what I hear happened to Primo Bimbo, because after what I saw today, how the Dictator was talking all this garbled nonsense and the way he was jerking around and quivering like a big piece of whale blubber, well to be honest, I couldn't shake the feeling that Satan himself had grabbed the guy by the balls and was yanking him straight down to hell. It just struck me somehow that the guy wasn't too long for this world. Maybe other people saw it that way, too, I don't know, but by the look on the faces of the people sitting there watching this dipshit I'd say they thought he was a goner in one way or another. They were all fucking stupefied. The whole thing was a fiasco, a meltdown, a shambles, it got so bad that the Dictator's aides had to finally run out and drag the guy away. They really had to manhandle him, too, really had to rough him up, he just wanted to keep standing there jabbering.

Not for all the world could I take my eyes off that television, Willie. My heart was pounding. I was all tensed up like waiting for what was going to happen next, the whole thing was so ominous, like there was some point of no return that things had gone beyond. Somewhere in the back of my mind a little voice seemed to be saying something, these words that I wasn't fully aware of and which were slowly dawning on me until they finally became clear—*the beginning of the end*! That's what the words were, Willie, and so if I had to draw any conclusions from it all I'd say the gig is up in more ways than one and that the Dictator is going down for the count and not getting up again. Of course it's anyone's guess in these crazy times, but for right now I'm going to have another beer, and while you're at it draw one for yourself, Willie, you're going to need it, I think.

TRIPWIRE CHATTER

Quickly now . . .

"Tell me, Ted, not that I've got anything real definite to back me up, but have you been hearing any strange stuff coming out of Virginia lately?"

"Maybe, the grapevine does seem to be lighting up a bit more than usual."

"I'm hearing there are a lot of subverted protocols these days. From what I understand, the ground is shifting under people's feet, if you follow me."

"Who have you been talking to, Roger?"

"The usual stock-in-trade guys, foot soldiers like me. They're all saying something is going down."

"Something is always going down, Roger, you know that."

"This is different. We're talking about strange requests, resurrected files, midnight cabals that seem to include everyday people randomly pulled off the street who are suddenly in meetings along with in-the-know bigwigs. It's really strange stuff."

"Pulled off *the street*?"

"Outsiders, you know, people who are just out there."

"And what bigwigs are these people meeting with?

"That's hard to say."

"Rumors, Roger, that's all. Over the years I've heard it all and more."

"But in all these years, Ted, there's never been a situation like what you've got now. The agency is jackknifing, I'm sure you know why—the issue of allegiance, allegiance has become a hot topic. There's a rift, there's all this talk about a Dark State. Rumors? Maybe, but just because you hear them it doesn't mean they're not true."

"Careful, Roger, go straight and narrow on this. My opinion on the Dark State is that it's nothing more than something that's been there all along."

"Then why don't we know what it is exactly?"

"It's a slippery component of the business we're in, I guess," says Ted with a long sigh. "I'm not sure what the Dark State is, but I do know if you don't hold steady you'll start seeing phantoms and phantasms popping up all over."

"Funny you should put it that way."

"Oh?"

"Ever hear of a guy named McPherson?"

"One of ours?"

"Yeh."

"I'm not aware of him."

"I'm not surprised, he's real old school, been out of commission for quite some time. I got the lowdown on this guy. We're lazy spies, Ted. We rely on a lot of high-tech gadgetry to do the job. We're twice removed, but this McPherson climbed right down in the dirt and lived there. Literally. Back in the days of all that communist empire bullshit, he once worked his way from Austria into Hungary in the middle of the night, somehow got through an electric fence by digging and crawling under it with a rubber blanket or something, just so there'd be no paper trail, no passport stamping, no airline tickets, no getting spotted by anybody. This guy was good at taking root, he had assumed a prearranged identity, seems to have relished it. Well, eventually after a lot of years he got out of the business and was more or less retired, and then, after a long stretch of being a nonentity his name pops up. Suddenly there's this little internal AMBER Alert to try to find him, or so I'm told. In any case, this guy likes to lie low. Where the hell is he? Nobody knows. But after enough digging and sleuthing they turn him up, yet to what end remains a mystery. No sooner do they find this guy than the case is closed. That's that. There's no record of contact, no communication channels. Somebody wanted to find him and they did. That's all anybody knows. There's no apparent followup, at least not on record. I'm not jumping to conclusions, people have their whims, I get it. You and I, we like snooping, we're spies, right? So maybe some female agent had a long-standing crush on this McPherson guy and wanted to track him down after all these years for old time's sake. Maybe. But here's the weird thing, Ted. A guy I know wouldn't let the thing lie. He got curious, and he's not just any guy, but a real diving bell. High, high clearance, and he decides to go down deep into the inner sanctum, just on a whim. He wants to see what's so special about this McPherson fellow. And you know what he finds? Nothing. Suddenly McPherson has disappeared into thin air, gone completely off the radar. No sooner do they find him and he's gone. Do you see what I'm saying? So this guy, the diving bell, I can't tell you his name, of course, he gets together a little ground crew to do some checking. They look into matters thoroughly, but no dice. McPherson really is gone. They find out that he simply left his apartment one day and never returned, left all of his possessions sitting there. His bank accounts were all closed. His retirement checks aren't being cut anymore. The more people look into it, the less they find. This is deep, deep cover, wouldn't you say?"

"I agree," says Ted, deliberating, "but as you mentioned, he was old school, there might have been something in his past coming back to haunt him, some long-forgotten issue. People in this trade hold a lifetime of grudges, Roger, you know that. People get killed. People point fingers. Some crazy agent from the Cold War might've have decided to go after him for some past transgression. McPherson might have been funneled off to some secret location for his own protection."

"I thought of that, I see what you're getting at, but there's something else that's been nagging at me."

"Which is?"

"It's the matter of timing. Whenever something really big goes down, you know how it is, people fly the coop, they turn into one big redaction, you don't ever see or hear from them again."

"So what are you saying went down, what is so big exactly?"

"I'm not sure if anything exactly went down."

"But you suspect it did."

"All I'm saying is that this McPherson happened to disappear not long after that fateful night when our fearless leader appeared on national television drooling and shaking, and then picking his nose, talking about how he wanted Harley-Davidson to start manufacturing golf carts and claiming that he knew more than anybody about space travel and pizza crust. You remember *that* night, don't you? I watched that clip over and over. Everybody in the whole nation saw it until his aides ran out and dragged him off the set, and since then if you try to find out what's going on with the guy you hit a brick wall—and I'm pretty good at finding out things. But nobody's saying anything. Nobody's talking. All his close advisors, anyone in the loop, they got their mouths shut tight, keeping all of us in the dark."

"It's pathetic," says Ted, shaking his head. "The whole world thinks we're assholes."

"That's not what I'm getting at."

"I know what you're getting at, Roger, believe me, and if you're right about what I think you're hinting at, then this is big, super big. I just can't get my head around it. I don't see how in God's name it's possible, how to pull it off—and how could this McPherson of all people do it? I mean, I can think of ways, but it's all too outlandish, though I grant you, something weird is definitely going on, something is under wraps."

"Yeh," laughs Roger, mulling matters over, a cold and distant look in is eye. "It's under wraps with a winding sheet, that's what I think, and don't you say you heard it from me, but a lot of the boys on the inside are closing ranks, they're making plans. If the Dictator flatlines they're going to go in guns a blazin', they're going to shut down this three-ring circus and set the nation up for democratic rule again."

X-RATED SPOILS

Q uickly now . . .
  Sitting in the back room of the State Street Grill in Clarks Summit, Pennsylvania, a writer recuperating from a broken arm sips a cup of black coffee while reading a magazine. Whenever someone enters the back room, he looks up, but then returns to an article about the Moroccan dictator Hassan II. Too many dictators, thinks the writer, too many useless and deadbeat kings. Then he pushes his coffee cup toward the edge of the table for the waitress to refill, his foot tapping expectantly on the floor, for he has come to the State Street Grill three mornings in a row now, waiting to meet his designated "contact."

Little does the writer know, he will not wait long. Several doors down from where he sits, a black Toyota Camry pulls into a parking spot and a man in a forest green jacket, gray pants and new Asics sneakers climbs out. The man is tall and thin, with mostly gray hair that is parted on the left. As he approaches the State Street Grill and climbs the front steps, he conveys the self-assurance of someone with a certain *savoir faire*, his pale blue eyes alive and engaging.

After entering the State Street Grill, this man, who may very well be the lately defected Russian double agent, Kolossus, looks around casually, and then is struck by a host of curious portraits on the walls, oil paintings of famous American actors all wearing the military attire of Russian generals from back at the time of Napoleon's invasion in 1812. Clint Eastwood and Bill Murray are among them, their uniforms replete with golden epaulets, the star of St. Vladimir and other medals. Taken aback, this man who might be Kolossus needs a moment to collect his thoughts, to refocus, as it were, after which, not seeing anyone around who seems to anticipate his arrival, he walks the length of the bar and into the backroom, where, facing him from a table near the window, there sits a lean and perhaps underfed man with a scuffed, brown leather jacket draped over his shoulders, his left arm held in position by the Velcro tabs of a sling. This man, as he looks up, knows beyond a doubt that the new arrival in the room is the person he has been waiting for, which causes him to raise his cup of coffee, as if to say, *Salud!*

Once the two men are seated across from one another, the writer waits for his companion to speak, who, after a moment, *does* speak, his voice having a warm and would-be ease about it, his accent sounding faintly British as he remarks that the winds can rise up out of nowhere these days, that it's better always to stay ahead of things. The writer, saying that he couldn't agree more, now offers the man something to drink. "Coffee? Tea?" Politely declining, the stranger regrets that he is pressed for time, but is glad for the opportunity to have met, at which point the writer feels something tap his knee under the table. Discreetly, the writer puts his right hand in his lap and then reaches out toward the object that has touched him, grasping what feels like a small manilla envelope lined with a thin layer of bubble pack. Once it is firmly in his grip—and out of the hand of the man across from him—he slips this envelope into a zippered pocket on the inside of his leather jacket. It is then that the man who is certainly Kolossus notices a look of inquiry on the writer's face, but this he curtails by saying: "A dot that cannot be connected."

Acknowledging this assessment, the writer quietly adds that dots such as these often act as free radicals, that it's in their nature to do damage. With a wry smile, Kolossus takes a breath, gives a nod and then stands up, but as he turns to leave he pauses, noting yet another portrait of an American actor in old-fashioned Russian military garb. Pointing at it, he says, "Look—it's Al Pacino," after which he walks out of the room and disappears.

SLUMMING WITH MINERVA

Quickly now . . .

Having taken up residence in a small but comfortable flat on the Amalfi coast, McPherson sits on a stone balcony overlooking the Tyrrhenian Sea. The sun is in his eyes as he gazes out at the wonderfully blue water, and with his mind wandering he thinks of long-ago battles of sword and shield and how the sweep of history has made such a distinctive mark on the land about him. History, thinks McPherson, will always continue to swirl about us, slaughtering innocent people at the hands of some bloodthirsty emperor while provoking the backlash of valor and retribution. It is never a pretty sight, but then again, in the greater scheme of things, he realizes, it is inevitable. There will always be those born to cock their guns and take a stand against the overlords who binge on power and believe themselves invincible. Indeed, it is always the same tug of war between the people and those who seek to control them, be it a military junta in Chile or Argentina, or butting up against Franco during the Spanish Civil War. Always there is some thug to fight who is only too eager to trample justice and human dignity, Hitler standing out as Exhibit A, the go-to guy for evil, for whom it was all in a day's work to force Slavs into slave labor or incinerate Jews by the millions, while Joseph Stalin, yet another one-man freak show, gleefully packed off millions of people to the meat lockers of Siberia, when he wasn't, of course, murdering them outright or starving them en masse. Where, asks McPherson, do such idiots come from? It is no wonder, he thinks, that things will inevitably boil over and that people will simply blow their stacks. Whether it was 1381, 1776, 1789 or 1917, the human time bomb of revolution will always ultimately explode—and yet it is never quite enough. The closure is never truly finalized, a point driven home by the fact that now, in the United States of America, a conniving and reckless dictator has taken over the halls of power, a fact which stuns and baffles McPherson, leaving him to conclude that something had broken down along the way, that some guard had dropped, and therefore, in the name of vigilance, he realizes it is imperative that the spirit of revolution never end, that it must continue every day, that it must honor every minute with just accord. Certainly a black man in America must realize this well enough, that the word "emancipation" might only serve to illustrate the ironic distinction between the map of good intentions and the actual territory of racism. Thus it is no surprise that in the 1960s the noble ideals of civil disobedience dissolved horrifically into chants of "Burn, baby, burn!" Such incidents, concludes McPherson, are simply inevitable when the arc of history lands that punch of human oppression so hard that things ultimately reach a breaking point.

Yes, sighs McPherson, thoughtfully, revolution must always continue in spirit, it must always assert itself. How else to prevent someone like the Dictator and his party hacks from demolishing democratic rule? Indeed, that the Dictator had obtained a foothold on power in the first place, that he had come so far in the scope and scale of his dictatorship is inconceivable to McPherson. But did this egomaniac really think he could swing a wrecking ball into the sacred tenets on which the nation was founded and not face repercussions?

Did he really think he could cast a noxious shadow of hatred and duplicity across the entire land and not spark blowback? McPherson knows, of course, that the Dictator is a fool, the political byproduct of a nation of fools, and so it is anybody's guess as to what the man actually thinks or doesn't think. All McPherson knows is that the tipping point is at hand and that the sane and stalwart keepers of the flame of freedom are rising up. How it will all play out, of course, remains to be seen, and as McPherson sips a cool glass of mineral water and gazes out at the blue horizon before him, all he can do is take satisfaction in knowing that he has done his part, that he has fulfilled his duty, however strange it might have been—enlisting the services of a guttersnipe of a girl who apparently possesses mysterious powers, who has all but snuffed out the life a fascist bungler now rumored to be on life support. Logically, McPherson is still smarting from the whole incredible train of events, events that will never add up or, what is more bothersome, that perhaps *do* add up in ways he cannot fathom. How can he possibly process it all, a pragmatic man like himself? Witches and spells, how can it possibly be?

With a resigned shrug of his shoulders, McPherson takes another sip of mineral water and tilts back his head, his eyes closed as he basks in the warm sun, his mind wandering as he considers that on such a day long ago women might have strolled along the quay before him with parasols open while boys scampered about flying kites. As his thoughts drift here and there, he reminds himself that there is still beauty and wonder in the world, that a person can still enrich the soul and savor the words of poetry and philosophy, that the magnificence of art is still there to behold. Thus he makes up his mind to travel north to Pompei sometime soon, and to see Herculaneum as well, where he plans to visit the House of Neptune and Amphitrite, where, perhaps, after all, he will hear old Triton blow into his conch shell and herald a better day.

Opening his eyes, McPherson now reaches out to a small table before him for his saxophone. Standing up, he brings the instrument to his lips and is about to play a tune when he notices that a woman in a white sundress has appeared on the balcony of the adjacent building. Standing there, her arms at her sides, she wears her long brown hair pinned back gracefully as it trails down her neck. McPherson never meant his song to be a serenade, but as he plays a slow and sultry version of "Blue Moon" the melody lifts itself through the air with much romantic nuance. When he has finished, the woman on the balcony turns to him and smiles, while McPherson nods politely, taking pride in the fact that his saxophone playing has improved immeasurably in the recent weeks.

LUCK OF THE DRAW

Quickly now . . .

By the time Jennifer Golembeski and Amber Lamphere left Smitty's Tavern it was near one in the morning. They had already clinked together a few gin and tonics and had eaten a couple of tasty bar pies, not to mention having played a good game of pool that garnered some admiring onlookers. The music that night was jazzy and mellow and richer than one might have thought coming from just a guy on electronic keyboard and a sax player, the two of them improvising in ways that carried Jennifer away. The longer the musicians played, in fact, the more she realized it was nice to hear music without any singing, without any bellyaching about broken hearts or whatever, just the notes being played, that was good, it was better that way, better for letting the music get inside you and really get to you, Jennifer thought, and when she expressed these ideas to Amber, she agreed wholeheartedly.

"It's true, Jen," she said. "There's even a song I heard on the oldies station that my boss listens to. I think it's called "Echoes of My Mind." It's all about how people should just shut-up. It's an ancient song. I like think the guy who sang it is probably dead. It was still a good song, though, all about this guy that just doesn't want to hear anybody chewin' his ears anymore."

The walk back to Jennifer's apartment that night took the young women past a boarded-up gas station and several vacant lots overrun with weeds, then down a crooked road that led to a block of shabby rowhouses that looked like they were weary of standing. Gazing at the darkened windows of these houses, Jennifer felt like a trespasser into the lives of the people within, the shadows having taken hold of those who slept while she was wakeful and alert and somehow compromising the quiet of their dreams. Because of this, she was inclined not to speak and to move quickly on her way, with Amber making an effort to keep up with her, the two young women walking Indian file as if on some secret mission, stealing along the streets deftly and silently.

Having noticed the change in Jennifer's mood, Amber addressed her in a whisper, "Jen, what's the hurry? Did something spook you?"

"I just want to get home."

"Did you see something?"

"No."

"What is it then? Do you have to take a piss or something? You can go in the bushes and I'll stand guard."

"I'm just anxious to get home."

Walking on briskly, the two friends covered nearly a mile and were breathing rapidly when the house where Jennifer lived came into view. Without a word, they approached the front door and then climbed the stairwell to the top floor. After unlocking the door to her apartment, Jennifer stepped inside, feeling the warm and stuffy attic air. As she turned on a lamp that sat on a small table by the door, the room lit up with a modest cone of light, as did the ripples of lathwork showing in the plaster walls. With Amber beside her, they both eased out of their jackets and Jennifer locked the door behind her. Then she walked into the kitchen area and turned on a light, stopping suddenly.

"Amber!"

"What?" cried her friend, instantly beside her.

"Somebody's been here, that's not mine," said Jennifer, pointing a finger at the kitchen table, where a black leather duffle bag lay.

"I'll say," agreed Amber with subdued wonderment, leaning closer to the duffle bag, "but . . ."

"But what?"

"Look, it's imprinted with your initials, right here under the handle, J.G., that's what it says."

Standing frozen in place and with her thoughts racing, Jennifer put a finger to her lips and quietly retrieved a carving knife from a kitchen drawer. Once armed with this weapon, she and Amber then cautiously checked the bathroom and the attic's only closet, making sure that no one lay in hiding.

"There's no one here, Jen, there's no place for them to go, and there's no bed to crawl under."

"But someone was here."

"Check your stuff and see if somebody robbed you."

After examining all of her belongings and the food in the refrigerator, Jennifer concluded that all seemed to be in order.

"What about your gin?" asked Amber. "Did they take your gin?"

"No, it's there, but what about *that*?" asked Jennifer, again pointing at the black duffle bag.

"I don't know, Jen. Maybe the landlord thought it was yours and let himself in to leave it there," ventured Amber.

"Right, like I'm always going out and buying leather duffle bags."

"It's very nice looking," admitted Amber, "but we need to see what's inside it. Maybe there's somebody's ID, something to tell us whose it is."

"And maybe it's boobytrapped."

"You're kidding, right?"

"I don't know," said Jennifer, feeling flustered, "let me just lift it up and see how heavy it is."

In a manner akin to picking up a newborn infant, Jennifer cautiously lifted the duffle bag and gauged the weight of it in her hands. "I don't think it's boobytrapped," she admitted. "It seems kind of bulky."

"Can you peek inside it?"

"It's zipped tight."

"Then just unzip it."

Very gingerly, Jennifer began to pull back the tab of the zipper, watching the little teeth disengage one by one until the soft, black leather slowly began to open, a gap in the duffle bag forming, growing wider and wider, not unlike the eyes of Jennifer and Amber, who on peering inside saw thick stacks of one-hundred-dollar bills, each one bound by a paper tab. Once the duffle bag was completely open, Jennifer lifted it up and turned it upside down, spilling the contents onto the table, the two friends watching as stacks of money came tumbling out, falling topsy-turvy in a pile. Next, after searching every inch of the duffle bag, after opening a small zippered pocket on the outside and exploring that too, Jennifer found nothing else and was left to stare at the windfall sitting there before her, softly saying, "Holy shit."

Amber, meanwhile, reached out and took one of the stacks between her fingers, holding it up and gazing at it. "It's real money," she said.

"It sure looks that way," agreed Jennifer.

Stunned and incredulous, the two friends now began to handle the green stacks more freely, looking at them front and back, bending them open to see if the hundred-dollar denomination on the top of the stack was replicated within. So crisp and smooth were the bills that there was something unreal about them. Holding a stack of cash up to her nose, Amber sniffed it and observed how clean the money smelled and "not like that punky smell of money in people's pockets." Jennifer meanwhile squinted at the face of Benjamin

Franklin, wondering if his knowing countenance held some clue as to where all this loot came from.

"Someone jimmied the lock to my door and got in here, Amber, and this is what they left," Jennifer stated with amazement.

"They sure did."

"But what do you think it means?"

"It means you're rich, Jen. You gotta get that money into a safe deposit box. You can't just take it to a bank teller, it's too much, they'll sic the bulls on you. You can spend only so much, just here and there, cash and carry, and don't keep going to the same stores either. Remember, they're watching everybody these days. Keep switching stores so you don't get too familiar to people and call attention to yourself. You need time to figure out how to handle all this."

"It's a lot of money."

"A lot of money, Jen."

"And it's here on purpose, it's no accident."

"So what are you saying?" asked Amber.

"I'm saying why is it here? Where did it come from?" blurted out Jennifer.

"As if you didn't know," said Amber. "Are you pulling my leg? You know where it came from."

"I'd have to say it's because of what I did."

"I'd say so, silly. They believe in you, Jen, that's what it means. We hear there's a meltdown going on with the Dictator. They say he's bleeding from the eyeballs and blowing lunch in a barf bag all day long. Everybody's getting wind of it—and you did it. They believe in you."

"And so you're saying *they* means the people that wanted it done?"

"Come off it, it's the guys! Mr. Wingtips! I could see right from the start he had a thing for you, and you pulled it off, that's what has them doing cartwheels. You're the cat's nuts, I'll say."

"And you're the dog's bollocks," laughed Jennifer, suddenly feeling tipsy as she twirled herself around and flung back her head, her eyes closing as she said, "Unbelievable."

"You got the power, girl," said Amber with admiration.

"But all this money," stated Jennifer, casting an eye over the green bundles of cash jumbled on the table, "I never put a price on anything, I never asked for anything, and you know it, and I don't want to be indebted to anybody either."

"Relax, you fought the Dictator, you fought him in the street, and those shithead goons of his walloped you, you've got a scar across your head to prove it. You'll be disfigured, and you did what those guys asked you to do, so you earned the money, that's all, you earned it because you're tried and true," declared Amber.

"I don't know what I am," sighed Jennifer, "something, I guess."

"Sure you are, and now with this money you can take those beach towels off the windows and buy real drapes to put up, and you can buy a box spring for your mattress and finally get that stupid slow leak in your car tire fixed. It's a lot of money here, Jen, and we need to count it. It must be thousands and thousands of dollars. Tens of thousands! Tens and tens of thousands," speculated Amber as she picked up a wad of bills and let it flick off her thumb like a deck of cards.

"But it's your money, too. We did it together, so it's even Steven."

"I didn't do nothin', Jen," Amber pleaded.

"You believed in me even more than those guys did."

"It's still your money, Jen."

"Amber, no, it's halves, it's got to be. If you weren't with me I don't know if I could have gone out there that night, if I could have really done it."

Amber smiled warmly at her friend while Jennifer, struck by a sudden impulse, turned to see if the scratch-off lottery ticket that had been stuck under a magnet on her refrigerator was still there. Seeing that it was, she experienced a tingle of excitement while the involuntary tug of a smile played on her lips. She considered that now might be the right time to rub off that GOLD RUSH ticket, but then, she instead reached out and took hold of Amber's hand, silently leading her to the mattress on the floor where they would often lie together. Without a word, the two friends looked into each other's eyes and undressed, embracing tenderly before eventually falling asleep.

Toward morning Jennifer began to dream. She dreamed she was pushing her way through the branches of a deep forest, stumbling and forging on until she emerged at the shore of a slow-moving river. Here she paused and walked down an easy slope to the water's edge, where she loitered about and began to skip stones. The stones around her were plentiful and she watched as they skimmed along the water's surface, leaving a series of little splashes. Eventually, she took a fig from her pocket and slowly began to chew it while gazing at the opposite shore, surveying a high cliff that stretched upward to a gloomy sky. Jutting out from this cliff were rocky outcroppings that contained just enough soil for a stunted tree or small bush to grow, but most apparent to Jennifer was an area where the cliff dropped off sharply, a sheer broad plummet on which a huge green skull had been spray painted. Under this skull the word TYRANT had been scrawled in large green letters. Despite being weathered and faded, the huge green skull stared down at Jennifer Golembeski with visible outrage, but Jennifer stood her ground and spoke to the skull with contempt, her words audibly on her lips that morning when she awoke, "You go to hell, scumbag."